A Down Home Christmas

LIZ TALLEY

Hallmark
PUBLISHING

www.hallmarkpublishing.com

Dedication

This book is dedicated to Common Ground Community, a vital ministry in the Cedar Grove community of Shreveport, Louisiana. Specifically, I would like to dedicate this book to Matt and Vickie Whitehead, two people who walk the walk every single day. This is also for Chuck, Terry, Mary Lauren, and all the boys who choose to work hard to make their lives better. Go, CG Chargers!

I would also like to thank Robyn Collins, songwriter extraordinaire. Thank you for sharing your talents with me and giving Kris the beautiful lyrics in the story. You are awesome!

Table of Contents

Chapter One

I *SHOULD'VE COME HOME BEFORE NOW.*

The thought buzzed in Kris Trabeau's head as his car bumped down the winding drive that led to Trabeau Farms. New potholes and overgrown trees greeted him, causing the guilt he continually stowed in the back of his conscience to rocket to the forefront.

At the very least he should have hired someone years ago to help his aunt. The old homeplace was too big for such a slip of a woman to take care of by herself—especially one with a broken leg.

But he knew his Aunt Tansy well. The fiercely independent woman would have sent whomever he hired on their way before the ink was dry on the check. Which was part of the reason he'd driven almost three hundred miles to Charming, Mississippi. It was beyond time to convince his stubborn aunt to give up on living alone and come live with him in Nashville.

Just as Kris crested the hill that would bring the farmhouse into view, a chicken flapped across the drive.

A chicken wearing a sweater.

"What the—" The words died on his lips as a huge beast loped behind in pursuit of the squawking fowl. A leash trailed behind the dog that seemed single-minded in its pursuit of the chicken.

Next came a barefoot brunette, waving her hands and screaming. "Heel, Edison. I said heel!"

Kris slammed on the brakes, the brand-new Mustang fishtailing before jerking to a halt. The woman's gaze flew toward him, her mouth dropping open, before she continued her mad dash to apprehend the dog. Kris unbuckled and climbed out of the car. "Whoa, hey, you need help?"

"I got it," she called back, disappearing down the hill.

Kris lifted his eyebrows and mouthed, *Wow*.

Then his aunt came limping as fast as her crutches would allow. She wore a track suit circa 1995 and a medical boot around her leg. "Think he's gonna get my Loretta, does he? Well, he's got another think coming, is what he's got."

Kris moved then, meeting his aunt who hadn't seemed to notice he stood in her driveway. "Whoa, now, Aunt Tansy. What's going on?"

"Oh, sugar, Edison's after Loretta Lynn again. That dog has taken a fascination with my chickens," his aunt said, her gaze fastened to the spot where the chicken, dog, and pretty brunette had disappeared. Then she jerked stunned eyes to him. "Wait, *Kris*? What are *you* doin' here?"

"Surprise," he said, throwing up his hands. "I thought I would visit for the holidays." *Even though I swore I would never come back.*

Aunt Tansy closed her mouth and wobbled a little. "For the holidays?"

Here in front of him was the very reason he needed to convince her to make a change. Tansy hobbling around chasing a dog was dangerous. She could have tripped again and done even greater damage to her healing leg. Or what if she had a heart attack? Heart disease ran in the family. Or someone broke into the house and Aunt Tansy couldn't get to his great-granddaddy's shotgun in time? So many horrible things could happen to his closest living relative, things he hadn't considered until Thad Cumberland, editor of *The Charming Gazette*, had called his manager and relayed the news that Tansy had fallen, broken her femur, and was in surgery.

The panic at the thought that she could've died alone in that house with things still unsettled between them had sent a load of guilt so massive, Kris had trouble breathing. Guest appearances, tours, and promotional opportunities had occupied too much of his time lately, and he'd put his personal life on the back burner—including his Aunt Tansy. He couldn't put off addressing her situation any longer. Thanks to the new contract, now he could afford to take care of her the way she deserved.

But, of course, he couldn't tell her his plan just yet.

Tansy's dark eyes flashed with something that made the guilt he carried wriggle inside him. Tansy had taken him in at ten years old when his parents had died in a plane crash, sending a terrified Kris from the flat plains of Texas to the gentle Mississippi hills. Living at Trabeau Farms with a maiden aunt he'd barely known hadn't been easy. But Tansy was a determined woman and hadn't given up on him, even when he threw a brick through the front window of Ozzy Vanderhoot's Old-Fashioned General Store or when he drank a six-pack and spray-painted a choice directive on the Charming, Mississippi, water tower.

"Well, boy, I'm glad to see you, but I ain't got time to sit here jawin' when Edison's chasing my Loretta. He may not mean harm, but he might scare her to death. Wait here. I'll be right back," she said, starting toward the woods to his right.

"Hold up," he said, taking her by the elbow. She felt too

thin. Looked too tired and old. How long had it been since he'd seen her? Three years? Maybe four? "You broke your leg. I'm sure you're not supposed to be running after chickens."

"I'm not running after chickens. I'm running after a dog."

"Let me get the dog…and the chicken," he said, carefully leading her to a flat patch where she could balance better. She looked so slight a stiff wind could likely blow her over.

Tansy didn't look satisfied. "You remember how to handle chickens? You're a fancy city boy now and all."

"I'm pretty sure I remember how to pick up a chicken," he said, with a roll of his eyes. Fetching eggs had been one of his jobs growing up. Of course, back then, his aunt hadn't named her egg producers and dang sure hadn't dressed them in sweaters.

"I suppose it's like riding a bicycle," she conceded.

"Probably. I'll be back in a sec," Kris said, before jogging down the slope that led to a wooded copse that held a small creek and good climbing trees. He'd built a fort in those woods when he'd first come to live with Tansy, and the remnants were probably in there somewhere.

He followed the sound of yipping dog and squeaking brunette, pushing through the brush that should have been dead in December but wasn't. Because it was Mississippi and unusually warm for December. Heck, sometimes they even wore shorts at Christmas.

"Ouch, ouch. Please, Edison. Stop. Stop!" the woman yelled somewhere off to his left.

At that moment, the sweater-wearing chicken flew by Kris's head and the dog came bounding after it. Kris ducked as the chicken tumbled by, crashing into the underbrush. He snatched the leash that bumped behind the dog, making the beast's head jerk around when he reached the end of the tether. The huge fluffy dog immediately started yipping at the hapless hen. A few steps behind, the brunette emerged, panting, her curly hair displaying bits of leaf and twigs. With her pointed chin, big gray eyes, and flushed cheeks, she looked a bit like a woodland fairy.

"Oh, thank goodness," she breathed, pressing a hand against her chest.

Edison, who looked like a cross between a Saint Bernard and Chow Chow, whined and strained at the leash. The chicken's sweater had caught on a broken limb and the poor thing flapped and squawked. Kris extended the end of the leash to the woman. She took it and jerked her dog back toward her. "Sit, Edison. And hush! You're scaring Loretta."

The dog sat, tongue lolling out, panting, eyes still fixed on the Rhode Island Red that flopped about pitifully in the brush. Kris went over to the bird and wondered how in the heck he was going to free the terrified Loretta Lynn without getting pecked to death. He started unbuttoning his flannel shirt.

"What are you doing?" the woman asked, sounding slightly alarmed.

"Trying to calm this chicken down."

"By taking your shirt off?" Her eyes grew wide as she looked from him to the chicken.

"I'm going to drape it over her so I don't get pecked. Then I'll try to free her."

"Oh," the woman said, tugging as her beast leapt against the restraint. "Good idea. Birds have a higher visual stimulus and covering her eyes should calm her down."

Visual stimulus?

He shrugged out of his shirt, glad he'd pulled on an undershirt to ward off the early morning chill when he left

Nashville that morning. Then he approached the chicken, who grew even more agitated as he moved toward it. Carefully, he drew his shirt over Loretta, then slid his hands around her now-clothed body, pinning her wings to her sides. The hen went still. "There."

"Her sweater's still hung," the woman said unhelpfully.

"I got it," he said, pulling the royal blue yarn free from the branch and looking back at the woman and dog. "Why is this chicken wearing a sweater anyway?"

"That's Loretta Lynn. Miss Tansy's pet. She likes to knit sweaters for her hens. She got the idea off Pinterest."

"Pet? She calls them pets?" Kris arched a brow. "And people make clothes for farm animals now?"

"Haven't you seen the videos of baby goats in pajamas? They're so cute." She paused and then shook her head as if she knew she'd gotten off track. "For some reason, Edison really likes Loretta. I think it's because she's very flappy."

Kris couldn't stop his smile. "Flappy?"

"Miss Tansy sometimes gives Edison dog biscuits, and he remembers. So when he gets loose, he comes here. Unfortunately, the chickens intrigue him. Maybe he prefers Loretta because she makes the most noise."

"That makes sense. He's a dog, after all," he said, turning back to the chicken. He carefully lifted and tucked her beneath his arm. The hen, oddly enough, seemed to sink in relief against his side. Poor Loretta Lynn. "There now."

"I'm so relieved she's not dead. Miss Tansy would have killed me and Edison." The woman let out a sigh.

"And who are you exactly?" he asked.

The woman pushed back the hair curling into her eyes and held out her hand. "I'm Tory Odom. I live next door to Tansy."

"You're one of the Moffetts?"

"No, I live in the cottage on the other side of Tansy," she said as he took her hand. It was small and capable-looking, like she could smooth a child's fevered forehead or hoe a garden equally well.

"Oh, the Howards' old place?" Last time he'd been home, he'd predicted a strong wind could topple what was left of the Howard place.

"I restored the cottage. It's really nice now." Edison took that moment to spring toward the bundle under his arms. She tugged on his leash and pushed him into a sitting position. "And you are?"

"Oh, I'm Kris. Tansy's nephew."

"The country music singer?"

Kris felt pride stir inside. He'd waited a long time to be known as a country music singer. Being named CMA's New Artist of the Year just weeks ago had cemented his position in the country music scene. He'd placed his award in the center of his mantel and made sure the accent light hit it perfectly. The award was the first of many he'd use to decorate the downtown Nashville loft he'd purchased earlier that year with the royalties on his first album. *A Simple Dream* had hit big last spring, but it had taken years of sweat, tears, and sore fingers from playing guitar for his dream to come true. He'd hit number one with two songs on his debut album and was in the process of putting together his second one. Of course, he still had to write some songs for it, but they would come. He prayed they would come. So, heck yeah, he was *the country music star*. "Star is kind of a strong word, but, yeah, I play country music."

"I didn't say star."

She *hadn't* said star. She'd said singer. He glanced away so she wouldn't see that he was embarrassed about the faux pas. He felt really stupid. "Right, right."

"I don't really care for country music. You could be a star and I wouldn't know it," she said, sounding like she offered an apology.

Her admission embarrassed him even more, and he found he hadn't a clue what to say to her. Maybe the sweater-bedecked chicken nestled beneath his arm paired with an ego smackdown had something to do with not being able to find the right words.

Or maybe it was the fact he'd not been able to find the words for the last few months.

And that was what worried him most.

Tory Odom was at her very essence a scientist, so she knew Kris Trabeau was exactly the sort of test subject that behavioral researchers would use to gauge the concept of attractiveness. People were more apt to trust others with symmetrical features as an indicator of being attractive. The man in front of her fit the description. Not only were his features symmetrical, but he also had broad shoulders, shaggy dark hair, and a scruffy beard. Normally she didn't care for a rough-around-the-edges look, but somehow it worked for this country music singer.

Then again, Tory also knew that good looks didn't amount to squat.

Kris's brow had gathered into a frown at her words about his not being a star.

That was rude, Tory.

"Uh, I don't listen to any music all that much, and when I do I like classics or Motown. No offense." She pulled Edison's leash as Kris pushed out of the underbrush. These woods extended toward a large lake on Salty Moffett's land. Salty and Tansy had a love-hate relationship and people said they always had. Tory had often wondered if it had to do with a relationship gone bad, but she'd never asked. Tansy was very private and not open to personal questions. Tory hadn't even known the woman had an injury until a week ago. Of course, that was mostly Tory's own fault. She'd been stuck in her own blue world and hadn't been out much herself.

"It's okay. I know not everyone listens to country music," Kris said, emerging into the clearing, holding back a limb so she could pass.

"Thank you," she said, studying the still green patch of clover covering the slope and praying there were no stickers. Her mad dash barefoot had been unwise, but when Edison had turned toward Tansy's and shot off like a rocket, she hadn't had time to go inside and put shoes on. She'd stepped on a pinecone and knew she'd scraped her foot.

Obviously, she and Edison needed to practice commands again. He'd done so well at obedience school but needed to have consistent practice. She'd slacked off over the last few months. Time for a refresher course on *sit* and *heel*.

They arrived back on the graveled drive where Tansy waited. When she saw Kris carrying the draped bundle beneath his arm, her shoulders sank. "Oh, no. Not Loretta Lynn."

"She's fine," Kris said, patting the hen beneath the shirt. "I covered her so she wouldn't see the dog and be scared."

"Oh, thank goodness," Tansy said, clasping a hand to her chest. Then she eyed Edison as he padded in front of Tory, tongue hanging, looking every bit as happy as a dog could look. Tory wished Edison would have the decency to be cowed, but no. Edison didn't seem to ever feel shame.

Tory shot Tansy an apologetic look. "I'm sorry, Miss Tansy. Edison has been doing so well at his obedience training that I let my guard down. He loves coming to visit you…uh, and the chickens. You know he would never hurt them intentionally."

Tansy sniffed. "He's a menace is what he is."

They all turned to look at the overgrown puppy with his shaggy coat, happy brown eyes, and smiling face. He looked nothing like a menace. In fact, he looked pretty adorable. He woofed and held up a paw.

"See? He's sorry," Tory said.

"Here, Aunt Tansy. Why don't you take your chicken back…to wherever you keep her." Kris handed the cloaked hen to his aunt.

Loretta flapped beneath his shirt but settled when Tansy cooed to her. "It's all right, Retta. You're safe now."

Kris shot Tory a look. She was fairly certain it was a "has my aunt gone bonkers?" look. Tory gave a slight shrug as Tansy hobbled off carrying the chicken. She'd also taken Kris's flannel shirt with her, leaving him clad in a thin t-shirt.

With Tansy gone and the drama of Edison chasing Loretta over, Tory started toward her house. Her left foot hurt from the pine cone scrape and she tried not to hobble. A person had to have some dignity after running like a wild woman after her adorable but obedience-challenged mutt. "Better get Edison back home. Nice to meet you."

"You need a ride?" Kris called after her.

"No. Edison would get your car dirty. He sheds a lot and that car looks…" She turned and glanced at his gleaming, granite gray Mustang GT. "Very well taken care of."

He narrowed his eyes as if pondering what the dog hair

would actually do to his leather interior. "It is, but you're barefoot."

"I made it here. I can make it back. But thank you for asking." Tory started across the large expanse of shaded yard, trying not to wince each time her foot struck the hard earth.

"Looks like you hurt your foot," Kris said, jogging to catch up with her. Edison's tail thumped and he grinned up at the country music singer like he'd found his new best friend. Edison was fickle that way. He loved everyone, and life was big fun. Chasing a squawking, flapping Loretta, Tammy, or Dolly around the farm was a great game. Maybe Tory needed to adopt a new friend for Edison. Perhaps he'd stop thinking about playing with Tansy's chickens if he had another pup to tug a rope with.

"I'm fine. Probably a thorn or a little scrape." She didn't want to put this man out any more than she already had. She was embarrassed of her disheveled hair, ratty sweatshirt and bare feet in serious need of a pedicure. Ever since Patrick had dumped her, she'd let her beauty routine slide. Chipped toenail paint aside, she didn't want to climb inside his fancy car with her hairy, drooling mutt.

"Let me drive you back. I insist." He placed a hand on her elbow, halting her.

"No. I can make it. It's less than half a mile."

"I know you can make it, but let me play the gentleman," he said, with a smile that made her stomach do a loop-de-loop.

Stop it, Tory.

"It's really not necessary."

"My Aunt Tansy would have my hide if I let you walk back barefoot. Come on. I can clean the seat if I need to."

Tory sighed. "Fine."

She hobbled beside him, praying Edison didn't do

something ridiculous like tear the leather seats or barf on the floormat. He was notorious for having bad timing. Once he'd done his business in the middle of the vet's office right when the pastor of Charming United Methodist had asked her about her parents who lived a few towns over.

Edison had been adopted from a local rescue. Tory had fallen in love with his exuberance and sloppy kisses on first meeting, but Edison's past as an untrained puppy sometimes reared its head. Still, even polite dogs had accidents...and drooled.

"You sure your foot is okay?" Kris asked, opening the passenger door for her. Her ex, Patrick, had never opened the door for her. He'd told her he believed in equal rights for women and that her arm wasn't broken, was it? Of course, opening the door for a lady didn't mean a man thought she couldn't do it herself. It meant he was raised to be respectful. But in this case, it might be merely because she had a thorn or something in her foot and was trying to manage her overgrown canine who just happened to adore a car ride.

"It's fine," she said, wincing as Edison bounded into the small backseat with the enthusiasm of a toddler at a playground. Kris clicked the front seat back and she lowered herself into the seat. The interior of the car smelled new and gleamed in the weak winter sunlight.

Kris jogged around and slid into the driver's seat. When he closed the door, the intimacy level went to threat-level ten. Tory shifted toward the passenger door to give herself some room. Kris smelled like pine trees and expensive cologne, both strangely inviting. She tucked her frizzy hair behind her ear and tried to make sure her elbow on the middle console was positioned beneath her dog's drooling mouth without invading Kris's space.

He backed up, the car thrumming with power.

"This is quite a car," she said, trying to make conversation and catch the drool with her arm.

"Yeah, I thought about a pickup truck. You know, country music bad boy and all, but I used to covet these bad boys when I was a kid. My parents had a ranch hand who had a vintage GT he liked to soup up and race all over the county. I thought that was the coolest thing I'd ever seen."

"It's nice," she said. Then she made a face. "You call yourself a bad boy?"

He laughed. "No, but I liked the idea of the image. Like I was tough. That sounds lame, doesn't it?"

"I guess everyone wants to portray something."

They fell into silence as he pulled out onto the highway. The farm across from Tansy's had multiple blowup Christmas lawn ornaments at the entrance. The festive balloons bobbed in the afternoon breeze. Edison barked as the towering Santa dipped toward them. Kris made a neat right into her place and roared down the graveled drive.

"Oh, you did do a great job with the house," Kris said when her small farmhouse came into view. Tory was rather proud of the fresh bright white paint and black shutters. A swing hung on the front porch and she'd put bright patterned pillows in it. Ferns hung in between the rustic beams she'd used to support the porch. "But where are your Christmas blowup decorations?"

His question had been teasing, but her response was the one she'd given everyone who had commented on the absence of her Christmas decorations. "I don't have any. I'm not doing Christmas this year."

With that, she opened the door, flipped back the seat to let Edison bound out, and said, "Thanks for the ride."

Chapter Two

TANSY TRABEAU GENTLY PLACED LORETTA into the opening of the fenced in henhouse. "There you go, sugar. Go have a nap or something. Ol' Edison is long gone."

The hen flapped her wings a bit and toddled into the henhouse like a drunken sailor. Patsy Cline and Tammy Wynette sat outside on the perches she'd mounted in the corners of the chicken-wired yard of the coop. Both of her pretty girls were still adorned in their knitted capes and seemed to be enjoying the December sunshine.

Tansy had gotten the idea of knitting capes for her chickens off Pinterest. She'd learned about Pinterest from Peggy Bradley at the beauty parlor. Peggy had a whole bunch of digital boards filled with hairstyles and cool ideas for multi-purposing things like faucet spouts and cola bottle caps. When Tansy had broken her leg tripping over a loose porch board a month ago, she'd decided to take up knitting again to pass the time she couldn't spend in her now overgrown winter garden. One of the Pinterest boards she'd run across had patterns for sweaters and capes for chickens. At first it seemed ludicrous, but since she had lost old Beau, her collie, a few years back, the only pets she had were her six laying hens. They were easy company and had their own personalities. With no one else to knit for, Tansy had decided to make her chickens some winter hen cozies.

She'd started on a sweater for Edison, but now she may just give his Christmas gift to some other cute mutt who would look good in red and green stripes.

Tansy hooked the door of the hen yard as Kris came roaring back up the drive.

Someone could have knocked her over with a feather when she saw her nephew standing there grinning in her graveled drive. The boy hadn't been home since he left many years ago. Oh, she'd seen him on occasion, driving up to Nashville, trying to amend the hard words she'd said to him the day he left the farm. They loved each other, sure, but the boy's career choice had always been the elephant in the room.

Every Christmas he promised he'd come home, and every Christmas Eve he would call with a reason he couldn't make it. Usually, it had to do with a gig. Or the fact he'd sworn he wouldn't come home until he had a record deal. Tansy knew the life he led well enough. She knew what a mistake it was to be a slave to money and fame. Hadn't worked out well for the love of her life, Jack Prosper, that was for dang sure. Regret plinked inside her when she thought about Jack.

If only...

The muscle car's engine died and Kris climbed out.

He was home now, and he wore success like he wore his Wranglers—comfortable and made for him. His white t-shirt against the Mississippi sky reminded her she'd tucked his flannel shirt under her arm. "I got your shirt here, sugar."

He jogged over, eyeing the huge henhouse she'd hired a local handyman to build for her. "Your chicken okay?"

"She'll live," Tansy said, shoving the wadded-up shirt toward him. She noted he wore a Rolex watch. He'd never been one for fancy things, but success made it easier to indulge in things a person thought he never would.

Kris took the shirt. "I ran your neighbor and her dog back home."

"That dang dog will be the death of one of my chickens. But it's my fault. I bought him dog biscuits for when he visited, but then he saw the chickens, and it's like he's obsessed."

"Tory said it's because they're flappy. He probably thinks it's a game," Kris said, pulling her into a hug.

"He's not a bad dog." Tansy closed her eyes for a moment and reveled in the embrace of the child she'd loved like her own, stowing away all the hurt from not seeing him in a while and ignoring the small ball of resentment that still sat between them. She regretted the words she'd said to him the day he left. No doubt he regretted his. They were both stubborn people and had allowed old hurts to hang around too long. Giving him a squeeze, she broke their embrace and leaned back. "So what in the devil are you doing here, Kristopher James?"

His brown eyes seemed shadowed with things unspoken. "Seeing you, of course."

She narrowed her eyes. "Why?"

Kris made a face and turned toward the porch. "Well, it's almost Christmas. Besides, you're my favorite aunt."

"I'm your only aunt."

"Still," he said with a grin, walking around to the front of the house and climbing the steps. He paused, wiggling the antique iron fencing that sat on either side of the wooden steps. "Rail is loose."

Tansy moved around to the front of the house, trying to see the farm that had been in their family for generations through Kris's eyes. The paint was flaking here and there, and the once crisp Williamsburg blue shutters had faded to periwinkle. The pale butter paint was rubbed off in a few places, and the bronze kick plate and matching door knocker were spotted with age. The old house looked a lot like Tansy, it had good bones and a definitive presence but could use a little work. She hadn't been able to keep up with maintenance like she thought she would. Sometimes it was easier to ignore a broken hinge or a dripping faucet.

Glancing at Kris, she could see that he wondered about the condition of the place, a place he'd never loved the way she wanted him to. Of course, he'd been heartbroken when he'd come to live here. Not to mention most teenaged boys didn't like the chores they had to do when it came to keeping a farm going. Kris seemed to not give much thought to legacy or heritage, or Charming, for that matter.

"The house needs painting," she said, needlessly.

"Yeah. And you don't have any decorations up. Not even a wreath. You skipping Christmas like your neighbor?"

"You mean Tory? She's skipping Christmas?"

"That's what she said, and by the look of things, you are, too." He came back down the steps and took her elbow. Kris had always been a gentleman. In that, his mama and daddy had raised him right. And she'd continued that respectful upbringing when he'd come to live with her years ago. Or tried to.

"Hard to climb up into the attic to fetch decorations when you got a busted leg." She carefully thumped up the steps, leaning on him. She'd left her other crutch by the front door. She couldn't wait to be done with the silly things, but she could tell her leg still needed a few more weeks healing before she could ditch the crutches. "Maybe you can help me put a few things up. I downscaled years ago and now only do a small artificial tree. Makes better sense since there's just me here now."

When her mother had lived at Trabeau Farms, they'd gone all out for Christmas. Festive garland draped across the eaves, huge poinsettia wreaths ordered from Millie's Teahouse hung on the doors, and a twelve-foot pine tree towered beside the holly-bedecked hearth. Starched, embroidered linens on the tables, red satin runners and her great grandmother's bone china on the gleaming sideboard. Her mother had placed the porcelain angel, which had traveled all the way from France with her great-great-grandmother, on the mantel and flocked her with cedar and wild berries. Tinsel, vintage large-bulb lights on the tree, and fresh gingerbread from the oven had always been part of their holidays. Once they'd even had a taffy pull in the kitchen. One Christmas, snow had blanketed the Mississippi countryside, and her Uncle Earl had taken them sledding. Christmas had been an excuse to pull out the finery and forget the cares of the world.

"Not sure how long I can stay, Aunt Tans. I booked a cabin over in East Texas for a couple of weeks. I'm recording my second album in January. If I want a few of my own songs on there, I have to get them written. Haven't been able to concentrate in Nashville, so I thought a long drive and isolated cabin might help."

"You're only writing a few songs for the album? Where are you getting the others?" she asked.

A shadow crossed his face. "Well, I'm with Strata Records now. They have their own songwriters. Willie Nash and Harper Keno are working with me on this one. They've been sending me songs they think will work. I got 'em narrowed down."

"Really?" Tansy was surprised, since her nephew had written or co-written all of the songs on his first hit album.

"They said they'd let me put a couple on there as long as there was room."

"*Let* you?"

Kris sighed. "You know how it is, Aunt T. Your group worked for a label back in the day. The bigwigs pull the strings. Anyway, my therapist suggested getting away from everything. She said maybe the solitude would get the creative juices flowing."

"Therapist?"

"Are you a parrot?" he joked. But his cheeks went pink and it wasn't from the cold. "I've been having some stress, you know, some trouble sleeping. I didn't want to rely on medications, so I'm trying therapy first. Anyway, I haven't been back to Big Horn since I was a kid. That's where my roots started."

Tansy's heart squeezed in her chest.

Of course, Kris hadn't returned to Texas once he'd come to live with her. Back when he needed family to step up, nobody in East Texas had said boo about raising a little ten-year-old boy. Oh, sure, now that Kris had hit it big in music, he probably had third cousins crawling out of the woodwork. Didn't matter. The boy was wrong—his roots weren't in Texas. They were here in Charming, Mississippi. Thing was, he didn't want to know where his roots were from. Instead he'd chafed against the ties that bound him to the farm. "You're going all the way to Texas to find yourself? Maybe you should just look at the ground here first."

Kris looked guilty. "I just needed some peace and quiet. I found a place on a lake. Figured with nothing but the hoot owls and the whitetail to distract me, I would get these songs hammered out in no time." Tansy saw the doubt in his eyes. A first album was written with passion, guts, and late-night epiphany. A second album was written with crushing pressure. Or maybe not so much since the label had its own agenda. She wondered about those songs, about the look on his face when he mentioned the label's direction for him.

Tansy wanted to pursue the conversation, but she knew when to give a person breathing space. She opened the front door. "Come on in. I hope you'll at least stay for supper."

"Yes, ma'am, I thought I would spend a few days, if that's okay. Maybe be of some help since you probably need a few things done around here." Kris held the door for her.

"I've managed quite well, thank you." She didn't want to sound defensive but couldn't help herself. Kris had been gone, too busy chasing his neon rainbow to fiddle with an old woman. What made him think she needed him now? Her bum leg?

The house was dim and smelled old. She'd closed the formal parlor off and spent most of the time in the kitchen watching the cooking channel and knitting scarves for either her church's charity or her hens. No need to heat or cool the entire place. Since she'd broken her leg, she'd started sleeping in the former housekeeper's room off the kitchen to save going up and down the stairs. She used the downstairs powder room to shower, ever thankful her daddy had insisted upon putting in a shower over her mother's protest that a powder room did not require bathing.

Kris followed her into the kitchen. "I know you've managed, but it can't be easy being out here alone. I've been worried about you."

But not worried enough to come see me.

Tansy struck the thought from her mind. Yeah, her feelings

had been hurt, but she'd been the one to tell him not to come home. He took her at her word. Besides, she knew he'd been occupied, living on the road, playing gigs every night, feeling the pressure.

Kris was home now. She should focus on that.

"Would you like something to eat? I've got some soup I can warm up. Tory made it. It's decent."

"When did she move in?" he asked, pulling out a ladderback chair and settling down at the table covered with skeins of yarn and last week's papers.

"A year or so ago. She teaches biology at the high school. Moved here from Jackson, but she's originally from Morning Glory." She knew that Tory and her fiancé had ended their engagement. She'd heard that several people had received a card in the mail that had relayed the news the wedding was off. Since that time, she hadn't seen Tory around much. Occasionally her neighbor came by when she was out walking Edison in the stretch of woods between them, but it was always short and impersonal.

"Oh, that explains it," he said.

"Explains what?"

"She said something weird about visual stimuli when I covered your chicken with my shirt. She's a science person." He said it like it was a disease. Tansy couldn't stop her smile.

She hobbled to the fridge and pulled out the vegetable soup Tory had made for her. "Well, I guess she's a bit odd in a nerdy way but nice enough. She adopted Edison not long ago and has been trying to train him. He's like a regular male and has a mind of his own....and an inordinate interest in chickens."

"Well, she's pretty."

Was that interest in her nephew's voice? "I thought you were dating Kelsey Swank?"

Kris looked surprised. "No. I went on tour with her, but she's with her guitarist."

"The gossip magazines linked you two." Secretly Tansy was glad. She'd watched Kelsey perform several times and, while the gal was pretty as a shiny penny, she had a slickness to her that didn't sit right with Tansy. She couldn't see down-to-earth Kris with someone who seemed, well, insincere and overly ambitious. Then again, her nephew had hit it big, so she wasn't certain that the shine of all that glitters had worn off on him a bit.

Kris made a face. "You believe gossip magazines?"

"Of course not. I just wondered. That Kelsey's a hot number."

"Well, I'm not seeing anyone. And I'm not interested in your neighbor. That would be weird. All I was saying is that she's attractive in a wholesome sort of way."

Tansy limped over to the stove. "I guess."

Kris jumped up. "What am I doing sitting here? Let me heat that up, Aunt T. You sit and rest."

"I can heat up soup. What do you think? I can't take care of myself?" Tansy pointed toward the chair. "You sit."

Kris hesitated, and she could tell he wanted to argue, but he turned back and sank into the chair. "I should have already sent someone to help you. You're getting too—"

"Watch it," Tansy interrupted, jabbing her pointer finger toward him. "And I'm fine. Don't need no one poking around here. I've taken care of myself for years and I ain't stopping now."

She felt his eyes on her. She was seventy-three years old but didn't feel it. Well, most days. Climbing onto the tractor to bush hog the back field and weed-eating around the old barn tired her out on good days, but most of the other chores she'd handled competently if not quickly. The broken leg had slowed her down, but she wasn't going to admit that to anyone. She managed, and the leg would heal.

"I'm not saying you can't take care of yourself," Kris said, his voice holding what she knew to be respect and caution. The boy wasn't stupid. "But the place is hard to take care of when you're...uh..."

"Careful," she reminded.

"What I'm trying to say is that I am here to help you do a few things."

"Good. I got a list," she said, pouring the soup into the pot and turning on the burner. "You can start by getting the bread from the bread box and popping it into the toaster. Tomorrow you can go into town and get what you need to paint the soffits and fix that railing."

Kris blinked a few times.

"Well, you said you were here to help me do a few things."

Her nephew nodded. "Uh, sure."

"Then like I said, I got a list a mile long, and since your hands work, I'll give 'em something to do. And while you're doing them, maybe you'll think up a song or two. That's how I used to do my writing. I put my body to work and my mind followed." Tansy sank into the chair opposite him, feeling quite suddenly that her get-up-and-go had gotten up and left. Her hopping after Edison had tired her out and her leg now ached.

Kris rose and walked to the bread box. "I've been stuck."

"Well, it's a good thing you've come home."

He turned and walked toward the toaster. "Why's that?"

"'Cause home is the best place to find what you've been searching for."

Kris set his overnight duffel on the bed—the same bed he'd slept in until he'd graduated from E.G. Roth High School—then sank into the rolling desk chair where he'd once done trig into the wee hours of the night. Never used stupid trigonometry yet.

His room hadn't changed much. Aunt Tansy had pulled down the sports posters and packed away his trophies, but the same navy coverlet and Civil War battlefield site posters still decorated the small bedroom. He switched on the familiar lamp on the bedside table and looked around.

Home.

His aunt had suggested this was the place to find what he was looking for, but he wasn't sure how that could happen. Being here made him feel like that angry boy who'd packed his bags and his old guitar and headed for Nashville, head full of dreams and a notebook full of songs he'd written. What a schmuck he'd been. He'd thought becoming a country music superstar would be so easy.

With his aunt's decree on how he was a fool ringing in his ears, he'd driven away from Trabeau Farms, his resolve unmoving. He'd come back and make her eat crow when he proved her wrong.

When he'd struck out for Nashville after four years at Mississippi State and a degree in Business Agriculture, his dream of getting a recording contract seemed highly probable and easily grasped. After all, his college band had booked gig after gig all over the south. They'd made decent money, which helped him put a down payment on an apartment and buy a second-hand truck that had less than 200K miles on it. His former bandmates wished him well as they settled into the careers their college majors dictated, and he drove away without a second glance in his rearview mirror, leaving behind what Aunt Tansy had declared to be his legacy. His aunt had not wished him well. She'd been madder than a wet hen.

He'd gotten a job waiting tables at a Nashville landmark bar, auditioned with a cover band, and registered as a songwriter. After a few short months, he'd put together a catalog of songs he'd written and managed to publish one with a reputable company. When Kilby Stewart recorded "Summer Daze," Kris thought his ship had come in. Unfortunately, the track ended up not getting any play time and his royalty check was less than his tips from waiting tables on a good night. Welcome to Bruising Reality 101.

Years faded into years, some better than others. He wrote some songs with some top-notch Nashville writers, even working with some of the industry's hottest talent, but nothing he wrote ever broke out. His first band, Southwind, toured and put together an album fraught with growing pains that went nowhere. He left that band and put together a new one called County Line and started touring, writing, and saving up for recording studio time.

Last year he put a solo EP on Soundcloud, started a hard press to build up his online presence, and called in a favor from Charlie Choo, the syndicated host at WSIX in Nashville. Charlie played his single "Good Time Baby" on the newcomers show and the requests started pouring in. His song downloads quadrupled in five minutes' time. Six months later he signed with Strata Records and recorded his first solo album, *A Simple Dream.* "Good Time Baby" went number one and stayed in the top twenty for three months.

And now he was set to record in a month or so, but everything felt intangible. His only lifeline was the ability to put his own stamp on the album, but his muse had packed a bag and left for an extended stay in No Words Land. A stay that might mean he'd have none of his own songs on the second album. A second album that would probably sound nothing like his first. A second album with songs that sounded more Taylor Swift than Toby Keith. Kris had a panicky feeling he might go from "up and comer" to "down and goner."

So, after talking to his therapist, he'd canceled everything on his calendar and booked a remote cabin in Texas where he prayed he could focus on writing, but before he could relax, he had to get Tansy squared away. He could no longer leave her here in a falling down house.

Sinking onto his boyhood bed, he dialed his manager Preston Kammer's office.

"Preston Kammer's office. Can you hold?" said the office assistant.

No. I can't hold. But instead he said, "Tell him this is Kris Trabeau, and I'll hold."

He listened to half a Marin Morris song before his manager said, "Hey, Kris, what's up, man?"

"I read the Martin endorsement proposal, and I'm worried that—"

"I'm handling it, KT. No worries," Preston said, sounding like he always did—confident.

"Yeah. Okay. But did you talk to Nick? Did you tell him I had some concerns about the demos they sent? I mean, I know those guys write hits, but those tracks just don't seem to fit me. I'm really worried, Pres. I mean, really—"

"What do you pay me for, KT?" Preston interrupted, "Let me do my job. Your label knows what fans want. They know what sells. How many hits have they had this year? Dozens upon dozens. We signed with them for a reason."

"Have you listened to what they sent? It sounds like pop."

"They think you can cross over, Kris. That's a good thing. Trust me. Trust them. Okay?"

"Okay." Kris sighed, wanting to feel soothed but failing to achieve the peace he craved. His gut had been in knots for weeks. Kris had gone through a ton of songs and none of the ones they liked for him felt right. His first album had been raw, yearning, reminiscent of George Strait's *Chill of an Early Fall*, one of his favorites, but the label seemed to envision something more current, upbeat with clever lyrics over profundity. So the songs he contributed had to reflect who he was and wanted to be as an artist.

"Where are you? Texas?" Preston asked.

"No. I had to stop in Mississippi."

"Why?"

"My aunt. Remember?" Preston had been the one to suggest The Hermitage Retirement community right outside Nashville in lovely Henderson, Tennessee. The facility boasted a movie theatre, dance classes, and a huge community vegetable garden. Dancing fountains out front paired with golf cart trails and four-star restaurants made The Hermitage a much-sought-after community for retirees. His Aunt Tansy would be safe at the gated facility that boasted around-the-clock care, a 24-hour physician on call, and security cameras. He just had to figure out how to get her to consider joining The Hermitage way of life.

"Oh, yeah. Teensy."

"Tansy. And you're sure they got my deposit? Because

there's a waiting list. I'm going to try and talk her into moving at the first of the year. At least by early spring."

"Done and done, worrywart. What's wrong with you? You're micromanaging a micromanager. Get some sweet tea and go sit on the porch. Isn't that what you guys like to do down there?"

Kris smiled. "Yep, right after we run our coon dogs and shoot at possums."

"You don't have to be sarcastic. You know I'm from Philly. I don't know a coon dog from a poodle." He heard cars honking in the background and could tell his manager had him on Bluetooth and was likely leaving his office and navigating Nashville traffic, which had swelled as Christmas approached. "I just looked at the email from the administrator at The Hermitage and your deposit will hold to the end of the month. They'll want a lease agreement signed and a move-in date scheduled by the first of the year. So get your aunt on board and those songs ready for the album. Tick tock, tick tock."

Kris hung up, his manager's words echoing in his ears. *Tick Tock. Tick Tock.*

He had half a song written. Half. And he suspected it needed to be scrapped.

"Kris?" his aunt called up the stairs. "I made some hot cocoa. Come on down and bring your guitar. I've been picking on something that you may like."

Her words were like a shot of calm to his troubled soul. Aunt Tansy had been the person who'd taught him to play the guitar, igniting his love for picking and composing. His aunt had written more than her fair share of the folk songs the Mississippi Travelers had recorded back in the mid-sixties, but she'd grown up adoring country music and knew more about the history of country, folk, and rock than anyone else he knew. She loved music, but she despised the music business. She'd been very vocal about what chasing that dream could do to a person. She'd told him it would bring him a bad end.

Still, maybe playing the way he used to with Aunt Tansy would help him get unstuck. Focus on the music and not the business. He needed to do what Preston had suggested. Leave the business to his manager. Kris had come to Trabeau Farms with a specific purpose, but maybe he'd also come here because he needed something more than a change for Tansy. Maybe here he could remember the origin of his music.

He grabbed his Martin acoustic case and headed to the door. "Coming."

Chapter Three

"LET'S DO THESE PROBLEMS ON the white board, Javarius. Maybe seeing it up there will help things click," Tory said, walking to the board mounted on the wall and taking a dry erase marker from the tray. "Adding fractions is harder than multiplying them, but once you have it, you have it."

Javarius plopped into the rolling chair, his brown eyes watching as she wrote the problem from his study guide on the board. He fingered the end of one of his braids and said, "I knew how to do it in class."

"You'll get it," Tory said, injecting confidence into her voice. She'd asked around about Javarius and the center director had relayed that he had moved more than ten times in his short life, had a constant stream of shifting guardians, and a dizzying array of disruption—all of which had affected his educational journey. Tory was determined to help him catch up as much as she could in the two hours she spent several days a week at Common Connection, a non-profit community center in Rankin County.

Tory had first started volunteering as a teen at a similar after school program in her hometown of Morning Glory, which sat twenty-two miles north of Charming. When she left Jackson to take the position of science department head at E. G. Roth High School in Charming, she was pleased to discover that Valerie and Mac Whiting had opened a similar facility there. Tory had immediately signed up to tutor during the week. She'd seen firsthand the results of the afternoon program on the youth in her hometown and knew that Common Connection could be just as effective. She'd been at the center for over two years and loved seeing her work pay off.

She uncapped the marker. "Okay, first thing we have to do is find the least common multiple."

"What's that?" Javarius asked, his forehead crinkling adorably.

"Hey, Tory, you got a second?" Valerie asked from the doorway of the tutoring room. The cacophony in the background made Tory hesitate. Javarius would get distracted by the children who'd already finished their assignments if she paused in her lesson.

"We really need to finish this."

"Won't take but a second," Valerie said giving her the patented Valerie smile that made everyone fall in line. No one could resist Valerie.

The center director had a wide smile, dimples, and beautiful dark skin. Her eyes shone with intelligence and compassion. She loved to wear bright colors and big earrings, and when she wore her hair up, it accentuated her elegant long neck. With a booming voice and eclectic taste in music, art, and Netflix choices, Valerie Whiting was Tory's biggest champion and closest friend.

"Here, J. Look up least common multiples, and see if you can figure out why we need to find them to do the problems on your sheet. I'll be right back." Tory picked up the basic math skills workbook and handed it to Jarvarius, who glanced past Valerie into the common area with eager eyes. He hated having to do private tutoring, but it was working. He'd pulled his grade up from a D to a C in just one month.

Tory followed Valerie past the children playing video and board games. A few of the other tutoring room doors were closed, indicating some of the college students from the nearby junior college were also privately tutoring a few of the other children. Valerie waited for Tory to step into her cheerful office, replete with paintings done by the center children during summer camp and a mason jar full of what actually looked to be weeds that had probably been gathered at the school bus stop that afternoon.

"What's up?" Tory asked, as Valerie closed the door.

Valerie sighed. "Well, the usual. Too much to do and too little time to do it in."

Tory smiled and sank into the chair across from Valerie's second-hand desk. "I know how that feels."

"So about Tinsel..." Valerie rubbed a hand over her face.

"I have my tickets. Think my mom might end up being my date." Tory had bought her tickets for the non-profit fundraiser to benefit Common Connection when they'd first announced the date nine months ago. Of course, she'd bought two—one for her and one for Patrick. By the time the benefit rolled around, they would have been married for two weeks. She'd bounced around the happy thought of bidding on the auction as Mrs. Patrick Odom-Jones. But that had been before Patrick had announced he was moving to Massachusetts. Before he'd relayed how his feelings for her had faded away. Before he wanted a blank slate, a new start, and a relationship with the biochemistry doctoral student he'd met at a symposium last year. Tory felt like she'd been hit by a garbage truck and left for dead on No-Longer-Your-Future Road.

The icing on the cake was when he gave back the key to

the house they'd painstakingly restored…and asked for her to return the diamond solitaire he'd given her.

That's why she wasn't celebrating this year.

No tree. No holly. No flipping eggnog. She just couldn't seem to find her normal Christmas cheer. Her mood for anything festive had left on the heartache bus and hadn't made its way back. But she wasn't going to miss the holiday benefit, mostly because she knew Valerie and Mac expected her to go.

"That's great," Valerie said, thumbing through a stack of papers. "Your mama's so sweet. She crocheted a gorgeous shawl for the silent auction."

"She's pretty great. So what do you need from me? Work the registration table or something?"

Valerie looked up. "Not exactly. I was actually hoping you'd be my co-chair."

"Co-chair? But Tinsel's in two weeks. *Two. Weeks.*"

"I know, but I can't handle everything. See?" Valerie picked up a check, her agitation growing. "Here's Vince Vermeer and the Twilights' check. It's been returned. You know why? He didn't realize that he'd booked us on the night he's supposed to play his niece's wedding in Jackson. Now we don't have a band."

"No band?" Tory repeated.

Valerie groaned and rubbed a hand over her eyes. "I know, and a lot of people come for the musical program. It's always fantastic with sing-alongs and cute dance numbers. Vince even dressed in a Santa suit and rapped ''Twas the Night before Christmas.' But now—now, we have…zilch. I just need you to take over the entertainment and the silent auction. That's it."

That's it? Tory wanted to run from the room. Go to the holiday benefit and drink watered-down punch? Check.

Squeeze herself into her one black cocktail dress? Check. Buy something she absolutely didn't need from the silent auction? Check. Be the co-chair? Um, not so fast. "Well, I don't think we can find a band that's not booked. It's Christmas."

Valerie gave her a flat look. "I know, but we have to. We can't just feed our guests pork tenderloin and hustle them for money. We need some sort of entertainment in order for them to open their checkbooks. This is our one major fundraiser for the year. The center has to have funds to operate. Without this annual event, we can't help the children we have, much less grow our community involvement."

Tory saw the panic in Valerie's eyes and every excuse she'd considered for saying no fled. Worry and stress etched the director's face, and it hurt Tory to see her friend so frazzled. "I guess I can try."

"Will you?" Valerie clasped her hands together and closed her eyes, her shoulders sinking in what looked like extreme relief. "I mean, I would be so, so grateful if you would help me. You're so good organizing things and pulling rabbits out of hats when we need you to. I knew you'd be perfect."

Tory sucked in a deep breath and then released it. "Okay, then. Um, I'll need the list of all the bands you've already tried. Oh, and the list of auction items. I'll get those things organized, touch base with outstanding contacts, and start calling around to see if we can nab a decent band for the event."

Valerie shuffled through the stacks on her desk. "Here's one folder—it has all the auction items we've collected and the names of people who still need to be called. Ignore the chicken scratch. And here's the list of bands. Not many really. Vince pretty much does it every year, but the mayor gave me a list a few years back."

Tory took the crumpled sheet, disappointed to see only five names on the typed list. She stood. "I'll start as soon as I get home."

Valerie walked around the desk and pulled her into a hug. "Thank you, Tory. I don't think you know what this means to me."

"I do. I know how hard you work, and I'm happy to help you." The word "happy" stuck in her throat but she choked it down. Her other words were true. Valerie and Mac had left a comfy home and good jobs to move into this community, so they could be available for the children in the neighborhood who needed breakfast or a ride to games or practice. She and Mac were practically surrogate parents for about forty kids in the rural part of Charming. Tory could make this small sacrifice.

Valerie gave her a final squeeze. "I'm so glad."

Tory caught sight of a huge box of chocolates out of the corner of her eye, along with a trashcan filled with little brown crinkly wrappers. "Are you stress-eating chocolates?"

Valerie glanced at the box. "Yep. Want some?"

Tory laughed. "Yeah, I think I might need a few."

Tansy tried not to panic at the sight of the brochure in the side pocket of Kris's duffel bag. She'd come upstairs to get a few things from her room, an emery board and a couple of wool cardigans now that the nights were finally cool. Kris's door had been ajar, making her heart happy. She pushed open the door and smiled at the wrinkles on the bed. The boy had never been a slave to neatness. His guitar sat in the stand by the window and his sunglasses and keys sat on the bedside table. Her boy was home. Finally. She'd just been about to turn on her crutch and leave when she saw the papers sticking out of his duffle bag. A shiny brochure with bright colors.

She'd pulled it out, not thinking twice about prying.

The Hermitage?

Sounded like a monastery. Or a haunted gothic mansion. Or, wait....an assisted living center?

She opened the brochure and saw the verbiage: 24-hour care, activities designed to keep aging parents active, Alzheimer's unit. Her heart dropped into her toes.

"What the devil's he thinking?" she said out loud.

But she knew.

Kris hadn't come home because he'd done the thing he said he'd do—make it in the business. He'd come because he thought she couldn't take care of herself anymore. Dang leg. She'd been so careful to make good decisions as she aged. She'd avoided salt, rode her stationary bike, and started using her step stool to dust the fans rather than balancing in the middle of the bed. One loose porch slat sticking up had sent her flying and crashing into the marble table holding her Christmas cactus. Her leg snapped like a toothpick. With no one to help her, she'd tried to crawl back into the house. She was lucky that Joe Addison, her mailman, had heard her involuntary screams each time she inched forward, and had driven his mail truck down the long drive to find her lying half in the house, half on the porch, nearly delirious with the pain.

Tansy shoved the brochure back into the duffle pocket and glanced at the door. She'd sent Kris out to the barn to check the battery on the tractor. The back pasture had needed haying for over a month, but when she'd tried to climb onto the tractor a few weeks back, she'd nearly fallen and broken her other leg. She suspected the tractor was dead from disuse.

Just like her. Not working. But she would be soon. She didn't need to go to a stinkin' retirement home that sounded like a horror movie hotel.

Tansy pushed the bag back into place and caught sight of an official-looking envelope behind the brochure.

She really shouldn't open anything more. To dig out that brochure was bad enough.

Tansy had always been intentional in giving Kris his privacy when he lived with her. She remembered how strangled she'd felt as a teen girl growing up with parents who had regulated every aspect of her life. They loved her, but the constant pressure of their proverbial thumb on the back of her neck had driven Tansy to do something she'd often regretted, run off with Jack Prosper and his cousin Vinnie. Oh, there was more to it than just trying to escape her parents' strict rules. There was the music. And there was the way Jack took her breath away.

But that was a lifetime ago.

Presently there was an envelope practically begging her to look inside. *Open me.*

She moseyed over to the window and spied her nephew lugging the spent battery to the old farm truck parked beneath the garage attached to the barn. Then she turned back to the bag. The envelope stared back at her.

It would be wrong.

But maybe just one peek. After all, now that she knew about the proposed retirement la la land for washed up old birds who tripped over porch floor boards, she needed to make sure there weren't other surprises awaiting her.

Quick as spit, she rushed to the bag, pulled out the envelope, and slid open the flap tucked inside.

The thick papers inside were from Sullivan-Lambert Realty. The first page had her name, the farm address—she ran her finger down—then Kris's name, and a 90-day guarantee. An agreement to list the farm for sale?

Her heart squeezed in her chest and panic burbled up.

Sell the farm?

Was he insane?

The front door slammed shut, and Tansy jammed the papers back into the envelope and tucked the flap back inside. Then she shoved the envelope behind the brochure for the senior living retirement place that frankly looked horrible. Who wanted to practice sun salutation on the front lawn? Or take shopping trips to outlet malls? Or play mahjong with new friends? Tansy didn't need new friends. She had plenty of old ones she didn't care to see, so why would she want to saddle herself with new ones?

Situating the duffel back on the desk chair, she hobbled toward the hallway.

"Aunt Tansy?" Kris said from the top of the stairs just as she pulled the door back as it was.

Drat. That boy was fast.

Tansy tried to look nonchalant and not like she was drowning in incredulity at what she'd discovered. Her heart galloped and she felt panic knocking against her chest. "Oh, hey. How's the battery?"

"Dead. I'll have to get another one." He glanced toward the cracked door of his room as if he suspected she'd been poking through his things. Well, she hadn't intended to snoop, had she? She'd just seen the top of the brochure and pulled it out without thinking. And because he'd obviously had some kind of intention of presenting her with that nonsense, she had to go through the envelope, hadn't she? Totally accidental snooping that was merited.

"I figured as much." She glanced at his room. "Oh, I just thought I heard something in your room. Came up here to get a few cardigans. Starting to get cool, thank goodness."

"Yeah, I could tell a cold front was coming in." He glanced at the open door. "I came inside to tell you that Tory and Edison are here with an apology. It looks like pound cake, which is a great way to apologize for her dog almost eating your chickens."

"He doesn't want to eat them. He's just lonely and thinks they're his friends. Loretta and the girls aren't interested in his kind of friendship. Let's go downstairs." She hobbled toward the stairs.

"Don't you need to get your sweater?"

Drat. That's why she'd made the difficult climb upstairs. Instead she'd found something that had taken the breath from her chest. She couldn't leave the farm. Somehow she had to make him understand that this land was part of who she was. But how to do that? Her mind raced, keeping time with her racing heart.

"Right. My sweater," she said.

A few minutes later, they went out onto the porch where a cold north wind and Edison danced around their feet. The dog looked at them as if they were his long-lost masters and he owed them a heap-load of doggy kisses. Kris smiled and patted the dog.

"Hi," Tory said, holding out a foil-wrapped loaf tied with a cheerful red bow. "I wanted to say I'm sorry for Edison scaring your chicken."

Edison barked and bolted down the steps, scooping up

a stick and running back with it in his mouth. His dancing brown eyes screamed "Someone play with me!"

"Well, that's fine, but you've got to keep him under control, Tory." Tansy said, taking the proffered apology. She didn't mean to sound so harsh, but her emotions were somersaulting around like mutant clowns. Her world felt close to spinning out of control, echoing *sell the farm* and *come be a part of The Hermitage life.*

"I know, Miss Tansy. I know," Tory replied, throwing up her hands as Edison bounded toward her, stick in mouth, unbridled joy evident in every movement. Everything about that dog was unbridled—unlike his owner who looked very put together.

Tory wore a long, cranberry-colored sweater, dark tights and high black boots. Big hoops dangled at her ears, tangling in her curly brown hair. The biology teacher was a lovely woman, something her nephew seemed to notice as his gaze fell on Tory.

Hmm. Now that was interesting.

"We're going to practice what he learned this summer a bit more. He's still a big puppy and learning." Tory grabbed Edison by his collar. "It's been a long day. Time to go, boy."

"You want some hot spiced tea?" Tansy asked, not even knowing why. She didn't really want company, but something about the way Kris responded to her neighbor had her wondering. Pair that with a niggle that had hatched inside her brain as she rummaged through her closet upstairs, and she was scooting a rocker toward Tory.

How could she get Kris to abandon his intentions for her and the farm? Years ago when he'd left, she'd acknowledged that her failure to support his hare-brained dreams had damaged his attachment to her and the farm. The farm had become something he'd tolerated because he had to, and in one fell swoop she'd made him resent commitment, duty, and heritage.

She had to change his view of their homeplace while proving to Kris that she could take care of herself. He didn't know it, but Trabeau Farms was his true home. There would be no selling of the farm. No Trabeau would *ever* suggest tossing over something that had been in their family for four generations.

Deep inside, her nephew had to have a sense of what family and home meant. Kris had gotten turned around somehow and couldn't find due north. Trabeau Farms should be where his compass always led him. And if she could convince him to stay for more than just a couple of days, maybe he could see why home was more than just a word.

But how would she do it?

And then she remembered her memories from the day before. Christmas at the farm. The only way to turn the boy the right way was to remind him of the rich past, and with Christmas a few short weeks away, putting on an old-fashioned farm Christmas would be perfect. The only problem was she would need to convince Kris to skip Texas...and she would need some help pulling it off. Maybe the cute brunette and the fluffy mutt were part of the answer.

"Uh, I'm not sure—" Tory began, looking at the rocker before casting a glance back at her car.

"Go on and have some spiced tea with Tansy," Kris said, nodding toward his aunt. "I'll toss this stick for Edison in the side yard and wear him out for you. Looks like you had a long day."

Tory's forehead knitted together. "It's that obvious? I had Quiz Bowl practice, then tutoring at Common Connection.

I guess one cup would be nice. It's finally getting chilly. Plus, Edison loves to play fetch."

"What's Common Connection?" Kris asked, picking up the stick, ripping Edison's attention from Tory to the slobbery pecan wood.

"It's where I volunteer. We serve low-income families in the county, and I work specifically with the children—tutoring them for skills they may have missed in school. I love it."

Edison barked excitedly making Tansy plug her ears. Dang dog.

Kris grinned. "I want to know more, but Edison is telling me I will have to wait."

For the next few minutes Tory sat next to her neighbor in the rocker, sipping the fragrant spiced tea that Tansy made every autumn the way her own mama had years ago. The first sip always made Tansy miss her mama with sharp longing.

"I know Edison's a young, sweet pup, Tory, but he needs to have some sort of containment. Not just because of my chickens, but because he could get hurt." Tansy glanced at the woman sitting in the rocker next to her. Tory had been watching Kris and Edison with a half-smile on her face. "I don't mean to overstep. I know we haven't been close as neighbors, but neighbors look out for one another no matter what."

"I know you're right, Miss Tansy. Patrick was supposed to have a fence put in, but, well, that didn't happen. I should have taken care of it myself, but I haven't been myself for the last few months."

"I'm sorry about that, too, sugar. Sometimes a man doesn't know what he has. They can be pretty obtuse as a gender." Tansy eyed her nephew as he took the stick from Edison and hurled it as far as he could throw. "But if I'm honest, I think you're better off."

"I know that now," Tory said, cupping her tea with both hands, her face growing wistful. "Oddly enough, my heart didn't seem to hurt as much as my pride. I had everything in my life planned out and then with one sentence from him, everything went up in smoke. I was hurt, that's true, but I'm getting over it. Sorry if that's TMI."

"Don't worry, darling. I'm a good person to talk to, if I do say so myself. Sometimes you never get over heartache. Other times you do. Sometimes you find something better comes along, and if you had stuck with your original plan, you would have missed the really good things life has in store for you. I know. I had my heart broken once upon a time, too. I think everyone has, so we all understand when it takes a while to get your feet back beneath you." Tansy couldn't believe she'd admitted to heartache. She never talked about Jack and their dust-up with the Travelers much, mostly because it still hurt, but she wanted Tory to know that she wasn't alone.

"Thank you, Miss Tansy. That helps. And as for the fence, I've already talked to the Fields brothers about building one out back for me, but it won't be until the first of the year. Honestly, I'm a bit overwhelmed at the moment. Valerie talked me into co-chairing Tinsel with her. Now I have to find auction items and book the entertainment. In two weeks. Our band backed out at the last minute, and Gilda Brooks' nephew won't donate anymore of her artwork. Those paintings were always our biggest ticket items in the auction."

Tansy sipped her tea, her mind whirling like the pinwheels she used to skip around with as a girl. Tory needed something. Tansy needed something too. Maybe, just maybe, she could work a deal with her neighbor.

"I have a proposal for you, Tory," Tansy said after a few more seconds of thought. "One that will give you what you want, and me what I need."

Chapter Four

THE NEXT DAY, KRIS DIPPED his brush into the paint as Tansy strummed her guitar on the porch.

"I like that progression," he said as he carefully swiped across the eave.

"This one?" she asked, strumming the guitar again.

"Yeah. It sounds really good, a solid intro."

"It's similar to the one my friend Velda Osborn used on her first album. I like the balance. Fast, fast, slow. Fast, fast, slow. It's like an invitation. Come with me."

"And where are we going?" he asked, falling back into the game he had played with her as a boy, asking questions as they put together songs. Sometimes his aunt would pick out an entire melody before considering the lyrics. Other times she found concepts she liked and wrote the words before finding the right notes to accompany them. He'd inherited her erratic songwriting technique. He'd even once dreamed an entire stanza of a song.

"What does it sound like?" she asked, playing the progression again.

"Like an invitation to a show. A circus. No, a rodeo. Something exciting."

"Mmm, maybe," his aunt said, playing a reflection of the progression. Slow, slow, fast. Slow, slow, fast.

Just as he climbed down to move the ladder, Tory pulled

up. He found himself inordinately pleased for some odd reason, like seeing Tory was a nice way to cap off a productive day. He also found himself a bit disappointed that Edison wasn't with her. Of course, the exuberant dog would likely knock over the paint and cover everything in sight with white paw prints. The dog had an abundance of enthusiasm that grew on a guy…but maybe not when he had a gallon of white paint balancing on a ladder.

"Hey," Tory called as she climbed from the car. She wore a black wrap dress that fit snug around her waist and a pair of wedge pumps. Her hair was twisted into an updo, which frankly he was opposed to. The riot of curls softened her no-nonsense, analytical personality. She could probably grow on him, too. If he were in the market. Which he wasn't.

His career was his mistress and she was a demanding one. He'd given up pursuing anything serious with women because all the ones he'd dated had demanded more time than he could afford to give. They wanted him on their arms to attend benefits or fancy parties, and while he could do that for a few nights a month, the rest of the time he needed to work. Drama with women had led to disruptive discontent in his life, so now he smiled for pictures with female fans and took the occasional friend to dinner. And that was it for socializing with the fairer sex.

The thought of pursuing a relationship at this point in his career seemed nuts. He had way too much on his current plate and dessert wasn't an option. His eyes were fixed on his goal.

"Hey, Tory." His aunt rose and set the guitar in the adjacent rocker. "I'll go get that guitar for the auction."

"Oh, it's a guitar? Great." Tory smiled. He swore it made his day seem a bit brighter. She had a beautiful smile with straight, even, perfect white teeth.

"What guitar is this?" Kris asked as Tansy disappeared through the front door.

"Your aunt said she'd donate something from her days in her folk band."

"Really?" Kris cocked his head. "Well, that's surprising. She's pretty attached to her old guitars."

"Well, it's for a good cause. We're doing a benefit for the center. It's called Tinsel. It's right before Christmas and there's a silent auction." Tory pushed back a strand of curly hair that had escaped her bun and shrugged. "Tansy and I are trading favors."

"Trading favors?" His aunt had several guitars stored in cases in her bedroom closet. She rarely got them out, electing to play the Taylor she'd bought when she bought his first guitar. He always thought it was because strumming her old guitars made her sad. He didn't know much about her days with the folk group Mississippi Travelers other than she was an early member who was replaced after their first couple of albums. There was a lot of resentment there, and he'd wisely skipped around it.

Back in the mid-sixties, Tansy had toured the country playing festivals and college campuses. But something had happened, sending her back home to Charming. And she never left again or talked about what had cut her career so short. He knew she'd been in a relationship with a guy named Jack, and that he'd been in the Travelers, because he'd found some old letters once when he was looking for pictures of his parents for a project. He could have sworn that the yellowed paper was stained with tears.

But Kris never found out what happened. His aunt shared her love of creating and playing the guitar, but she'd been dead set against him ignoring his college degree and the farm and going to Nashville. They'd had a horrible fight the night before he left. He had never seen his aunt so furious. She'd told him Nashville would break him, and that if he went, he didn't need to ever come back.

He now understood she thought she was scaring him straight, but back then her lack of faith in him had broken something between them.

He'd left more determined than ever to prove to his aunt that he wasn't scared to try like she'd been. He'd said those words to her, watched the color drain from her face, and vowed that he *would* come back, but it wouldn't be until he had a fat contract in hand.

He hadn't expected it to take so long though.

Tory cleared her throat, jarring him out of the cobwebs in his mind. "Tansy wants to decorate for Christmas this year. Oh, and bake some kind of cookies her grandmother always made. And something about a home movie compilation. Essentially, she needs some help and I need a good auction item that will bring in money."

"Why does she need you to help her? I'm here. Well, for a while anyway."

"Because you've got your hands full with painting and fixing the porch railing," Tansy called out, pushing out the screen door while trying to balance on one crutch. In her hand, she carried one of the black guitar cases he'd often studied in the back of her closet. It was an electric guitar case, one of only two she had.

Kris hopped off the ladder, jogged up the steps and took the bulky guitar from his aunt. "Let me help you. What kind of guitar is this, anyway?"

Tansy stared at the case in his hand. "One that should bring a couple thousand dollars at least. Maybe more if you have anyone there who knows anything about music. Go ahead. Open it."

Tory climbed the steps and moved to stand beside him. He sucked in a deep breath, enjoying her girly scent. She smelled like springtime. Kris set the case on the marble table between the rockers and unlatched it. When he opened the case, he smiled.

A white Fender Stratocaster.

"Cool," he breathed, running a finger over the bridge. "What year?"

"1963," Tansy said, her voice snagging on emotion.

"Wait, there's an autograph. Jimi who?" Tory leaned in and peered at the whimsical signature.

Kris looked up at his aunt. "Seriously? A Jimi Hendrix signed Stratocaster?"

Tansy shrugged. "It'll bring in good money."

Tory snapped to attention. "Miss Tansy! You can't donate that! It's priceless."

Tansy smiled. "I can do what I want to do. I told you that if you would help me put on a Trabeau Farm Christmas, I would donate an auction item that would be a big ticket. That thing's been sitting in my closet for years not doing one dang bit of good. What am I keeping it for? To gather dust? Jimi wouldn't appreciate his guitar being shut up like that. Things have a need to be used, and when they're not, they lose some of their magic. Whoever buys it may not play it, but they can let people participate in some way in the music Jimi made on this guitar."

"This is crazy." Kris shook his head, amazed he'd not known she had this guitar. Well, he'd known, but not that it was Jimi Hendrix's guitar. "What did he record on this one?"

"I don't know," Tansy said, plucking one of the strings. "It was a studio guitar. He recorded a lot of stuff up in New York City at Juggy Murray's studio. They kept this one and another like it there for when he came in."

"How did you get it?" Kris asked, looking down at the chipped paint on the edges. This was a guitar that had been well-used. He liked them this way – ones that had been played up one side of a studio and down the other. The passion poured into it transferred to the next person. This guitar had been the vehicle for greatness. "I mean, you knew Jimi Hendrix? You never said anything."

"Some things are better left in the past, honey." His aunt's eyes grew misty and Kris wondered for the umpteenth time what had happened long ago to his aunt.

"But your past was…kinda cool. You knew icons in music."

Aunt Tansy's mouth twitched. "I crossed paths with a few people who went on to become quite famous. Jimi loved music. His guitars became living things in his hands. It was something to see him play."

Dampness glistened in Tory's eyes. "Miss Tansy, you can't do this. It's too much."

"Hogwash. I just told you that I can and will. It should fetch a good price, so advertise what you have. Tickets are still on sale, and if you can get Dandy Grigsby to do an article on the guitar, you'll sell a few more to some collectors. Usually, I would say don't let them drive up the price so that regular folks can't afford it, but since this is for your center, I say let them duke it out."

Tory gave Tansy an awkward half hug. "I don't know how I will ever pay you back for this. What I'm doing isn't enough."

Tansy patted Tory's back. "It's exactly what I want to do. And tomorrow we'll get started on the decorations. I'll get Kris to pull the boxes down from the attic so we can go through them. My mama kept everything, so some things will likely need to be tossed, but there are gorgeous glass antique ornaments and embroidered tablecloths and napkins. Oh, and my great grandmother's porcelain angel. It's been so long since I did a real Christmas."

Tory dropped her hands. "I may not be in the spirit of things, but going through all those boxes actually sounds fun. I'm definitely getting the better end of the deal."

"So you say now," Tansy said, closing the cover of the guitar.

"I'll give you twenty thousand for it," Kris said, unable to rip his gaze from the case. It was a lot of money, but it would go to a good cause. And he'd have a Jimi Hendrix-signed guitar, one that the man had wailed on.

"Oh, no you don't," Tansy said, wagging a finger at him. "You want it, go to the auction."

"But I won't be here," he said.

Tansy raised her eyebrows. "Maybe it's a good enough reason to stay. Seems to me that you haven't been here in so long you've forgotten what home is. Tory's going to help me recreate a good old-fashioned farm Christmas just like my mama used to do, and maybe you'll find you like celebrating Christmas at the farm. And since Tory's in charge of the auction and entertainment, you can give her some suggestions. I'm sure some of your fancy Nashville friends would donate something, right? Or maybe you know a band that doesn't mind traveling south for a good cause?"

Kris looked at Tory. "You need some help?"

Her face pinked, which was cute. "Well, I wouldn't want to impose, but honestly I'm under a time crunch. The event is next Friday night."

"Yeah, I'd say you have a ticking clock." Just as he did

on writing the songs for the album. That was a huge piano hanging over his head by an unraveling rope. "I can make a few calls. Maybe score some tickets to some shows? And I know a few bands, but I'll be honest, most don't schedule gigs that close to Christmas, and if they do, they've likely been booked for months."

"Yeah, I'm sensing that," Tory said, shrugging her shoulders. "I made a few calls today and my short list is now non-existent."

"Give Kris your number, darling. He can be good at getting things done. He's a lot of things, but lazy ain't one." Tansy snapped the guitar case closed.

"Sounds like a good lyric," Kris said, pleased at his aunt's words. Which were true. He didn't sit on anything, which was good and bad. Sometimes it led to him pushing too hard. Which led to falling off a ledge and landing hard. He'd done that too often throughout his career. Hustling, hustling, hustling only to end up with nothing to show for it.

"I've been told I'm good at lyrics," Aunt Tansy said with a quirk of her lips.

Tory held out her hand.

"What?" Kris said,

"Give me your phone and I'll put in my number, that way you can text me the info."

Kris entered his password and surrendered his iPhone. "I'll make some calls, but don't get your hopes up."

At the moment he uttered those words, he realized that he could likely be her backup. Of course, that would mean canceling his rental in East Texas and staying in Mississippi. He wasn't going to do that. He needed some peace and quiet in order to find the words, the sound, all the things that seemed to be missing from the songs his label had sent his way. The sinking feeling in his gut urged him to give Tory help without sacrificing his original goal of solitude.

"Don't worry. I'm used to disappointment," Tory said. She wrinkled her nose. "Well, that sounds sort of pathetic. I guess what I'm saying is I expect I won't find a good band on this short of notice, but any help you can give is appreciated."

"So if you don't find a band, do you have a backup plan?" he asked.

"Well, I heard Mavis Parks took some belly dancing lessons and is up for showing off her moves. And Bubba Howell plays the banjo but only knows two songs so it could get repetitious. Oh, and my mama said my daddy is available to read some of his poetry—*Musings of a Mail Carrier.*" Tory shook her head, her gray eyes sparkling in a charming way. "It could be a humdinger of a Tinsel this year."

His aunt looked pointedly at him. He knew what she wanted. She expected him to bail Tory out by volunteering to sing for her. But she might as well take that pointed look and direct it back at herself because she was a musician, too. Of course, she'd professed stage fright and wouldn't even sing in the church choir much less go on stage as a solo act. Didn't matter though, he wasn't going to be here next weekend.

"Well, I better leave you to your painting. Edison needs to be fed." Tory handed his phone back to him and lifted the guitar case.

"Let me help you," Kris said, taking the case from her. His hand brushed against hers and he had an odd inclination to tuck the curls that had escaped her updo behind her ear. Weird, but not unexpected. She was attractive and he was a guy who hadn't really thought about romance or kissing a girl in a while. Okay, he'd thought about it but hadn't acted on anything.

Tory surrendered the case to him and followed him to her sensible car. "Thank you for helping. That's nice of you."

"I'm pretty sure Aunt Tansy would tan my hide if I didn't do what I could to help this community. It's a good thing you're doing. I can't promise anything, but I'll do my best." He set the guitar in the backseat, wishing he didn't have to let it go. He really wanted that guitar.

"Still, it's nice of you," Tory said as he straightened.

He turned toward her and smiled. Her eyes softened a little, her lips parted. Interest. Which pleased him as much as it alarmed him. Because he liked her and was so tempted to touch her. But he wouldn't.

His goal for being in Charming was clear—get Aunt Tansy to agree to move to Nashville. And if he could talk her into selling the farm, all the better. Sure, the farm had been in their family for a long time, but it was no longer a working farm and it would be a drain on finances and too much trouble to keep it up. Change happened. And it was time to move forward and embrace the future he'd made for himself, and bring Aunt Tansy along with him. The Hermitage would cater to her every whim. She could finally take the pottery classes she'd always dreamed about and have good nutritious meals instead of the cheese and crackers he suspected she ate most days.

"No problem," he said, stepping back so she could slide behind the steering wheel. She clicked her seatbelt, and he shut her door, slapping a hand on the top of the car as she fired the engine.

Tory backed out of the drive and he gave a little wave before turning back to Tansy, the porch and the painting awaiting him.

"You could have volunteered to do the entertainment for

her. You know that would bring hundreds more people to the benefit," Tansy said, resettling herself on the front porch rocker.

"And so could you," he said, climbing back up the ladder and picking up the brush that had semi-dried while he'd been chatting.

"I don't perform anymore. You know that," she said. She picked the guitar up and started strumming the earlier progression.

"Well, I'll be gone. I'm going to Texas. I have to," he said.

Aunt Tansy mumbled something that sounded like "We'll see about that," but that could have been the wind in the dying day.

Chapter Five

"I READ THIS ONE ALREADY," BRIA Smalls said, her pointer finger emphatic as she stabbed the cover of the book. "And all these others. I read 'em all."

Tory smiled. "Well, you're just a super reader, Bria."

Bria Smalls was a tough cookie to figure out. Sometimes she barely spoke at all, others she seemed almost resentful. Today was the latter. Her golden-brown eyes crackled in indignation and she crossed her chubby arms, sinking down into the bucket chair of the reading room. Likely it wasn't just the lack of books that bothered her. "We never have any good books. These are baby books."

Tory perused the offerings. "Hmm…I do believe you're right. Maybe I can do something about that."

She'd been trying to figure out a gift for the center's students. With so many kids, she couldn't afford individual presents, but a few new books for the older children and some puzzles for the younger ones could be the perfect solution.

Of course, Tory had shoved that particular to-do to the back of her list the moment she agreed to help Valerie with the benefit. That afternoon before coming to the center, she'd called every band on the contact list Kris had sent her that morning and had come up empty-handed. Most of the bands or singers were very regretful. They thought it was a terrific cause, but they were obligated elsewhere. She had gotten one maybe. But the lead singer was pregnant and her due date was the exact date of the benefit. Didn't seem promising, and she couldn't imagine the poor woman trying to entertain the crowd while simultaneously trying not to go into labor.

Bria interrupted her troubled thoughts, her eyes narrowed. "*You* gonna buy them?"

"Buy what?"

"New books." The "duh" was understood.

"Maybe I will."

"Are you rich or something?" Bria asked.

"No. I'm a teacher. I'm pretty sure that's the opposite of rich," she said, giving Bria a smile that she hoped might soften the girl. Bria's expression didn't change.

"Most teachers are pretty rich. They drive nice cars and wear good clothes," Bria glanced down at her own faded uniform shirt. The hem of her pants was frayed and her tennis shoes had seen better years. The child had been placed in the foster system when her mother had gone to prison for possession and distribution on a third offense. Tory didn't know the foster family caring for Bria, but she knew the child's life wasn't easy. Guilt flooded her. She wanted to wrap her arms around the chubby eleven-year-old but knew her hug wouldn't be welcome.

"You're right in a way, Bria. I'm very thankful I have a job and can afford a car. Because that car brings me here where I can hang out with you."

"Why you wanna hang with us? I wouldn't." Bria shuffled her feet against the carpet, averting her eyes from Tory.

"Because I love you guys and I want to help."

"Oh." Bria seemed to fight against showing any emotion. Most of the kids at the center were good at running from goodness and hope, as if it were too much to ask for.

Tory rose from where she crouched by the bookshelf. "Why don't we work on some reading practice tests in the computer room? You're good at those, and it will earn you another star for today."

Bria shrugged. "Sure. I guess."

They went out in the chaotic common room where a few kids played video games, a few worked on cleaning out their backpacks with Valerie, and two of the boys were dancing to music thumping through a cracked iPhone.

Jay and CJ were essentially old-school breakdancing, laughing at each other as they showed their moves, which were honestly pretty good. Tory high-fived them as she moved past them, opening the door to the computer center.

Only three kids were in there—Brittany, Jaylyn, and Shay—and they were watching YouTube and singing along with a popular female singer who looked familiar, but who Tory couldn't place.

"Ladies, you're supposed to be working in here," Tory said in her teacher voice.

Their voices trailed off as they clicked off the YouTube video.

"Sorry, Miss O," Shay muttered, her eyes downcast.

"I know," Tory said, pulling out a chair for Bria. "It's hard to concentrate on work after a long school day, and your voices are so pretty I'm tempted to let y'all go on singing. But since this is a study room, I think I better not."

"We just needed to see something real quick," Jaylyn said, picking at her painted nails. "We're just practicing for the talent show in January."

"Oh, there's a talent show?" Tory asked, logging in on the computer so Bria could do some practice on standardized testing. Bria ignored the girls. Mostly because those three hadn't been very inviting of the often frank and not as friendly Bria. Tory had been trying to include all the girls in a few activities, so the trio of more popular girls could see beyond Bria's bristly nature.

"They're having a talent show at the school," Brittany said, tossing her hair over her shoulder. "We got an act together. The prize is $150. We're gonna win it."

"Great," Tory said, absentmindedly, because her mind had started spinning. *What if...*

Bria logged into her account and started the program. Tory slid in next to her, doing a mental accounting of the center's students. Eric played in the school orchestra. Clarinet, maybe? Jack was quite the comedian—he could do impersonations of tons of celebrities. His impressions kept everyone at the center laughing when he handed out snacks. The two break-dancers, the girls' trio, and maybe a few others recruited from the high school could fill in some spaces. The drama club was practicing *Bye, Bye Birdie* for a winter production. Perhaps a musical number from that? Charming was loaded with talented kids. Maybe, just maybe, she could provide entertainment for Tinsel after all.

But it would be really hard. Two weeks to put together a variety act? And how to sift through who would be good enough to participate and who might be, well, grasping at straws with their talent? And would people think it was hokey? Or would they find it heartwarming to see the very kids they were helping be part of the benefit?

"I have to go speak to Valerie, Bria. I'll be right back to go over any incorrect answers with you." Tory stood and held the door while the other girls shouldered their backpacks and left the computer center.

Valerie was in her office putting a bandage on Jeremy's

knee. "Hey, Tor. Jeremy got on the wrong end of a wrestling match. Which is why we don't allow wrestling matches, right?" She looked pointedly at the boy wiping dampness from his face.

Jeremy nodded. "I'm sorry, Mama Valerie."

She squeezed his leg and stood. "Go on and tell the other boys to change for practice. Mr. Mac will take y'all to the gym in about fifteen minutes."

Tory sank into the chair. "I have an idea that might sound a bit crazy but just might work."

"For what?"

"Tinsel."

"Oh my gosh, Tory, that guitar! Mac near about fell out of his chair when I told him."

Tory had been excited, too. The guitar had the capability to bring in serious money that was much needed by the center. Of course, she'd had to promise to help Tansy put on an old-fashioned family Christmas to get it. Tory wasn't so sure why the woman was so set on dragging out everything her mother and grandmother had stored in the attic, but Tansy seemed very intent. Tory suspected it had something to do with Kris. The older woman had said she needed to "show him the value of home" and "why Trabeau Farms was so special."

The whole thing made Tory wonder why Kris had come to Charming. Something in her gut told her it was more than just checking on his aunt.

Valerie clapped her hands. "Mac called the paper this morning. Dandy said he'd do a write up for tomorrow. Can you believe?" Valerie opened her box of chocolates and rooted around the empty brown papers, withdrawing a rounded one and popping it into her mouth. "Ahh."

Tory blinked. At times it was hard just keeping up with

Valerie. The woman's mind jumped from subject to subject at an alarming speed. "Yeah, I'm excited, and her nephew is a country music singer—"

"Kris Trabeau! Everyone knows him. He won an award a few weeks ago. You know his song. 'If you thought you were taking me down, you didn't know it was my kind of town'—"

"Valerie," Tory interrupted Valerie singing, snapping her fingers in front of the director's face. "Focus."

Her friend started laughing. "Sorry. I love that song."

"Anyway, Kris said he would try to get us a few more things for the auction."

"Wait, you *talked* to him?" Valerie's eyes lit up. "Wait. Is he here? In town?"

Boy, was he. Kris Trabeau was right next door and the reason Tory had agreed so quickly to help Tansy decorate and bake. Wait. No. She was not helping Tansy so she could be near Kris. Tory was being a good neighbor, building a relationship with the older woman. And it was for the guitar. She'd agreed to help Tansy in order to procure what she needed for Common Connection. Had nothing to do with the handsome singer.

Nothing.

"Yeah, he's here for a visit, but that's not why I'm here. I have an idea."

"Go on," Valerie said, leaning back in her chair, swiping another chocolate.

"So I've called umpteen bands and no dice. But as I walked through the center, I had a brainchild—what if we let the kids perform?" As Tory said the words, she realized it sounded a bit ridiculous. The Tinsel guests expected cocktails, sweet tea, pigs in a blanket and a nice holiday show to loosen their wallets.

"*Our* kids?"

"Yeah. Like we could showcase their talents. We have a trio of divas out there who can harmonize really well. We have comedy, a clarinet, a jazz ensemble, and I'm pretty sure the drama club at E.G. Roth will help out. If we get six or seven acts, that should do it. And Mac can be our Santa. You might need to let him have some of those chocolates though."

"Mac as a singing Santa?" Valerie laughed.

"You rang?" Mac asked sticking his head into the office. Mac stood well over six foot, lean, with salt and pepper hair, a goatee, and a propensity to smile at everything.

"Tory wants you to be Santa at Tinsel."

"I can do that," Mac said, snitching one of Valerie's chocolates. She swatted his hand and gave him the eagle eye but smiled as soon as he grinned at her. Their obvious love for one another warmed the cockles of Tory's heart. And because Tory was a biology teacher, she knew cockles were the Latin corruption of the word *cochleae cordis*, which were the heart's ventricles.

"And she wants the kids to be the entertainment," Valerie said.

Mac looked at Tory. "Perfect."

"You think so? You don't think our crowd would be too stuffy for old-school rap?" Valerie asked.

Mac laughed. "I don't think these kids even know what old-school rap is. I think it's a terrific idea and we can offer up a small payment since we don't have to pay a huge sum to a band. A gift card for each performer would be nice. They can buy Christmas gifts for their families."

This is why Tory loved Common Connection. The center wasn't about merely giving away basic items families needed to live. No, Common Connection fostered pride and self-worth—a hand up, not a handout.

"How are you going to pick the ones who will perform? If there's a gift card up for grabs, they'll all want to do it." Valerie folded her hands and sat her pointed chin atop them. Her gray-green eyes looked tired and the hair she'd pinned up fell in raven chunks around her face.

Tory smiled at her. "Rest easy. I have an idea for that, too."

Chapter Six

WHEN KRIS CAME IN FROM painting late that afternoon, he nearly tripped over the box blocking the front door. "Whoa, what's going on in here?"

Tansy and Tory sat in the middle of the living room that had previously been closed off. Dust cloths still covered the Victorian settees and walnut tea cart, but the heavy drapes had been pulled back so what remained of the day's light bathed the space in a persimmon glow. Boxes upon boxes surrounded the women, who were unwinding lights and unwrapping Christmas decorations.

"What does it look like?" Aunt Tansy said, from her perch on a folding kitchen chair. She set a box of metallic balls aside. Tory took them and stacked them near where she sat cross-legged on the floor. "We're sorting through all the Christmas decorations from the attic."

"You got all this down?" he asked, directing his question to Tory. She wore a green shirt that had an image of what looked to be Edison on it, along with black yoga pants and bright yellow and blue running shoes. Her hair was braided, but wispy curls rebelled, falling around her face. "I would have done it for you."

"None of the boxes were heavy," she said, setting the lights she'd been working on aside.

"I called Johnny Potts and told him you would come out and get the tree this evening." Aunt Tansy wore a brightly patterned shirt and leggings, a Birkenstock on her socked foot and her iron-gray hair in a braid down her back. Haight-Ashbury personified.

Kris gave an inward groan. "Tree? Like a real one?"

"Bingo. I'm doing the kind of Christmas my mama used to do, which means we need at least a ten-footer. You can use the truck. Take Tory with you because I don't trust your judgement."

"Oh, Miss Tansy, I'm sure you don't need me to go along. Kris can pick a good tree." Tory glanced at him nervously.

He didn't like making her feel that way.

Tansy waved a dismissive hand. "The one time my mama let Papa fetch the Christmas tree, we ended up with a fifteen-foot Scottish pine that got sap all over creation. Nope, I'm sending a woman to do a woman's job."

Kris grinned at Tory. "Don't worry. I won't bite."

"I know," the biology teacher said, shoving herself up from the floor. "It's just that Edison has been home alone all this time, and—"

"Take that beast with y'all. They allow dogs," Tansy said, placing a lid on a nearby box. "Kris will have to take the truck anyway. Edison can shed and drool all over it, and it won't matter."

"Okay, fine," Tory sighed.

The day before Kris had been certain she was somewhat attracted to him, but now she acted like she'd rather be strung up by her cute toenails than spend time with him. Wasn't like he didn't shower or wear deodorant. Or drooled as bad as her dog.

Maybe she was nervous because they would be out in

public. People would want to talk to him. Maybe even take pictures. That could be it.

He'd much rather have a shower and a sandwich, but Tansy was the kind who would not rest until he did what she wanted. Kris had spent all day painting, wondering why he was doing the job rather than hiring the work out. But he knew why. The work was soothing, the swish and swoosh of the brush over the soffits and shutters oddly calming, allowing his mind to wander, to open, to fall into that space where words, melodies and movement dovetailed into a something that had shape. His aunt had been right when she'd said occupying one's hands often emptied the worry clogging the mind.

As he worked, the world moved around him. No dinging texts or city noise. No emails, phone calls, or incessant checking of his ranking. Just cardinals chatting from weathered fence posts, pine trees rubbing together as the cold front blasted in, and chickens clucking happily from their henhouse yard. Simple things. Country things. Things he'd forgotten to miss.

"Let me grab the keys." He went to the kitchen, snagged the old truck keys, and met Tory on the porch. The afternoon had given way to evening. That was the way of winter, a light switch flipped to darkness. "Let's fetch your furball. Taking him Christmas tree hunting should be a blast."

Tory smiled. "His love for pursuing dog biscuits and fashion-forward chickens is part of his charm. A Christmas tree lot filled with children is probably Edison's idea of heaven."

Fifteen minutes later, they pulled into Potts Christmas Wonderland. Edison sat between them on the bench seat, huffing and drooling in excitement. Every time either of them spoke, the dog's tail thumped a happy beat against the cracked seats. Kris parked beneath an oak tree festooned with lighted balls.

In the distance, the Potts farm had been fashioned to look like a Dickens Christmas village, replete with fake snow clustered around globed lights. A Christmas train ringed a giant lit Christmas tree, and small children shrieked in the cars clacking around the track. A hot cocoa stand sat near the entrance to the Christmas tree farm, a staging point for a tractor with a trailer ringed in lights waiting to take visitors somewhere, most likely the glowing acreage around the rows of Christmas trees.

"Wow, I didn't remember the Potts doing this much when I was a kid."

"You should have been here for the pumpkin patch and corn maze. They did a special on it on one of the Jackson news stations." Tory clipped Edison's leash on and opened the truck door. Christmas music assaulted them. "Oh, joy. Christmas music."

Not just Christmas music, but the Chipmunks' Christmas song.

Yikes.

Kris climbed out, not bothering to lock the truck. There was nothing to steal unless someone wanted some rusty tools or an old John Deere ball cap. He met Edison and Tory around the front of the old blue truck. "It looks crowded. I wouldn't expect people to be here on a Tuesday night."

"Well, there's a live nativity every thirty minutes, so it's pretty popular," Tory said, moving toward the entrance. "Let's hurry and get this over with."

"You really don't like Christmas, do you?"

"It's not that. Uh, I'm...just hungry." She shrugged one shoulder.

"So why aren't you doing Christmas? Is it a religious thing or something?"

She jerked her gaze to his. "No. I just…well, it's hard to explain. I guess I'm not in the mood this year."

"Oh." *Brilliant response, Kris.*

Tory stopped but Edison kept going toward the entrance. She stumbled but righted herself before Kris could extend a hand to steady her. "If you want to know the truth, it's because of Patrick."

"Patrick? Who's he?"

"My ex."

Something pinged inside him. "Oh, you have an ex… boyfriend? Husband?"

"Fiancé." Tory closed her eyes and shook her head before opening them again. "Look, I'm sorry I brought it up. We were supposed to be married last weekend—a holiday wedding. Instead he took a job in Massachusetts without telling me and broke off our engagement. Christmas this year has been hard to deal with, and I just want it to be over with already because all this," she swept a hand around the faux Christmas village and laughing children, "reminds me of what didn't happen for me."

He wanted to say something that would make her feel better—something profound, but he didn't know what a guy was supposed to say to something as raw as her admission. He clasped her arm. "That really sucks. I'm sorry that happened to you."

She looked up at him, ignoring a whining Edison. Her brown eyes softened. "Yeah, me too." Then she turned and let Edison drag her toward the lit entrance.

Kris stood there for a few seconds as she walked into the crowded mini-village. Then he followed her, hoping that not too many people would recognize him. He wasn't that famous, but he was a native son who'd made good. Mayor Hamilton had already sent two missives asking him to be the Harvest Parade marshal and receive the key to the city. Charming residents were proud to have him from their small town.

"Woo hoo! Mama, look what the cat dragged in," someone hollered from across the open space in front of the tree farm. Kris turned to see Tug Mitchell hurrying his way, a grin a country mile wide on his bearded face. Tug had been the right guard on the offensive line, making holes for Kris to crash through back in high school. He'd also been one of Kris's best friends.

"What's up, man?" Kris said, reaching out to shake Tug's hand. But Tug was having none of it. The hug his old friend gave him lifted him from his feet.

"Well, I'll be danged if you ain't finally come home and ain't called me yet, son." Tug sat him down, slapping him on the arm with a massive swipe.

"Sorry, Tug. I should have, but Aunt T's got me busting my hump out at the farm. I'm here fetching her Christmas tree. She's insisting on putting one up this year." Kris turned to smile at Tug's wife, feeling bad that he hadn't thought to call Tug and Honey. "Hey there, Honey."

"Well, you rascal," Honey said, slamming into him and squeezing him like a boa constrictor. Kris laughed because that's how Nora Lee Goodman Mitchell, aka Honey, had always greeted him.

"Mama! Who is that?" a voice said from behind him.

Honey released him but not before smacking a kiss on his cheek. "Lord have mercy, Ava. I'm just saying hello to the best country singer this town has ever put out."

Kris laughed. "I'm the only country singer this town has put out."

"We put you out alright," Tug joked.

Honey's eyes danced as she drew her daughter to her. "Ava, this is your daddy's best friend from childhood, Mr. Kris Trabeau. We haven't seen him in so long I'm surprised I even recognized him."

"Trabeau?" Ava's voice rose an octave. "He's the one you and Daddy listen to on the radio."

Kris smiled and bent down, offering his hand. "Nice to meet you, Miss Ava. Your daddy sent me some pictures of you when you were a baby."

Ava ducked her head, suddenly shy. She looked like Honey with her blond-streaked brown hair and blue eyes. She wore skinny jeans and shearling-lined boots. Adorable in a gap-toothed, freckled little girl way. "Hi."

Kris stood, trying to avoid Edison jumping his way. The dog looked ecstatic at the jubilant greeting from his friends, as if he too were part of the clan. "Down, Edison."

The dog paused mid-leap and dropped to all fours.

Honey's gaze zipped to Tory like a missile to a target. "Well, I see you've brought friends with you."

Kris pressed Edison into a sitting position. The furry hound grinned at him, enormously pleased at the attention. "Do y'all know Tory, uh, what's your last name again?"

"Odom," Tug finished before Tory could say. "We know Tory. She teaches at the high school. My youngest sister is a cheerleader there. Lila Mitchell?"

Kris noted Tory looking taken aback at Tug and Honey's assault on him, but she delivered a polite smile. "Of course. She was in my AP Biology class last year."

Honey's eyes narrowed. "Weren't you engaged to Patrick

Jones? I think I met you at a Maritime Biotech party last year."

Tory flushed, her hand reaching for Edison's soft head. "Yes, of course. I remember meeting you."

"Dodged a bullet with that one, didn't you? And I must say you scored big on the trade in," Honey said, eyeing Kris and winking at him.

"I'm not—" Tory said, looking panicked.

"We're not—" Kris said, simultaneously.

Honey laughed, pulling out her cellphone. "I'm just joking with y'all. You're too easy, Kris."

"Tory's my aunt's neighbor. She's helping Tansy decorate the house so my aunt sent her with me. Auntie T doesn't trust me to pick out a good tree."

"Well, I wouldn't—" Tug said, turning to his wife when she jerked his arm. "What?"

"Lord, we gotta go, Tug," Honey said, sliding her phone back into her pocket. "Ava has homework and I have to make a cake for work tomorrow. It's Hugh's birthday."

"How long you in town, son?" Tug asked.

"A few more days. I'm heading to Texas after that." Even as Kris said the words, he wondered if solitude in an East Texas cabin was going to happen. He still hadn't broached the topic of selling the farm and moving Tansy to Tennessee, and he still had a good bit of work to do on the farm. The upside was that the mindless labor had loosened his writer's block.

And then there was the intriguing woman standing next to him. Maybe it was her self-imposed ban on Christmas or the startling vulnerability in her voice when she talked about her ex-fiancé. Or maybe he just liked her and her silly dog. Something pulled at him, and though he knew that wasn't a reason to stay, it might be enough to cancel the cabin.

Or not.

"I'll come by before you leave. Text me." Tug followed his wife and daughter out the exit.

"They seem like nice people," Tory said as she turned back to the tree farm.

"They are the best people," he said, falling in step with her. "I sometimes forget how much I like being around my old friends. Seems so long ago, yet not really."

Tory smiled at him. And Edison might have drooled on his boot. Didn't seem to matter because he felt lighter for the first time in forever.

Huh.

Surely he'd been happy before now? Everything with his career was finally going right.

Except it's not your career to control anymore. They're making you dance to their jig.

"We better get the tree and get back. It's getting late and we'll need to find the stand." Tory walked up to the booth that sold tickets and spoke into the round open circle. "We need to buy a tree. Can we get someone to help us?"

"Sure." The woman behind the glass wore an elf hat and a Christmas necklace that blinked. "You're gonna hop on the next ride out. Feel free to grab some hot chocolate and get into the holiday spirit while you wait."

"Grand." Tory turned and rolled her eyes. For some reason, her attitude about Christmas both amused and challenged him. He'd never been head over heels about the holiday, but he liked it enough to want her to celebrate in some small way.

"I'll spring for hot chocolate," Kris said, digging his wallet out of his jeans. "Do I need to buy some for Edison?"

"Lord, no. Dogs can't have chocolate, and besides, he'd get it on everyone within six feet of us." She reached down and patted the beast who sat at her feet looking utterly delighted at everything around him.

Kris fetched the hot chocolate, signed a few autographs, and after a few pictures with fans, he made it back to Tory. "Here you are."

"Thanks," Tory said. She accepted the now-lukewarm chocolate. "That must be annoying."

"What?"

"All those people pestering you all the time." She sipped the hot chocolate, getting a bit of the foamy, marshmallow-y stuff on her nose. It could have been a cute moment. Him wiping the smudge off her nose, leaning down, and...

He handed her a napkin. "On your nose. Right here." He tapped his own nose.

Tory swiped at her nose.

"I don't mind that much. It's part of it. My fans got me the contract with the label. It's a crazy world out there in the music business, and without fans you can pretty much hang it up. So, nah, I don't mind. I feel like I need to give back to people in some way. Snapping a picture or taking the time to listen to someone complimenting me is easy to do."

"I'm glad you feel that way," Tory said, taking another sip of her drink. "Because it makes it even easier to ask you for the favor I need."

Chapter Seven

TORY HAD BEEN WAITING FOR the right time to ask Kris to help her with the auditions for the Tinsel variety show, and since he seemed to be in the right frame of mind, sharing his views on giving back to the community, it seemed the best time. She nearly blew it when she hesitated in going to the tree farm with him, but for some reason the thought of being in the intimate space of the truck with him had given her pause. Or maybe it was the idea that this whole thing felt like a first date or something.

Truth was, she wasn't ready to feel the way she felt.

Interested.

The interest wasn't merely because Kris was attractive and successful. No, Kris intrigued her more and more because he seemed to be a genuine person. She liked the way he pitched in to help his aunt and the way he paid attention to her overly enthusiastic dog. Kris wasn't afraid to roll up his sleeves and do hard work or throw a slobbery stick. Besides, he'd made her laugh a few times. Her laugh felt rusty, but it also felt good to use it again.

"A favor?" he asked, somehow looking even more handsome in the festive Christmas lights strung above them. The Potts Farm looked like Santa had upchucked everywhere. No escaping festivity here, but for some reason she didn't mind it at the moment.

"I have this idea I'm not sure will work, but it could," she said, eyeing the people out-and-out staring at them. Correction. Staring at Kris.

"What is it?" he asked. He sipped the hot chocolate like it was a fine wine. Slowly, as if he savored the flavor on his tongue. The action made her look at his mouth. At his lips. How would they—

No. Focus and stop letting your mind wander where it shouldn't.

"I called all of the bands on the list you gave me and came up zero for zero. Only Devon Michaels had availability, and she's due to deliver her second child any day now. So I was hoping—"

"Look, I know what you're asking, and I can't be your—"

"Oh, I know," she interrupted his panicked protest. "I wouldn't presume to ask you to do that, though I have to say it would bring people in. Lots of people around here seem to like country music." Tory paused and took a sip of her hot chocolate. Edison had parked his behind right on her feet as he watched with great interest the people around them, many outright staring at Kris, as they toted adorable toddlers with their faces painted or juggled the funnel cakes that permeated the air with deliciousness.

"Well, it *is* my target market," Kris said.

"Right, um, so I'm thinking about having the kids provide the entertainment. We have some who are good at singing, one who is in a jazz ensemble, one who's so funny you could bust a stitch laughing at him, you know, if you actually had stitches. I think people would respond to them and be forgiving if it's not up to our normal standards. I mean, who's going to be upset at a twelve-year-old doing an impression?

I'm hoping that seeing the kids up close and personal, seeing the potential they have, might loosen our guests' wallets."

"And you're going to do all this in a week and a half?" His tone said it all. She was crazy cakes.

"I know. It sounds daunting, but—"

"Don't get me wrong," he interrupted, holding up a finger. "It's a nice idea, but the timing is an issue. Auditions, rehearsals, and putting a show together takes time. You're short on that."

"I know." She couldn't stop the disappointment from her voice. She'd thought her idea was better than hiring a sub-par band that people hated. One of the local junior college students said he played with a few guys, and they did some covers but focused mostly on techno metal. She wasn't even sure what that was.

"So what's the favor?" Kris asked.

She turned to look at him. "Huh?"

"You said you were going to ask me a favor."

"Well, if you think it won't work then there's no need." For some reason Kris shooting her idea down seemed to hurt more than she expected. She'd thought he'd be all in, but then again, she didn't know him well enough to expect enthusiasm for her idea.

"Now wait a minute, let me think," he said, strolling to a trash receptacle and tossing his empty cup. He waved at a few people who shyly raised their hands and came back. "If you had the auditions on Saturday morning, that would give you a week until the benefit. The kids auditioning would have to have talent, poise, and potential, but they wouldn't have to be perfect in the auditions. Kids are fast learners and sometimes braver than adults. They could practice for a good week before rehearsals. If you keep the number of participants to, say, six, and get a decent emcee, you can fill an hour."

Hope welled inside her. "That's all we need. We usually do a live auction at the end and then a sing-along to send everyone off."

Kris mulled that over. "It could work. So again, I ask, how can I help?"

"I want you to be the audition judge."

"You want *me* to do it?"

"Well, I need someone impartial and someone who recognizes talent. You fit the bill, plus you're leaving in a few more days, right? So you don't have to worry about those who don't make the cut letting the air out of your tires or egging your house."

Kris's eye widened. "You're kidding, right?"

"Of course. They wouldn't do that." The tractor with the lighted trailer pulled up. A large family climbed out, carefully lowering their bound tree. The mother held an adorable baby, and the father held the hands of two young boys who chatted excitedly about stringing popcorn. This was what Christmas was about—family spending time together, silly songs, bedecked Christmas trees. The sight touched her and made her yearn for things she'd thought to one day have. Things she thought she and Patrick would have.

Patrick. The thought of her ex still rubbed her the wrong way, and now she felt embarrassed that she had uncharacteristically told Kris she'd been dumped.

Tory had met Patrick at a charity golf event to raise money for City Green in Jackson. The cute scientist was running the putting contest and looked hopelessly out of place wearing a bow tie and plaid jacket. Honestly, he looked like the crew of *Caddyshack* had dressed him. Turned out Patrick knew next to nothing about golf, but he did know a heck of a lot about molecular biology. When he discovered Tory had a Masters in biology and was interested in biosynthesis, he'd peeled away from his assignment, bought her a wine spritzer, and spent the next hour talking academia with her. She hadn't minded a bit because she knew nothing about golf either. Her friend had talked her into the scramble and they'd used none of her shots anyway.

Patrick and Tory had dated for an entire year before he proposed to her. He'd said they were meant to be, and she believed him. They liked the same TV shows, loved going to the symphony, and had adopted Edison together. They were perfect. Until Patrick got the offer from MIT to do research in genome biology…and hadn't even told her about it for three weeks. They'd offered him a professorship and a place on the research team—a team on a Nobel Prize-winning trajectory. She'd expected him to discuss it with her before he took the job. He didn't. When she'd been upset about it, he'd broken the news that he wasn't interested in her going with him. Or maintaining their relationship at all.

Oh, he'd said it was him. Not her. He had doubts about the institution of marriage. Wasn't even sure if he ever wanted to make that sort of commitment. He'd felt pressured by her all along. Then he asked for the ring back. The beautiful solitaire she cleaned every week and stared at for much too long.

The last she'd heard, he'd run off to Vegas with the doctoral student and gotten hitched. According to their mutual friend, he'd not even had the decency to be drunk and impulsive. Patrick, her stable, predictable, cautious ex-fiancé, had done something so out of character it had felt doubly insulting.

So much for not wanting to be married.

But whatever. She was over him, if not completely over the

humiliation of being dumped a week after their engagement announcements went out. *Cancel that save-the-date, folks.*

"So Saturday morning?" Kris asked, jarring her from thoughts of her brilliant, handsome snake of an ex.

"Yeah. I sent a text to the drama teacher at the high school. She'll send an ensemble to do something from *Bye, Bye Birdie.* The band director has committed the jazz ensemble to do a few numbers from their Christmas concert, and the other acts will be the kids from the center. So we only need four or five. We talked to the kids at the center today, and they are excited. There will be some who aren't accomplished enough—we'll give them other roles, but there are others who could be really good. I just don't want to be the one to pick them."

"Okay," he said.

"Really?" she asked, excitement fluttering in her belly. This was going to work. It had to. "You'll be our judge?"

"One of them. We need two more. One from the center would make them less nervous."

"I can do that. I mean, I can make that happen. Thank you so much," she said, feeling the urge to hug him. But she wouldn't. It would be too much, too tempting to press herself against him.

"Sure."

The man driving the tractor whistled. "All aboard, folks. Beautiful Christmas trees are awaiting you here at the Potts Christmas Farm. Step right up!"

"Time to get that tree," Tory said, tugging Edison up. "Let's go, Edison."

The dog issued an excited bark before dragging her onto the trailer that had hay bales on each side as seating. Tory laughed and it struck her that it was the first time in forever that she'd actually had some fun.

With a country music singer at a Dickens Christmas Village.

Life was certainly strange.

Tansy held the door while her nephew dragged the bound tree inside the house. Immediately she was assaulted by memories of her father doing the same, her mother fussing about needles in the carpet, her daddy's gravely laugh making her and her older sister Jenny giggle. There had been so many Christmases full of joy, full of promise, full of hope.

And then Jenny died from pneumonia when she was thirteen.

No more laughter.

But Tansy didn't want to dwell on the tragic past. She wanted to revel in the nostalgia of good Christmases...and pray that her plan worked. "Careful, Kris. Mind the drum top table with Jenny's figurines."

"I've got it," he huffed.

Tory followed him inside, rubbing her hands together. "We left Edison in the truck. He would have tried to help us too much."

"He certainly made the tractor driver nervous. I mean, a dog and all those trees..." Kris said, looking up with twinkling sherry eyes the color of her baby brother's. Her brother Robert had been born when Tansy was twelve, two years after Jenny had passed. Robbie was like a gift from above, a small apology for the heartbreak of her sister's death. Robbie had come into this world howling and had proceeded to both delight and irritate Tansy. But she'd loved him like he was her own child, toting him around town on her hip, buying him sweets when tears slid down his plump cheeks, and cherishing the fact that she no longer had to dwell as a child alone in a silent house full of grief. Kris had gotten all the best characteristics of his father.

Tansy chuckled and picked up the corner of the sheet she'd given Kris to set the tree on and started dragging it toward the Christmas tree stand she'd found in the attic. One leg looked wonky, but it would hold fine. She hoped. A bedecked tree crashing to the floor would be no fun to deal with. She needed that tree to stand regally, laden with Christmas past, a symbol of what the holiday was all about—memories and a little glitter.

"Here, let me," Tory said, rushing to take the sheet from her.

Twenty minutes later they had the tree in the stand, fresh water in the bowl, and the scraggly branches trimmed so that the Douglas Fir looked perfect.

"Tomorrow, we can finish going through these ornaments and get the tree decorated. I'll put a pot of stew on and we'll all eat together," Tansy said. She was enormously pleased at how things were going. If she could keep that twinkle in her nephew's eyes, she might convince him to give up solitude for a family Christmas. And if she could show him how the Trabeau family had always done the holiday right, she could remind him who he was and why the farm had to stay in the family.

It was a total bonus that Kris had taken a shine to Tory, whether he realized it yet or not.

"I might be a bit late. I have a lot to do at the center. Kris is going to help us with our entertainment for Tinsel before he leaves town." Tory brushed the stray pine needles from her yoga pants and studied the tree critically.

"Oh?" Tansy arched an eyebrow at her nephew.

He shrugged. "Tory's going to let the Common Connection kids be the entertainment. I'm going to be one of the judges who will choose the ones who are good enough... uh, to perform, that is."

Tansy smiled. "Well, that's a real good idea, Tory. I think people will like that."

"Are you going to the benefit, Aunt Tans?" Kris asked, leaning over to pull the white sheet from beneath the tree.

"Don't do that. Leave it. When Christmas is over, it will be easy to get the tree out without getting dried needles everywhere," she said, nodding at the white sheet. "Bunch it up so it looks like snow around the base. That's why I got a white sheet."

"Clever," Tory said, leaning over to do as she suggested right when Kris did. They bumped heads.

"Ouch," Tory said, rubbing at her head, her face suffusing with color.

Kris grinned. "Didn't hurt. I'm a hard head."

And he was. Wouldn't be easy to convince Kris to forget about his plan for her and the farm, but it was doable. A little fake snow, a lot of Christmas cookies with sprinkles, and a well-placed piece of mistletoe would do the trick. She hoped. Because she wasn't moving to The Hermitage or selling Trabeau Farms. Her head was way harder than his.

As for Tinsel, Tansy hadn't planned on going. Truth be told, she didn't like getting out since she broke her leg. Life was easier in the space she lived at present, and though she'd spent many years working in her community, the upside to her broken leg was the down time she'd gotten to enjoy her own company. Her need for companionship was met by the ladies at her beauty parlor, coffee with the mailman, and the occasional conversation with Salty, who rode his ATV over when he got an itch for talking to someone other than himself.

The three of them stood—Tansy half-standing as best she could—and looked at the tree. A volley of urgent barking came from outside.

"Oh, no," Tory said, uncrossing her arms and scooping up the canvas bag she'd left on the plastic-coated sofa. She ran to the door.

Kris followed her out the front door and Tansy thumped behind him, her heart racing as she considered Edison once again riling up her chickens. Lord, at the rate their feathers were dropping from the stress of that dog, she'd have to make full-body sweaters for the poor darlings.

Tansy came around the side of the house to find Tory petting Edison beside the chicken coop. Her chickens were nowhere in sight.

Tansy's stomach sank, but she didn't see feathers scattering the ground. "Where are my—"

"They're safe," Tory said, rubbing Edison's head while she cast a wary glance toward the scraggly brush on the edge of the property.

"Relax, Aunt T. They're all in their house roosting. Edison here just chased off what looked to be a coyote. This time, Edison was Loretta Lynn's hero. He somehow wriggled out of the back window of the truck and put himself between the coop and the coyote."

"You're telling me that silly mutt protected the coop?" Tansy asked.

"A regular Sir Lancelot," Kris said, laughing as Edison pranced about looking quite pleased with himself.

Kris's laugh sounded about as good as anything she'd heard in a while. He knelt down and rubbed Edison's ears.

Tansy didn't miss the way Tory's gaze softened at Kris doling out a rewarding lovefest on her big puppy. There was something definitely there between the two of them, and she knew exactly how to use that to her advantage. The more Kris enjoyed being at the farm, the better her chance at changing his heart.

"Well, I suppose he deserves a treat," Tansy said, turning back toward the front of the house. Edison barked his agreement and chased after her. His fluffy hair brushed her legs and she used her crutch to push him back. "Don't trip me, mutt."

Edison trotted ahead. Just as she reached the corner, she glanced back at Kris and Tory standing by the coop, the moonlight giving enough glow for her to see the sparks.

Yep, in this fight for her farm and future, she had an ace in her pocket.

An ace named Tory Odom.

Chapter Eight

TORY HURRIEDLY TOOK EDISON OUTSIDE, hopping from one foot to the other, blowing on her hands while he took his slow, sweet time doing his business. Edison leisurely smelled every bush, every tree, and every tiny rock he could reach from the long retractable leash.

"Hurry, buddy. It's cold out here."

Edison looked up and wagged his tail, and then moved with the speed of a sloth toward the next bush that awaited a christening.

The day had been a good one—she'd done a lab with her students and even had a few tell her they enjoyed it. The Holy Grail of teaching—kids who actually liked a lesson.

"Eddie, please, hurry and do your business. I'm freezing out here."

Edison did as bid and trotted her way, looking longingly toward the woods that led to Tansy's farm.

"I know, boy. You were a hero last night, but tonight we're decorating with very breakable ornaments. Your help will not be appreciated. Now, heel."

Edison's head sank as if he understood her words, but he did as bid. She'd spent the last few days making sure she used the correct commands and was consistent in Edison's training. It was paying off.

Tory let her fluffy chicken protector back into the house,

shivering in delight when she stepped into the warmth. The adorable cottage featured the original hardwood floors, Craftsman-style wood molding, dark beams across the pitched ceiling and a gorgeous set of bookcases that flanked the restored fireplace. She'd chosen simple furniture that she frequently had to vacuum for dog hair and Tiffany lamps that cast a cozy glow. She loved her house. She and Patrick had planned to add onto it, intending on having two children. Patrick had wanted only one, but he'd capitulated when she'd shown him the studies on the positive benefits of siblings. Well, maybe *capitulate* wasn't the right word. Maybe he didn't bother to argue because he wasn't planning on marrying her anyway.

Tory dashed the bad thoughts away. *Not tonight, Satan.*

After all, she had a Christmas tree to decorate. Fa-la-la-la-lah. La-la-la-boo.

"Is it weird that I'm actually looking forward to this?" Tory said aloud, earning a crook of the head and low whine from Edison. "I'm supposed to be wallowing in heartache and ignoring Christmas. But I don't feel like doing that anymore."

Edison woofed and lifted a paw. *Come to me. Pet me. Adore me.*

Tory dropped a kiss atop his head. "Never mind. You wouldn't understand. You celebrate everything."

She grabbed the bag holding the bread she'd bought from Extraordinary, the new bakery that had opened last year, and pulled on her fleece jacket. Since she'd decided to stretch her legs and walk through the woods down the old path to Tansy's, she added the gloves and scarf her mother had made her that fall. They were a soft angora, blue to match the flecks in her eyes, and smelled like the lavender lotion her mother used. Winter had decided to make an appearance, driving away the warm fall and blessing them with cool, crisp air that made the stars brighter and her breath cloud as she stepped onto the porch. "Be good, Edison. I'll be home in a few hours to snuggle with you on the couch. Keep my spot warm."

Edison jumped onto the couch and sank down, setting his big head on his big paws. He sighed and continued looking adorable.

Tory went down the porch steps, inhaling the smell of burning leaves. Ten minutes later, she stood on Tansy's porch. From outside, she could smell the stew and hear Christmas music. Kris answered the door and, for a moment, her heart leaped into her chest.

Don't be ridiculous, Tory.

"Hey," he said, opening the door in invitation. "It's getting cold out there. Brr."

"Yeah, finally," she said, stepping inside, pulling off her gloves and unwinding her scarf. She'd worn her hair down today and it tangled in the scarf.

"Let me help you with your jacket," he said as she slipped the navy polar fleece from her shoulders. His hands were warm when they grazed the back of her neck. She stepped away and told herself it was a natural response to stimuli rather than a response to Kris's specific touch.

Tansy hobbled into the foyer. "Soup's on."

"I'm starving," Tory said, smiling at the woman who before the past few days she had rarely spent any time with. Tansy had always seemed polite, but when Tory first moved into her house, she'd been too busy to think about getting to know her neighbors. When Patrick was in her life, she'd spent most of her time with him, failing at making many friends in Charming. And then when he'd left, packing his car in the middle of the night, she'd been too upset to reach out to anyone. If she hadn't had Valerie at Common Connection and a few of her teacher friends, she might have gone back home to Morning Glory. Slowly but surely, she'd climbed out of her funk, and last week the caterer and event planner for Tinsel, Wren Daniels, had asked Tory to join her book club. Tory didn't read much popular fiction, but if it meant having wine and companionship, she'd give it a go. Now she had a neighbor she could visit, maybe even count on to loan her a cup of sugar. That felt nice.

"I haven't made a stew in forever, so if it's terrible I'm blaming it on my bum leg," Tansy said, thumping toward the kitchen.

"Don't worry, I tasted it. It's fine," Kris said, hanging Tory's jacket on the antique hall stand that dominated the foyer.

They gathered around the round table in a kitchen that had seen better days but somehow felt perfect. The stove was an antique, one of those people paid a lot of money for, and the red teapot and embroidered tea towels gave it vintage charm. The cabinets could use fresh paint, and a marble countertop to replace the old worn tile would go a long way in updating the space, but even so, Tansy's kitchen was like her: matter of fact, genteel, with a pop of the unexpected.

"I brought some bread from the new bakery in town. I thought a seven-grain would be good with stew." Tory held up the bag.

Kris took it and pulled out the wrapped loaf. He set about cutting it into gorgeous hunks of grainy goodness and then set it in the toaster. Tansy sank into a chair and poured a glass of iced tea. "Sit."

Tory sat, accepted a glass of tea, and folded the soft cloth napkin stitched with redbirds onto her lap.

"Now, while my nephew finishes things off, you tell me about yourself. I know you're from Morning Glory, but little else. So shoot."

Tory nervously cleared her throat. She hadn't been prepared to be grilled. "Uh, well, I'm a teacher. Biology. I went to a small liberal arts college in Arkansas and worked on my Masters in microbiology at the University of Maryland. I thought I would go into research, but after a while, I got homesick and decided to come back to Mississippi. I fell into teaching and I love it. I worked in Jackson, but I longed for small-town life. There were no jobs in Morning Glory, but the school board was looking for someone to head the science department here so...here I am."

She went on to talk about her parents, her hobbies and how much she loved tutoring at the center, all the while sliding glances at Kris—pouring himself a glass of iced tea, buttering the toasty bread that made her mouth water, gathering ceramic bowls that he filled with savory beef stew. Tory tried not to look at the man who seemed to fill the kitchen. There was something about him, about the way his hair curled against the flannel shirt collar, about the way his Wranglers fit so perfectly. His actions were efficient, his jaw clean shaven...

"You shaved your beard," she said, in the middle of telling Tansy about adopting Edison.

Kris looked over his shoulder. "Yep. Aunt Tansy has an aversion to facial hair, and I like to start over every now and then."

"But all your fans love your beard," Tory said.

Kris tossed her an amused smile. "You know what my fans like? Thought you didn't like country music."

Tory burned with embarrassment. Okay, so she'd looked

up some stuff on him a few nights ago. A scientist's job was to examine and draw conclusions. She was being inquisitive, not nosy.

"I'm his aunt and I could give a rat's patoot what his fans say. I'm the original fan and I'm opposed to anything that covers his nice-looking face," Tansy said.

Kris rolled his eyes and brought the bowls to the table as Bing Crosby crooned about a white Christmas. He handed her one, winked, and pulled out his own chair. "Let's eat it while it's hot."

Twenty minutes and two helpings later, they pushed back from the table and made their way into the living room to decorate the tree. Someone had removed the covers from the couch and the room looked freshly dusted.

"Kris hauled away all the junk this morning and cleaned up a little for us," Tansy said, maneuvering her crutches around the coffee table covered with magazines from ten years before. Porcelain flowers scattered the table and a mantel clock chimed the hour.

"It looks nice," she said, surprised Kris had been able to clean so efficiently. She hadn't been around too many guys who were so accommodating. Her father mowed the grass and used duct tape to fix most of the issues her mother found, and Patrick had never lifted a finger that she could remember. The man had sent his laundry out and paid someone to mow his Jackson townhouse lawn. He seemed to be above such minute things. "Where do we start?"

"How about these?" Kris asked, toeing the box nearest him.

"First the lights," Tansy said, sinking onto the Victorian sofa.

The old-fashioned bulbs looked dangerous to Tory. "Are those safe?"

Tansy's expression narrowed. "They're the ones we've always used. They work just fine. I tested all of them."

"But if you get LED bulbs they'll put out less heat and will last longer," Kris said.

"And look wrong. Just because something's old doesn't mean it can't still be as good as it once was. You can't just toss things away like they mean nothing for something new-fangled and…energy efficient." Tansy's words seemed shaded with more than conviction over a strand of old Christmas lights. Again, something inside Tory raised its head. *What was all this really about?*

"Sure." Kris said, taking the lights from Tory, giving her a quelling look. "They're good for one more Christmas."

Tansy nodded and then eased down into a chair. "So y'all get those lights on and I'll start unpacking the ornaments."

Tory followed Kris to the tree and they began the process of twining the big-bulbed lights into the fragrant branches. Tansy competed with the old Christmas standards coming from the living room radio by remarking on every single ornament. "Here's one you made, Kris. I brought this one from Texas when I came to pick you up. Come look."

Kris would hand the lights to Tory and go to his aunt, smiling fondly as she held up the messy handprints stamped on a glass ball. "I forgot you kept some of my old ornaments from when I was a kid."

"Your daddy would have wanted them here at Trabeau Farms and not in some estate sale, tossed aside. It belongs here, at our home." Tansy looked up at Kris, weighing the effect of her words.

Kris shrugged and came back to Tory. He gave her a look

that said *I don't know what's going on* and then proceeded to shove a strand between two branches in the middle of the tree. Tory wisely said nothing because there were undercurrents here she didn't understand. But something was afoot.

Kris looked up at the top of the tree. "I'm tall, but not that tall. Let me grab a step stool."

A minute later, he planted an ancient-looking step stool beside the tree. Tory eyed the beat-up stool. "I'm not sure you should climb on that."

His mouth twisted. "You're much lighter than I am. How about you climb up, and I'll stand beside you just in case it decides to collapse?"

Tory looked at the stool. "I guess I can try."

The stool squeaked as she stepped up, but it held. She took the loop of lights and started threading them through the branches as quickly as she could. Kris's solid presence gave her confidence to lean far left to pass the strand around the tree so that Kris could grab it on the right. The process worked fine until the last pass, when she stood high on her tiptoes to make the final loop. The stool groaned, shifted, and she felt the metal give. She clutched at air as she tilted sideways.

"Eek!" Tory saw her world tilt, but Kris clasped her around the waist and caught her. Her clawing hands found his shoulders and her body crashed against his. Her foot was tangled in the bent stool top, so she kicked free making the stool fly toward the tree.

"That was nearly disastrous," he said, holding her against him for a second longer than necessary before righting her onto her feet.

Tory's heart had thundered at the near fall, but now it beat hard against her ribs at being so close to Kris. His soft flannel shirt was still knotted in her fists till she forced herself to release the fabric and step away. She refused to look at him because she didn't want him to see how affected she was by his touch. For a fleeting moment, she wanted to step back into his arms, feel his solidness against her body, inhale the scent of woodsy cologne mixed with the fresh scent of the tree.

"Thank you," she said instead.

"Lordy be, you nearly took out the Christmas tree," Tansy said, from her seat in the wing-backed chair.

"Aunt Tansy, here's another thing that needs to be replaced or fixed. If you'd have used this stool when no one was around, you could have broken a hip." Kris picked up the now-bent metal stool and set it aside.

"I wouldn't have used it in that condition," Tansy said, refusing also to look at her nephew. Maybe that was where a woman's vulnerability lay, in the eyes, and Tory understood the older woman not wanting Kris to see the truth.

The country music star arched an eyebrow. "You don't throw anything out and you refuse to buy things that make sense. Like new Christmas tree lights...or a better stool."

"Don't you fuss at me, Kristopher James. I'm too old to be talked to like a child." Tansy wagged her finger. "Besides, you're ruining our fun Christmas tree decorating party with negativity. Tory's fine."

Kris glanced at her. "You okay?"

"Of course."

"Come over here and look at these ornaments. They're painted glass. These were my grandmother's ornaments," Tansy said, lifting a box with ornaments nestled into tissue paper.

"So you haven't put these up in years?" Tory asked.

Tansy's mouth flattened. "I decorated, but it was on a smaller scale—a tiny tree with ornaments from a discount store and a few wreaths. These decorations here seemed too special to pull out for just myself. But this year, I have Kris home and I'm feeling more festive than normal."

Kris's face said it all. He looked about as guilty as a hanging judge watching an innocent man be dragged to the gallows. Tory started to say she thought Kris would be leaving soon, but he gave her a look that had her biting her lip. "Well, I think ornaments as pretty as these should never be left wrapped up and getting dusty in the attic. I'm glad you're going all out."

"Maybe they'll help you feel more in the spirit, too." Tansy began to sift through the ornaments, some of them mercury glass which were pristinely kept and likely worth a small fortune. There were also fuzzy plastic Santas, knitted stockings, and ceramic candy canes. One by one, she began to hand them to Tory and Kris.

"These are so pretty I'm afraid I'll drop them," Tory said, double-checking the hooks.

"Put them on the tree, darling. That's where they belong," Tansy said, leaning back and folding her hands, almost in anticipation of the big event—the decorating of the tree.

She and Kris began hanging ornaments, hearing the story behind each one. "That one your Aunt Glory gave to my mama. She got it in Germany." or "Those came over from Ireland. My great-great aunt crocheted them for Mama." and "Your father broke the Lord a Leaping when he was seven. That boy was always breaking something."

Tory found she loved hearing the old stories of Christmases past as she and Kris hung the decorations. At some point Kris began to sing along with Nat King Cole on "The Christmas Song." His baritone was rich, full, and so gorgeous she nearly dropped the five golden rings ornament. Valerie would have a cow if she knew Tory was decorating a Christmas tree with one of her favorite singers and being serenaded at the same time.

On the second verse, Tory joined in.

Her voice was choir quality at best, but it was Nat King Cole and the Country Music Newcomer of the Year...and a Christmas tree.

Kris's smile got bigger as they decorated and dueted, rolling right into "Walking in a Winter Wonderland."

At the end, Tansy clapped. Tory laughed. "I know I'm a bad singer."

"You're not a bad singer," Kris said, hooking on the last ornament. "You're just not a *good* one."

She laughed. "Very true, but I don't care. It was fun."

Kris smiled and her heart may have flipped over. *It was fun.*

"Time for the angel," Tansy proclaimed, sounding very pleased for some reason. Tory hoped it wasn't because she and Kris had been...flirting? No. It wasn't flirting. It was getting caught up in the spirit of things. Fuzzy Santas and bright bulbs did that to a person.

"How are we going to get it up there? We bent the stool," Tory said, taking the porcelain angel with her red velveteen robes and gossamer wings from Tansy.

"Kris can hold you up there. You don't weigh much," Tansy said.

"My scales would disagree with you," Tory joked.

"I got an idea." Kris dropped to his knees in front of the tree and then propped one up, making a flat surface.

"No way."

"Come on, I bet you were a cheerleader and did this all the time," he said.

"Um, no. I was the yearbook photographer. I took pictures of crazy people who did things like this."

"It'll be easy, and we'll have that angel on in no time at all." Kris patted his thigh. "Don't worry. You can put your hand on my shoulder to steady yourself."

Tory really didn't want to step on his knee and balance that close to him. The closeness was too much, especially when she already felt hyperaware of him. She darn sure didn't want to bobble beside him, relying on him to keep her from crashing into the tree. The vulnerability factor was eleven on a ten-point scale.

He must have noticed her hesitation. "Come on. Otherwise, I'll have to go get the ladder out of the barn. We can do this."

And now she felt silly because it was just stepping up and shoving an angel onto the tree. People did stuff like this all the time. Did she want him to think she was chicken or force him to go out to the barn and get a ladder? "Okay. I'll try."

She placed her foot on his thigh, glad she wore her soft-soled running shoes. He curled his arm around her knee and said, "Okay, step up. I got you."

Tory pretended she was getting into a saddle, but when she stood, she wobbled. He wrapped his arm around her leg and caught her free hand with his. "Gotcha."

Now she was standing on his leg with both feet and holding his hand.

"Stick it on there," he said.

Tory felt sturdier with Kris holding her so firmly. She reached high and jammed the angel a little harder than necessary onto the top of the tree. "Is that good?"

"Perfect," Tansy declared.

Tory stepped backwards a bit too quickly, bumping against

Kris. She realized he still held her hand at the exact moment the lights went out.

"Oh," she said, surprised at the sudden darkness.

Suddenly the lights to the tree clicked on, bathing the room in a glow. Tory looked over her shoulder at Tansy, who'd risen and obviously turned off the lights just as she stepped off Kris's thigh. She held a remote clicker for the lights in her hand, probably her one concession to modernizing her Christmas decorations.

"Whoa," Kris breathed beside her, giving her another squeeze around her waist before he dropped his arm. Tory let go of his hand too. "That's amazing."

And Tory couldn't help but think that was the exact word she would have used to describe this night…amazing.

Chapter Nine

"LET ME WALK YOU HOME," Kris said as he handed Tory her coat.

She took it and shrugged it on, wrapping her soft scarf around her neck. "Don't be silly. It's not even half a mile."

"It's dark out. I don't like you walking alone."

"We live in the safest place in the world. I think the last time the sheriff actually had to leave the counter of Mabel's was when Ray Ray Martin shot Roy Dell Moffit with a BB gun after mistaking him for a raccoon messing with his garbage. This is why I love living in a small town. I don't have to worry about walking home at night, especially since there's a perfectly good path between our properties."

"What about the coyotes? We had one last night skulking about."

Tory's confidence seemed to fade, and concern flickered in her eyes. "I didn't even think about that earlier."

"Yeah, so let me walk you home. It's a nice night, and you can tell me more about growing up in Morning Glory. We used to play them in baseball. They always had a good team."

Tory nodded. "Okay."

Kris felt oddly pleased to pull on his jacket and take a moonlight stroll through the scruffy pine woods that separated the Trabeau farm from the small cottage. He grabbed his jacket and opened the door. "Aunt T, I'm walking Tory home. Don't want her going alone since we had coyotes about."

That morning Kris had driven into town and purchased a set of outdoor lights that were triggered by movement. A quick check of the coop's chicken wire assured him that the dwelling for Tansy's brood of hens was secure. He hoped the lights coming on when predators skulked about would be enough to keep the chickens safe. This sort of threat was another nail in the coffin of certainty that Tansy needed to move to Tennessee with him. The coyotes and bobcats that roamed the piney woods of Mississippi were rarely a threat to humans, but Tansy was older and presently unable to move quickly. She had his granddaddy's shotgun, but if she were caught outside, she could be in danger.

"Okay," Aunt Tansy called back.

They'd left his aunt tidying up the ancient boxes that had held the ornaments. She seemed pleased by the way the parlor looked with the tree glowing in the corner and the holly and magnolia branches he'd gathered earlier that day lashed together to form a swag beneath the mantel. Tansy had woven some faux branches of berries she'd bought at the dollar store within the greenery and sat the porcelain angel in the center of the mantel. She'd directed him to spray paint large pine cones with gold that she scattered across the mantel and then added two bright red candles on either side. All there was left to do was hang the stockings.

When she'd unwrapped those, he'd gotten a particular ping in his chest. Years ago when he'd come to live with her, he'd been devastated by his parents' death. He'd hated the farm, the town, everything in life. His anger had been dark and hard like volcanic glass. His sharp edges had emerged in the form of volatile outbursts, and he thrived upon the discord he caused. He'd broken things, tried to run away, and essentially made Tansy's life a living hell. That first Christmas he'd remained cold in his bed upstairs, a raw ball of hurt. He'd grieved that he was here in Mississippi and his mama who'd always made Christmas breakfast casserole and fluffy homemade cinnamon rolls was dead in the ground. His daddy who always held one special present back and constructed a crazy game of clues in order for Kris to find the last gift was right beside his mama. He'd cried that morning and turned the covers over his head in hopes that he could disappear and not have to pretend to be happy about Christmas morning without his parents.

Eventually, he'd gotten up and pulled on sweatpants and a T-shirt. Padding down the stairs, he'd found the downstairs empty. A fire blazed in the hearth and presents sat unopened under the tree. Music spilled into the room from the radio in the kitchen, and he assumed his aunt was making breakfast because the scent of bacon tickled his nose. He walked into the parlor, his gaze finding a stocking with his name on it.

His mother had made that stocking. She'd sewn it for him while he was still a baby in her belly, and she'd proudly hung it up each Christmas Eve. He moved across the parlor and lifted it from the nail Tansy had hammered into the decorative edge of the mantel.

Inside he'd found no candy or fruit. No nuts or kitschy socks. No gift cards.

Instead, his aunt had filled his stocking with old photos and framed, handwritten stories. Most were of his father. Silly snapshots of his dad as a boy wearing a cowboy hat or posing in his skeleton costume at Halloween. The stories were funny vignettes, memories of a boy who'd tried to dress the dog in matching socks or climbed the water tower and wrote his initials. He pulled out drawings his father had done. A cartoon he'd doodled of Bugs Bunny. His old leather wallet with initials stamped on the outside. A rodeo belt buckle from high school days. Photos of his mother and father when they'd started dating. Finally, he pulled out a ring box. Inside was a solitaire diamond.

"One day you'll want to give that to someone as special as she was," his Aunt Tansy said.

He turned, dragging a hand across the dampness on his face, to find his aunt standing in the open doorway. She'd been crying, but her smile was full of the warmth he'd been lacking in his life for so long. "This was my mother's."

"Yes, it was," Aunt Tansy said, walking toward him. She had a cup of hot cocoa in each hand. She sat his on the floor beside him, lowered herself, and picked up a photo. "This picture was taken on your mom and dad's first date. I think it was a fraternity party. You know your father. He loved to dress up."

Kris swallowed hard and took the picture from her. His parents, dressed like Fred and Wilma Flintstone, were laughing, their hands joined. "Why did you do this? I've been..." He couldn't even say what he'd been because the sobs that he'd pressed down inside himself were rising to the surface. He emitted a keening sound as tears slid down his cheeks.

Tansy reached out a hand and cupped his face. "Because you are a part of him. The very best part of him. I loved your father like he was my own child. He brought joy into my life at a time I really needed someone to make me feel like living. You're what's left of him, and he would want me to remind you of who you are...and help you understand that though life is hard, it's worth the living. I know you're hurting, and that's okay. I get it because I hurt, too. Thing is, Kris, we have to keep moving forward. We have to find the good in life and hold tight to it."

Kris bent over and lay his head in her lap. He cried buckets on that floor Christmas morning. Tansy rubbed his hair and murmured endearments. When Kris finally lifted his head, he felt like a different person. He looked up at his aunt and said, "I'm sorry, Aunt Tansy."

She smiled one of the prettiest smiles, brushed his damp hair from his forehead, and said, "I know you are, angel. Now, I have something for you that I think will help."

Pulling him to his feet, she led him to the Christmas tree. Reaching behind the greenery to the back corner, she pulled out a guitar. A big red bow sat atop the acoustic Fender, and as he took it into his hands, he knew he'd found something he was meant to do.

"You're awfully quiet," Tory said.

Kris snapped back to the present. To the cloud of his breath in the night air, the crunch of leaves beneath his feet, and the woman walking next to him. "Sorry. Lost in memories."

"Coming home can do that."

"Except this never really felt like home to me. I mean, yeah, Aunt Tansy is, like, my home. I've been remiss in remembering that, but I guess I never really considered Charming a place to belong to. I lived in Texas longer than I lived here."

"What was that like? Texas, I mean."

He looked up at the stars glittering above them and thought about the house he'd grown up in. "There were a lot of cows."

Tory's laugh made him happy.

"Seriously, I grew up on a cattle farm in East Texas. It's different than what most envision as Texas. It was hilly with pine trees and pastures. Actually, it's similar to here. My life was good there. I had a horse named Little Lou and a dog named Domino. My mom baked brownies for my boy scout troop and wore a shirt that said *Kris's Mom* when I made baseball all-stars."

"Must have been hard losing them so young."

"Yeah, it was." He'd been soaking in memories and didn't want to talk about the sad boy he'd once been. "So, what about you? I heard you telling Tansy all about college and teaching, but you didn't talk much about your childhood. What was your childhood like?"

"Average. I was a quiet, nerdy child who liked to read and collect leaves and bugs. My older brother was popular, handsome, and likely to have been one of your teammates in all-stars if he'd lived near you. He didn't understand me...or like me much."

"I can't believe that."

"We get along, but we never built the kind of relationship your aunt obviously had with your father. I wish I'd had that, but he lives in Oklahoma with his wife and two children now. I'm supposed to go there for Christmas...or rather my parents want me to." She shrugged her shoulders and crossed her arms, tucking her hands beneath her arms. While the temperatures weren't below freezing, being a thin-skinned Southerner meant anything below fifty degrees merited a coat and gloves.

"You're not going? Because you're skipping Christmas?"

She issued a small chuckle. "Well, I've been running from Christmas, but between your aunt and this new Tinsel co-chair position, the holiday keeps dragging me back into its frivolity."

"Frivolity. Huh, that's a good word," he said in a teasing manner.

"Feel free to use it in a song," she said, smiling.

"Speaking of running from things. I need to try and focus on my writing." As soon as he said the words, he wished he hadn't. The problems with his new album were a dark cloud that kept following him around.

"That's my fault. I keep asking you to do things. And I was just about to ask you to help me with the script for Tinsel."

"I'll do it."

"No, I can't keep depending on the kindness of neighbors, or in your case, my neighbor's guest, to bail me out just because you're in the entertainment industry. You've done enough."

Kris felt himself get sucked into the vacuum again, but it was a place he wanted to be. He didn't mind obligating himself to her. For some crazy reason, he wanted to be near Tory, and if that meant advising over a script, he'd do it. "It won't take long to write out."

"Maybe not, but I'll do it. I've already searched for information about hosting a variety show. My friend Wren suggested I watch old footage of television variety shows. I loved watching *The Carol Burnett Show* when I was small. They did reruns and I rarely missed it, which was strange because I was such a serious little girl and never wanted to be in the spotlight."

"But you liked slapstick comedy?"

"She was a genius," Tory smiled, pounded her chest and did a Tarzan impersonation. Then she laughed at herself. "I can't believe I just did that."

Kris smiled. "You're pretty good at that. Practice a lot?"

Tory rolled her eyes. "Ha, I told you I was a dork. I

practiced it too much as a child. My parents worried about me."

He couldn't seem to stop smiling. "About that script…you sure you don't want help?"

"Yes. Work on your songs. I'll pull a script together, type it up, and maybe see if Tansy will read it and make suggestions."

They emerged from the path between the two pieces of land. At that moment, the moonlight met her in the clearing, illuminating her face. He loved that her hair curled around her face and the way her eyes looked so mysterious. She wasn't classically beautiful, but instead held an ethereal loveliness, reminding him of an ancient princess or a woodland sprite. Or Tarzan.

That last thought made him smile because he liked that she was a bit dorky…and funny…and so real.

He tore his gaze from her so she wouldn't know how much he wanted to touch her. Maybe reach out and cup her soft cheek or draw her close so he could inhale the clean scent of her shampoo. His hands still remembered the feel of hers when earlier she'd balanced on his thigh to place the angel on the tree. When she'd stepped off, he'd caught her against him, and he wanted to do that again. Her lips would be sweet. He had no doubt.

But he wouldn't.

Because he was leaving and she was a woman still healing from heartache.

They reached the steps, and from the depths of the house, he heard Edison bark. "I hear your beast."

Tory chuckled. "A beast that is all bark and no bite. Do you mind if I let him out? He'll need to do his business, and if he sees you leaving, he'll follow. I think he has a crush on you."

And I have one on you.

But Kris wasn't going to say that because he wasn't sure if that were wholly true. He felt something for Tory, but he wasn't ready to give a name to it. "Go ahead. I feel the need to scratch a dog's ears." *So I won't try to kiss you.*

She jogged up the steps, fished her key from her pocket, and opened the door. Edison burst forth like a geyser. The dog's eyes found Kris, and then the pup was upon him, jumping and licking.

"Down, Edison," Tory said in a firm voice.

Edison immediately dropped to a sitting position and looked over at Tory as she descended the steps of the house.

"Wow," Kris said, looking down at the pup who had actually obeyed a command.

"We've been working on commands that Edison seemed to have forgotten. He passed obedience school with an A+, so he knows how to behave. Okay, boy," she said, flicking her hand in dismissal.

Edison scampered off, running zigzags across the yard as if he were on a scent. They both stood silently watching him as he delighted in every smell.

"He's a good dog," Kris said finally.

"You're really good with him. Do you have a dog?"

Kris shook his head. "Wouldn't have time to take care of one. I've lived most my life on the road, and even now, I'm gone so often it wouldn't be fair to a pet. One day when I settle down, I'll get me a dog like Edison, a big, fluffy doofus who will fetch me sticks and drool on my pillow."

Tory turned to him. "You should do that. I can't tell you what joy he's brought into my life. Everyone needs someone to love them the way a dog does. Dogs don't care if you mess up or if you have a bad day. They still have snuggles to give."

"Yeah, I guess they do."

Edison loped back, sat at her feet, and smiled up at his owner as if he were validating her point. Tory reached down and rubbed his ears. "So, I'll see you on Saturday for the audition, right?"

"I'll be there."

Tory rubbed her arms. "Well, good night, Kris. Thank you for walking me home."

"You're welcome. Thanks for helping us with the tree." He stepped back, moving toward the path.

"For a Christmas skipper, I enjoyed it. It was a lovely night. Thank your aunt for me. I'm not sure if I told her how much I enjoyed dinner."

He held up a hand as she turned and led her dog to the porch. Edison turned around and watched him but didn't leave his mistress's side. He didn't blame the dog. He wanted to stay beside her, too.

Chapter Ten

KRIS DREW A SNOWMAN AT the top of his judging sheet and reminded himself he wasn't dealing with professionals here. The kid who was going to perform magic tricks for his audition was having trouble with the frog that was supposedly part of his act. He'd chosen a tree frog for some reason, and as soon as he opened the mason jar with the air holes punched in it, the frog had sprung out, causing momentary terror to ensue at the auditions.

The high school had let Community Connection use the auditorium for the auditions, and now they had a tree frog embedded in the velvet curtains framing the stage. Tory had commandeered a ladder, but the higher she climbed, the higher the frog went.

The blond boy, who wore a dress coat along with a cheerful red bowtie, looked worried. His adorable little chin even wobbled a bit. "Miss Tory, he's scared of you."

As Kris watched he was reminded of the way she'd felt in his arms when she'd tumbled off the step ladder. He'd liked the way she fit him. Which was even more reason to get his butt to Texas and stop messing around with...these weird feelings

"Cole, why in the world did you bring a live frog?" she called down to the kid.

"Because I couldn't catch a rabbit," the child said very matter-of-factly.

Next to him, Valerie stifled her laughter. "Oh, Lordy, that child is a mess."

The other judge was Mason Gardner, a local pediatrician and son of the mayor. His blue eyes twinkled as he watched Tory shake the curtains again. "This is way better than a round of golf."

Kris snorted. "I feel like I'm on the set of *The Little Rascals*."

"Welcome to my life," Valerie said with a grin.

Tory looked over at them and then back at the boy. "Let's just leave the frog for now and hope it comes down. Cole, can you do your act without him?"

The boy shook his head and the tears started for real. Valerie sprang into action, bolting from the judges' table and hurrying to the stage. She wrapped the little boy in her thin arms. "Baby, you don't have to worry. Just do your other tricks, okay? And even if you can't perform for us at Tinsel, you can wear that bowtie and help me. Can you do that? Be a helper?"

The child nodded and Valerie returned to her seat. She leaned over and whispered, "This poor angel is too fragile for this sort of thing. He's got home trouble, so catching that frog and getting it here is probably the biggest magic he can manage."

Kris felt his heart stretch at the thought of the child catching a frog and putting on a bow tie, yearning for some small success. He was sure he couldn't select what child got to perform and receive a gift card. Maybe he'd donate gift cards for the ones that didn't make the cut. It was the least he could do because he knew one thing for certain—Kris Trabeau wasn't cut out for being a dream crusher.

Ten minutes later, Cole managed to get his flowered wand, exploding deck of cards and extended chain of brightly-colored scarves from the stage. He'd cried one more time, and it was obvious he couldn't be a contender. But Kris had to give him credit for making it through the audition, even when he stopped to consult YouTube on how to finish a particular trick. It was heartwarming, adorable, and a trainwreck all at once.

"Next we have Quincy Jefferson and his high school jazz ensemble performing 'Walking in a Winter Wonderland.'" Tory started the applause.

The kids scattered around the auditorium clapped and whooped. The center kids had shown up to offer support, and Valerie and Mac had bussed them over to the high school so they could both cheer and heckle their friends. Seemed the heckling was expected, and only one small boy had tried to run off the stage and punch his friend. Mac quelled the sudden outburst, and within minutes the two boys were back smiling and laughing with each other. All the rough and tumble bars Kris had played over the past ten years had nothing on the Tinsel auditions. Dodging broken beer bottles and fist fights was a piece of cake compared to comments from the peanut gallery.

Quincy and his ensemble were dressed in white shirts and black pants and their rendition of the classic carol was perfectly performed.

"I wonder if they can do more than one song?" Valerie asked, marking a fat "yes" on her judging sheet.

"We have only two other yesses at this point so I think that's a good idea," Mason whispered.

Kris glanced back at the other judging sheets. They'd had ten auditions so far and they'd ranged from ridiculously unprepared to tragically awful. The three preteen girls had sounded good singing a current tune, and the boy who did impressions was enormously talented. But both acts would need to find different material if they wanted to related the potential donors who would be in the audience.

Last up was a lone girl. She had braided hair, a rounded face, and a faded t-shirt stretched too tight across her stomach. Her whole body seemed to tremble. Tory walked over to her, rubbed her shoulder and then whispered into her ear. The child nodded and flattened her mouth in determination.

"This is Bria Smalls singing 'Grandma Got Run Over by a Reindeer'."

The child inched to the microphone while in the background the campy Christmas classic started. Bria tried to catch up and then stopped and shook her head. Tory poked her head out. "Sorry. Let's try again."

The music started and this time Bria started on the right note. Her voice was strong, but her performance tenuous. She seemed both uncertain of the words and using the microphone, pulling back and sometimes moving too close. In the middle of the song, she quit and stepped back shaking her head again.

"I can't," Bria said loudly over the silly singing before walking off the stage. Tory looked disappointed but let the child go.

And with that, the auditions were over. So far, the judges had said yes to the jazz ensemble, the comedian, the trio of girls, two break dancers, and a kid who played the guitar well enough to strum "Jingle Bells."

"Well, I think this will work, don't you?" Tory said when

she approached them. She wore her curly hair in a ponytail and the requisite curls had escaped to tease her flushed cheeks. The heater was doing overtime, which transformed her into rosy perfection.

"I think we'll make it work," Valerie said, stacking her judging sheets. She looked over at him and Mason. "And don't worry. The children who don't perform will still be part of the event. No one is truly getting cut, just finding something that better suits their strengths. We like to teach them that everyone has his or her own gifts."

"But won't they feel bad?" Kris asked, still not comfortable with cutting children, but at the same time he knew having Cole do magic would be... uh... not entertaining.

"Our center doesn't work that way. We work hard to teach them life skills. Sometimes in life you don't get what you want, but you can find success in another way." Tory gave them all a warm smile. "Thank you, Mason and Kris, for being our guest judges. The kids loved seeing their doctor at the table."

Mason grinned. "I'm happy to do it. They're great kids."

The pediatrician's eyes slid over Tory with what looked like interest, and that bothered Kris. Not to mention, she hadn't said anything about anyone loving him being there. And *he* was a musician. A popular singer.

Kris stood, his concerns about the children quickly turning to anger at himself for feeling like chopped liver beside the handsome doctor. Why was he feeling insecure and petty? Tory was his aunt's neighbor. No need to let inferiority creep in just because he thought she was pretty. And nice. And smelled like a spring breeze in a countryside meadow. He was leaving tomorrow—the next day at latest. Or the next. As soon as he had a talk with Tansy about the farm and the new digs closer to him. As soon as he got Tansy to sign on the dotted line. Who Tory Odom did or didn't smile at wasn't any of his business.

Valerie had already taken a picture with him and gotten his autograph for five or six friends, but she couldn't seem to stop looking embarrassed when she looked at him. "And you, Kris Trabeau himself, judging our auditions. That's crazy. Just crazy. Thank you for taking the time to do this. It's so nice of you."

"Of course." He held out his hand to Valerie. She took it and then he pulled her into a hug because that seemed only right. "And thank you for doing so much for these kids. Taking a few hours out of my day is nothing compared to what you do."

"Mason," Kris said, holding out his hand, "I promise not to hug you."

Mason smiled and Kris tried to remind himself that the guy was nice. And not his competition. "Good to meet you. Can't wait to tell my golf buddies I rubbed elbows with a celebrity."

"Kris, can I talk to you before you go?" Tory asked.

"Sure."

Valerie and Mason left—Valerie to gather up the raucous bunch who were now running up and down the aisles of the theatre, and Mason to do whatever handsome doctors did on Saturday afternoons. Tory stood and gestured toward the door that led to the hallway.

"Is something wrong?" he asked when they stepped into the darkened corridor.

"Oh, no." She shooed the thought away with a wave of her hand. "I, uh, wanted to thank you for your help. The tickets for the concerts and the package for the Nashville tour are amazing. You've been so generous."

"I'm happy to do it."

"Uh, so I wanted to ask you one more favor. I know, I know, I have already asked you for so much, but I think she needs you."

He arched a brow, not because he was put out, but because he was a bit worried about what that might be. Like he suspected she wanted him to stay through Christmas for his aunt's sake. Yeah, Aunt Tansy had been dropping hints about how nice it would be to see him on Christmas morning and how much writing he could probably get done if he stayed in Charming. That the town was pure inspiration. Well, he wasn't sure about Charming being, well, that charming. If he recalled correctly, it was rather lacking in the inspirational category, but he wasn't going to surrender his intention to take a break from the world. His therapist had insisted measured solitude and meditation were key practices for successful people. Kris needed to try what she'd recommended because he had only one shot at putting his stamp on the new album.

"Bria's a bit of a tough cookie. She's in a hard situation—a foster family—and has a lot of anger. But, anyway, she has a gorgeous voice, don't you think?" Tory asked.

"Yeah, she does."

"I talked her into auditioning. She didn't want to. I had overheard her singing a few times and knew she was talented, but she said she wasn't good enough."

"She's good enough, but it was the wrong song choice and she wasn't confident."

"I know. Her younger brother picked out her song." Tory paused and seemed to measure her words. "So I'm bringing her out to my house today on the pretext of helping me select some books for the center, and I thought maybe you could talk to her about being scared of performing. I mean, maybe if someone like you who has made it thought she was good, she might believe it, too. And she's definitely good enough to sing in the show. I think we could make a special accommodation for her."

Her request surprised him.

She must have taken his silence for hesitancy. "I mean, if you're still here. I don't know when you're planning on leaving. Tansy said she thought you might decide to stay."

"I'm not staying. I have somewhere else I have to go, but here's the thing—Bria didn't finish her audition."

Tory's shoulders sank. "I guess you're right. Bria is just so…well, her self-confidence is nonexistent. I thought maybe if someone who was in the music business gave her some praise she might believe in herself. Stupid idea."

"It's not a stupid idea. Everyone needs encouragement, and some need it more than others. Aren't you and Tansy making cookies tonight? Some secret family recipe?"

"Yeah, we are supposed to. Jingle Bell cookies, I think."

"Then ask Bria to stay and help. I'll talk to her, maybe help her pick a better song. Then she can do it for Valerie and Mac, and they can say whether she can perform or not. Seems like they want all the kids who want to be involved to have a role for the event."

Tory smiled and something warmed inside him. He was becoming addicted to making her smile.

"That sounds perfect, and though Bria will not say making cookies makes her happy, I know she'll love helping us. She loves to be needed and feel special." Tory rubbed her arms in the chill of the hall.

"Then I'll see you tonight," he said, opening the door to the auditorium, letting the warmth of the large space penetrate the chill of the hallway. "Seeing you is getting to be a habit."

Tory's face flooded with color. "Habits aren't bad things."

"No, they definitely aren't."

Chapter Eleven

T ORY SET THE BOX OF books into the trunk of her car. "These are great choices, Bria. Now let's go over to Miss Tansy's and make some cookies."

Bria sat in the front porch swing, earbuds in place. She popped them out. "Why we gotta go to that old woman's house to make cookies? You got an oven."

"Because I promised to help her bake her mama's fruit cake cookie recipe, Jingle Bell cookies."

"Those sound nasty." Bria stood and grabbed the windbreaker she wore as her coat. Tory made an internal note to look for some fleeces that would no doubt go on sale after the holidays. So many of the center kids needed warm coats and jackets. For once she was thankful that Mississippi didn't have long months of subfreezing temps.

"Come on and try not to be so…umm, honest," Tory said, sliding into the car. Bria trudged down the stairs and climbed inside.

"I thought you're always supposed to be honest," Bria said.

"Not when you can be kind instead," Tory answered, backing out of the drive, her eye going to the Christmas wreath she'd hung on her door. It had been an impulse purchase when she'd stopped to buy the candied fruits and bourbon needed for Tansy's recipe. She'd declared she was skipping the holiday, but surely a simple wreath of holly wasn't breaking her vow.

Okay, it was, but she liked the way the cheerful red and green looked against the stark, polished white and black of her cottage. Her vow had been stupid. Patrick wasn't worth skipping Christmas.

When they arrived at Trabeau Farms, Tory turned to Bria. "Honey, these are my friends, so just think about trying the cookies."

Bria's mouth went flat. Tory had seen firsthand the girl didn't like to be told what to do.

"Come on. They might be good. Besides, Miss Tansy's nephew was a judge yesterday. He's a country singer and he said he would talk to you about another song you can perform at Tinsel."

"Nu-uh, I ain't doing it. I don't want to get up there and have people laugh at me like they did." Bria's chin jutted out in defiance.

"You're very good, sweetheart."

"But I ain't doing it." She opened the car door and climbed out.

Tory did the same, glancing at the girl over the hood. "Just be open to talking to him. He's a famous singer. People pay to hear him sing."

Bria looked at her and then looked away. "Maybe."

Kris came to the door and held it open as Tory brought in the grocery bags filled with the ingredients Tansy had requested. "Good evening, ladies."

"Good evening, Kris," Tory said, turning back to Bria. "This is my friend Bria."

"Nice to meet you, Bria." Kris took the bags from her. He was dressed in worn Wranglers, a soft denim shirt and cowboy boots...and looked like he could be on the cover of *Country Music Today*.

"I already saw you today," was all the little girl said as she pushed into the house and looked around.

Kris lifted an eyebrow.

Tory gave a slight shrug. Bria wasn't exactly polished in the art of conversation.

"Come on in. Tansy's in the kitchen sorting through recipes. She's already hand written copies of all her mama's best recipes for me, as if I'm going to actually cook them. Been at it for an hour."

"You don't cook?" Tory asked.

"Not if I want to actually eat." And again, the man's smile did funny things to her. "I thought maybe we'd order pizza for dinner tonight."

"Cool." Bria popped her earbuds back into her ears.

"Oh, no you don't," Tory said, tugging one back out.

"What?" Bria's eyes grew aggravated.

"You're getting points for helping neighbors. No earbuds."

Bria's ensuing sigh was both exaggerated and expected. There was a constant struggle at the center to deliver structure and expectation while balancing self-expression and autonomy. They awarded points to the kids for participation, helping out around the center, and being involved in the community. At the end of each month, points were totaled and those with enough points got to go to the movies or roller skating in Jackson. It was a system that rewarded good choices and it worked.

Tansy was in the kitchen wearing an apron and sitting on a high stool, her injured leg propped on a lower one. "Hello, Tory. Oh, and who is this you've brought to help me?"

"I'm Bria," the child said, studying Tansy's leg. "What happened to you?"

"I broke my leg. It's got pins in it."

Bria looked at Tansy's leg. "Sounds like it hurts."

"It did. But not anymore. It's nearly healed." Tansy stacked the recipe cards. "You gals ready to bake Jingle Bell cookies?"

Bria shrugged and Tory pointed to the bags Kris had sat on the table. "I got the ingredients you asked for."

Tansy gave a nod. "Perfect. Now, Kris, you sit here at the table with Bria. Here's a chopping board and knife. I want you to cut the candied fruit into small pieces. Bria, you can break these pecans up while he does that."

"I'm not baking," Kris said, looking alarmed. "I have to do some work...um, on some promotion stuff and I really need to look at—"

"Of course, you're going to help. We're doing a Trabeau Christmas and that means Jingle Bell cookies. It's a tradition we've let go too long." Tansy's tone brooked no argument. "Plus, it's fun to bake cookies."

Kris sighed. "I guess you aren't taking no for an answer."

"You're learning," Tansy quipped, rising from her stool with a wince and using her crutches to take her to the bar where she switched on the radio. Burl Ives crooned about silver and gold as Kris sank into the chair and toed the opposite one back for Bria. The girl sat.

Tory went to the ceramic bowls sitting beside the measuring cups. The colorful bowls were just like the ones her grandmother in Kentucky used when Tory spent several weeks in the summer with her. They'd always make banana bread and divinity. Good memories. Tansy handed her the recipe, Tory tied on one of the vintage aprons Tansy had lain over the kitchen chair and started sifting the needed flour.

Ten minutes later they had a stiff batter and Bria had started telling Kris about her favorite singers. They talked about rap music and R&B, and Kris shared his favorite singers in those genres. Then he asked Bria if she'd listened to country music. Tory smiled when Bria admitted to not liking country music much. She then told him she'd looked him up on the internet, much like Tory had done herself. Kris asked the child about playing instruments and then asked a seated Tansy if she would get her guitar and play a few chords.

Tory worked adding cinnamon and a pinch of salt, all while sneaking glances at the handsome man trying to get the girl to open up. But it seemed when it came to music, Bria was eager to talk.

"I ain't never listened to country music much. I hear it sometimes in stores."

Kris nodded. "It's a true American musical expression, much like jazz. Or rhythm and blues for that matter. Sometimes you hear the 'country' in the way a singer sings a song. Like you can take a Christmas song and make it sound country by the way you sing it. Or by the instruments you choose to play. Or the arrangement of the song."

Tansy came back into the kitchen, carrying her guitar. "Dang, my leg is bothering me tonight, but I can still pick a little. Tory, go on and add those fruits and the bourbon to the batter."

"So this has turned into Tory making cookies, and y'all making music?" Tory joked.

Bria looked at her. "I've heard you sing. Better stick to cooking."

Kris laughed and Tory muttered, "Cheeky child."

"Bria, you're a talented singer, that's true. But you chose the wrong song for your voice today. You have a soulful voice. That requires singing something that showcases what you can do. Aunt T, can you play a Christmas tune that has more depth?"

Tansy strummed the guitar for a few chords. "Let's see. Oh, yes, the perfect one." She started strumming something that made Kris laugh. Tansy looked up with a twinkle in her eye. "What?"

"Of course you chose this one," he said, before launching into "I'll Be Home for Christmas."

His voice was so gorgeous it made Tory stop stirring and turn to listen to him sing the beloved Christmas classic. Even Bria's mouth fell slightly open. And when Tansy joined in, harmonizing on the chorus, Tory felt tears prick at her eyes.

Good lord have mercy, they were amazing.

When they finished, both she and Bria burst into applause, which almost seemed to startle both Kris and Tansy.

"You *are* really good," Bria said, with a hint of hero worship in her voice.

"Thank you," Kris said, his sherry eyes warm as he looked at the girl sitting across from him. "You ready to try?"

"I can't sing like that," Bria said.

"Oh, you can. You haven't had anyone to teach you how to sing. Your voice is as good as mine easily. I've just had a lot of practice. I work on singing almost every day, doing notes, scales, modulations, all sorts of singer-y stuff."

Bria looked doubtful. "You're crazy if you think I'm that good."

"Show me." Kris sat his phone with the words cued up next to Bria. "Here are the words. Follow along as best you can. Doesn't have to be perfect."

Tory wanted to set the batter aside and watch the child work with Kris, but she knew it would likely make Bria self-conscious and unlikely to sing. So she scooped up the nuts Bria had crumbled and mixed them into the batter before adding a touch of lemon zest. Kris started the song over and began with the first verse. Tory peeked over her shoulder at Bria's stoic face. Kris nodded at her and she softly began to sing.

Bria's voice had weight, but it was also pure and sweet. This time Tory didn't bother to try and hide the tears gathering in her eyes. Her heart was touched by the obvious delight in Kris's eyes when the child joined her voice to his.

And it was beautiful.

Tansy joined in on the chorus, adding harmony, and even though Bria stumbled with the unfamiliar lyrics, Tory had never enjoyed a Christmas carol more than standing in a borrowed apron in her neighbor's kitchen listening to a country music star duet with an eleven-year-old girl. The most unlikely of circumstances had delivered the most beautiful moment.

When the last note ended, Tansy looked at Bria. "Sugar, you have to sing this for the benefit."

Bria ducked her head. "I can't get up there in front of strangers and sing."

"We're strangers." Kris pointed out.

"Yeah, but you know, that's different. We're just chilling here, baking cookies."

Tory cleared her throat. "Correction. *I'm* baking cookies."

Tansy's snorted. "Kris, go over there and help Tory. I'm taking this young lady into the parlor. We're going to talk and sing a bit right by that pretty Christmas tree we just decorated. Y'all make the cookies."

"Wait a minute," Kris said, making a face at his aunt. "You said these were a family tradition. You said I had to help, but you don't have to?"

"Can't you see I got a broken leg?" Tansy snapped, giving Bria a wink and a jerk of her head. "Come on, sugar."

Bria giggled and then followed Tansy from the room.

"So much for traditions," Kris said, looping a frilly apron around his neck. "Do these ruffles match my eyes?" He batted his pretty amber eyes at her.

Tory rolled her own. "Sure do, Julia Child. Now help me scoop these onto the baking trays." She handed him a scoop, enjoying the gaiety of the moment. Patrick hadn't even infiltrated her thoughts in the last few days, and her heart felt lighter than it had in…well, years. She should have been stressed over organizing Tinsel and working on the script, but with Wren Daniels volunteering to make the auction bid sheets and the kids from the center already practicing for the big night, she felt like things were falling into place.

Now, if she could just get Bria to agree to sing the final number, her plan for the entertainment portion of the night would be complete.

"These have a lot of bourbon in them. Can we get tipsy on fruit cake cookies?" Kris asked, using the melon scoop to place the dough onto the baking trays.

"Most of the alcohol dissipates when it meets heat. Alcohol has a higher boiling point than water, but some still remains. So while it's possible to get buzzed if you ate all this dough, it's improbable."

Kris laughed. "Spoken like a true scientist."

Tory shrugged before putting the first pan into the old-fashioned over. "I am what I am."

"That's a good mantra, one that seems easier to remember here."

Tory leaned back against the counter. "In Charming?"

"Yeah, my life is so different now, but somehow when you go back to who you were before, things feel simpler." He set the scoop back into the bowl and picked up the tray. Putting it into the oven, he turned to her. "I'm not sure I like feeling that way, like who I was. Still, oddly enough, it's comforting."

His words invited questions and a particular intimacy. "Everyone feels a bit like a child when they go back home. I do, too. But you sound a little sad about remembering who you were."

He paused for a moment. "Everyone has a few regrets, but there's nothing I would change. Except maybe the way I left. Tansy never wanted me to pursue music. She and I…well, we had a difference of opinion over what I should do with my life. I left mad. She was pretty angry, too."

"But you succeeded."

"Yeah, but I can't tell you how many times I almost quit and called her to tell her she was right. But somehow the stars and my prayers lined up. This year has been crazy, and everything I ever wanted is right here in my hand."

Icy fingers of reality cupped her heart. She'd do well to remember that Kris Trabeau wasn't some local guy. He wasn't a guy to mess around with. "That's a big dream."

"Yeah, it is. But it's exactly what I want to do. What I've always dreamed of doing—making it in Nashville." He looked at her. "What about you? Did you have ambitions?"

"Other than molding young minds for the future?" Okay, she sounded prickly, but not every person on the face of the planet wanted fortune and fame. She loved being a teacher, being part of something greater than herself. She loved her little cottage, the gentle quiet of lazy mornings, the way people here in Charming smiled and waved at you.

"I didn't mean…sorry. Of course, you love what you do. I see that in the way you interact with the Common Connections kids. You're probably an amazing teacher." His face looked stricken at his bumble.

"It's okay. I knew what you meant. At one point, I wanted to work in research, but the reality of doing lab work day in and day out didn't suit me. My first teaching job in Jackson was a hunch, a blip of homesickness I couldn't ignore, and on the second day of teaching, I knew that's what I was meant to do."

"What about the first day?"

"I threw up in the bathroom," she said, laughing at the memory of how nervous she'd been.

Tansy kept one eye on Bria and the other on her nephew and her pretty neighbor in the kitchen. Those two were looking mighty chummy and that warmed Tansy's heart. Her nephew had never had a serious girl when he'd lived at the farm. Oh, sure, he'd take a girl to a dance or sneak off to Jackson to the movies, but he never devoted much time to romance. She had no clue what he'd done in college, but between a demanding course load and gigging at events, she couldn't imagine him balancing a serious relationship. And then he'd spent all that time on the road, chasing his neon rainbow, stubborn as a dang mule.

Lord, Kris reminded her of Jack.

So determined. So committed. So short-sighted.

Success was a double-edged sword—one misstep and a person could come away broken. That's what she was so afraid of when he walked away from her and Trabeau Farms full of fire and determination. She hadn't wanted to see the result of his failing...or the result of his success. There were so few people who could handle what the music business threw at them. The road to fame had always been littered with casualties, and Tansy hadn't been able to stand the thought of watching yet another man she loved crash and burn.

Bria cleared her throat, causing Tansy to rip her gaze from her nephew flirting with her next-door neighbor to the child in front of her.

"Would you like to learn a few chords?" Tansy asked Bria.

"Nah, I don't know anything about guitars. I just like singing." Bria looked uncertain as to why she'd been summoned to the parlor.

"Why do you like singing?"

"I dunno. I guess it's, like, I feel good when I sing. Like I can be anyone." The child paused, shifting her gaze away. "That sounds stupid."

"No, it doesn't. That's exactly how I felt when I sang. I felt like a story came through me. I was merely an instrument like this guitar. My job was to make whoever was listening feel every note, every lyric."

Bria fingered the crystal bluebird Tansy's sister had loved so much. "You were a singer?"

"A long time ago I sang with the Mississippi Travelers. We were a folk band who had the unfortunate fate of starting when folk music was dying."

"What's folk music?"

"Well, it's not like what Kris sings. It's sort of traditional, like old-fashioned, but the messages were very…modern."

"Oh, sounds weird."

Tansy laughed. "It was a little weird, but important. Or at least it was to me. I left the band to come home and take care of my mama. She was sick and I was tired of being away from home. I never went back. Well, one time I thought I would, but it didn't work out."

"So you just quit?"

Tansy didn't want to talk about the past…or at least her past. Being in the Travelers was a part of her life she both cherished and regretted. When she'd told Jack she had to go home mid-tour, he'd given her an ultimatum, the band or her mama. Exhausted, tired of endless miles of road, and worried sick about her mother, Tansy had told Jack she had to go home. He, on the other hand, got angry at her and packed up the band.

A month after her mama passed, she tracked the Travelers down in Louisiana. She begged Jack to let her come back. He said she'd have to try out again. She sat in on a gig, but when she saw Jack kissing another woman in the wings, she froze. She couldn't sing. All Tansy could manage was to zombie walk off the stage and out the door. The band went on to replace her with the woman Jack eventually married. Her heart, her career, her dreams had been crushed. She put away her guitars and didn't pick one back up again until another child had come to live with her.

"I guess I did quit, but I never stopped loving music and the way it made me feel. I no longer perform, but I still sing. Sometimes to my chickens. Sometimes to the rain."

Bria made a funny face, but then she seemed to grow contemplative. "I sing to my stuffed animals. They're the ones my grandmother gave me before she died. That's why I got to live with the Miranda family now. No one else left to take care of me or my brother."

Tansy didn't know what to say to the child. Her heart hurt at the thought the child felt so alone. "That's tough, Bria. And not fair. But there are things you can control, and things you can't. Still, you're in charge of what you choose. You can decide a lot of things for yourself. Whether you study or not.

Whether you're kind or not. Whether you help others...or not."

Bria sat quietly for a moment. "You're talking about Tinsel. Singing because it's something I'm good at and can do for others. Mama Valerie always says that. You know, that we all have different talents and we have to figure out what they are. Like I'm not good at math. Or folding clothes."

"But you *are* very good at singing, and your talent can be a blessing to others. Your gift can touch their hearts, make them want to help Common Connection."

"I'll think about it."

"Good girl," Tansy said with a smile. "Now let's learn the words to 'I'll be Home for Christmas' just in case."

As she struck the first chord, she noted how big her nephew's smile was as he joked around with Tory. So far, he hadn't broached the conversation about the farm and her moving to the palace of old bones, a.k.a. The Hermitage. Maybe she'd been too rash? Perhaps the brochures and real estate agent documents were happenstance. Like he'd grabbed them on a whim or something.

But she didn't think so. He'd made too many comments about her inability to care for herself and the state of the farm. He'd also asked too many questions about the hunting leases she had on the land and the size of the farm. Tansy was certain his plan was to put the farm up for sale and move her closer to him so she could do sunrise yoga on the front lawn.

And that scared her. Not only because she didn't want to move away from the place she loved but because Kris had failed to develop one of the most important things a person can develop, deep roots. A tree couldn't stand without them, and she didn't want the one person she had left on this earth to topple over during a strong wind. The key was making Kris fall in love with Charming and the farm. She had to make him see that the intention he'd come home with wasn't worthwhile. Tansy wasn't up for another decade or so of disagreement.

That meant she needed to stick to her plan. And the fact that he'd developed an interest for the neighbor only strengthened her case for getting him to stay through Christmas. And if he stayed, perhaps this battle with her nephew would be one she would win this time.

Chapter Twelve

THEY HAD ONLY SCORCHED ONE batch of cookies, and that was because he and Tory had started telling stories about their childhood and forgot to set the timer. Tansy had fussed at them, reminding them that these cookies were more expensive because the ingredients were many, but she'd tempered it with an indulgent roll of her eyes when he'd given her a hug and a promise to buy more if she wanted him to.

His aunt had always been a sucker for a hug and flattery.

Still he had no clue how he was going to finagle her consent to sell the farm and move closer to him. And he was running out of time. He'd already gone five whole days without bringing it up. The one time he'd tried to talk to about the acreage of the farm, she'd changed the subject quick as a jackrabbit. He loved her independent spirit and would miss the beauty of the farm, but sometimes a person had to let things go—especially when it made sense to do so. In the long run, making this move would be better for his aunt. Change was always hard, but it had to come.

"Bria, let's show Kris and Tory how well you can sing the song now," Tansy said, nodding at the table. "You two sit there and don't eat any more cookies. I have to give some to my hair stylist and Katie Lou down at the post office. She loves Jingle Bell cookies."

Kris filched one more. "Katie Lou can make her own."

Tansy playfully smacked Kris's hand and whisked the plate of cookies off the table. "Sit."

Bria looked at them and ducked her head. "I don't want to do it."

"Yes, you will. Now we've been practicing for good reason. I'll start and you join in." Tansy started strumming the opening chords, determined the child would do as she wished. Tansy's voice was still good, not thin and wavering like so many older singers. Her singing brought back so many memories. Good ones. Evenings on the porch, singing hymns while watching squirrels tango around the pecan trees. That one flu-ridden night he'd been so fevered and she'd sung James Taylor to him while wiping his head with a washcloth. The way she'd taught him to square dance, yelling out the words to "Turkey in the Straw." He was so thankful for his aunt. She deserved to have what she'd given him, security and love.

Bria reluctantly joined in, her voice growing stronger with each word of the tune. He was fascinated by the purity of Bria's voice and the effortless way she could move from one note to the other. Her range was incredible, her tone perfect, her vulnerability endearing.

He glanced over at Tory. Tears of pride glistened in her eyes, and he felt something in his chest catch. *Uh-oh.*

This woman was too easy to like. There was so much about her he admired, like how she didn't fill silence with babbling and the way she delivered her opinions with gentle conviction. She had a great sense of humor, a kind heart, and a smile that made him want to bask in it like a lovesick fool.

No, he could not go there.

He was leaving. Soon.

But you don't want to leave. You want to stay.

When Tansy and Bria finished their duet, Tory brushed the tears from her cheeks and started clapping wildly. "Bravo, bravo!"

"That was incredible. Bria," he said, clapping his hands, too. "So you'll perform for Mac and Valerie? You have several days to practice the words."

Bria shook her head. "I don't want to. I mean, I know I should want to. I mean, I do want to help, but I can't get up there by myself and sing. I'd be too scared."

"What if I do it with you?" Kris asked.

Oh, no.

What had he just done? He wasn't staying. In fact, he was leaving tomorrow. Or at least Monday morning. He had songs to write, solitude to indulge in, and Texas deer to contemplate out the window.

"Yes." Tansy clasped her hands and Kris wanted to reach out and snatch the words he'd just said back.

"I thought you were leaving," Tory said, her voice sounding...hopeful? He wasn't sure, but he wanted her to want him to stay.

"I was. I am." He spread his hands. "I booked a place, but I think maybe staying here in Charming through Christmas makes sense. I can always go to the Texas cabin the day after Christmas. I want Bria to sing, and if she needs someone to accompany her, that's something I can do. Besides Tansy and I still have unfinished business, uh, you know, stuff around the farm."

"And now we can have a true Trabeau Farm Family Christmas. You'll come, Tory. And Bria, you, too. We'll do a round of carols on the standup piano. I'll make my mama's Christmas ham. Oh, and maybe a gingerbread house on Christmas Eve. Do y'all know how to—"

"Whoa, now, Aunt Tansy, slow down," he interrupted, pressing his hands toward her. "Tory and Bria have their own families."

Just as Tory was about to respond, the doorbell rang.

"Who in the devil could that be?" Aunt Tansy wondered, setting down her guitar.

"I'll get it," Kris said, winking at Bria who looked worried at unexpected company.

When he yanked open the door, he started laughing. Tug, Honey and their daughter Ava stood on the porch. Tug wore reindeer antlers and a red foam nose. "Start singing, Honey. They have to give us wassail if we sing."

"We don't have wassail, but we have coffee and Jingle Bell cookies. Come on in and spare me the singing," Kris said, stepping aside so his old friends could come inside. Their arrival felt like a confirmation that his impetuous offer to stay and play the guitar for Bria was the right one. He'd get his solitude on the back end of this self-imposed break from the craziness of his world. Surely his therapist would stamp her approval on spending more time with his aunt. *And,* a little voice whispered, *more time with Tory.*

Tansy clapped her hands when she saw Tug and Honey. "Lookee here, I haven't seen you in a month of Sundays, boy. And you brought your sweet wife and girl. Come on in. We have cookies."

Ava's eyes grew big and she knotted her hand in her mother's sweater. Bria had already sidled up to Tory and looked at everyone with unsure amber eyes.

"It's okay, Ava. This is Miss Tansy. She's almost as fun as me," Honey said, unwinding her daughter's fingers and going to the table where Tory and Bria were. "Hello again, Tory. Who's your friend?"

"This is Bria." Tory made introductions and Kris was relieved to see Bria sit down and study Ava whose golden-streaked hair, Nordic eyes, and freckles were the opposite of her own dark braids, smooth rounded cheeks and deep eyes. He could see a wariness in Bria's eyes.

Kris poured his friend some coffee and handed Tug some of his aunt's fruitcake cookies. Two bites and Tug was moaning in appreciation.

"These are so good. How you make 'em?" Tug asked.

Tansy eyed the dwindling stack of cookies. "You can find out when y'all make another batch. I feel like I did when I used to send you boys out to pick berries for a cobbler. Y'all ate as many as y'all brought back."

Tug grinned, crumbs peppering his beard. "I had many a bellyache but that never stopped me from your cobbler, Aunt Tansy."

Tansy's eyes danced and Kris felt satisfaction slide into his bones. She, too, needed this. Heck, he needed this. To feel a part of something, to bask in the glow of friendship and a sugar high. To be of use with Bria, who had seemed to have warmed up to Honey and Ava and was relaying a story about Tory and the frog at the auditions. His belly was full, his heart warm, and his head remarkably filled with images that tugged at him. Images, ideas, feelings, emotions that he needed to write down because they could be transferred into words. And words could become a song.

A Christmas song.

His album was slated for an early summer release. Didn't make sense to capture the fellowship of the season for his album, but still the way the kitchen smelled, the people gathered round the table nudged him to capture the moment, to find the words that said how these feelings sustained a person the whole year through. This was a glow that would last…this was way more than just Christmas. It was more than just family. More than friends.

More than presents, more than carols, more than Christmas.

His thoughts galloped, racing to get in front of each other, and even as Tug chatted about how many lights Salty had used on his front yard display, Kris found himself reaching for the notepad lying beside the kitchen telephone.

"Oh, you're going there, huh?" Tug said as Kris began to scratch down words, images, and emotions. "I forgot how you used to do that. Crazy, dude."

But Tug smiled, a wide grin splitting his fuzzy beard. He took another cookie and went to the table, leaving Kris to jot down all the good stuff that had come to him. Aunt Tansy caught his eye, and in the faded depths he could see her happiness.

A flash of something hit him.

Kris had denied himself this because he'd been a stubborn fool. He had been determined to make Tansy eat her words about his career choice. So much so that he'd stayed away, maybe even to punish her. Oh, sure, she'd come to see him play the Grand Ole Opry and they'd spent some birthdays together, neither one of them saying anything about the hard words they'd exchanged the night he left. But he'd persisted in letting hardness sit between them. Because he had to be right.

Is that why he wanted to move her closer? Why he wanted her to let this life go and come live his? Did he feel like he'd won that right? No. He wasn't that selfish.

Moving Tansy near him was about giving her a new, prettier life. A life where she didn't have to worry about leasing the farmland so she could pay the light and water bill. He wanted her safe and cared for. Yet looking now at her, sitting in the middle of the fellowship, chopping bits of candied cherries, he wondered if he'd been wrong. Not about being able to handle his career, but about Trabeau Farms and all it represented?

Lord, he felt confused about everything.

"Come play the guitar for us, Kris," Honey called motioning him toward the table and hooking the stool with her foot. "I wanna hear some Christmas songs. Tory says Bria is a good singer. She and Ava can sing for us. Tory and I will make more cookies."

Tory glanced at him, looking a bit deer-in-the-headlights. She likely wasn't used to bossy women like Honey and Tansy. He rather liked the contrast of Tory to his friend's wife. Tory was more a safe harbor, strangely calm and inviting in the tempest of the kitchen, while Honey was a bit of a general. Tory rose, surrendering her chair to Tug who sank down, cradling the chipped coffee mug in both bear paws. Honey joined her at the counter, tapping her foot as Kris took the guitar and started strumming "Jingle Bells."

For the next half hour while Tory and Honey made more cookies, with Tug sneaking a bit of bourbon for his coffee, the rest of them sang, a motley Christmas choir.

Kris tried to focus on enjoying the happiness. The smell of the cookies baking, the way the old guitar fit him, and the weathered hands of his aunt keeping time reassured him that he'd made the right decision to stay in Charming for the holidays. Question was, were his other decisions also right. Moving Tansy? Selling the farm? Holding back on something more with Tory?

The pretty biology teacher was not the kind of woman a man trifled with. His attraction to her wasn't a good enough reason to invite her into being hurt again when he left and couldn't sustain a true relationship.

Why can't you?

He knew the answer to that—he was too busy, his life too different from the quaint one in Charming. He'd go on tour to promote the new album over the summer and into the fall. He'd be stressed, tired, and distracted. Women never liked a guy who was not wholly into them. He'd learned that pretty quick. They liked the idea of being with Kris Trabeau, but they never liked the reality.

Still, there was something about Tory that made him want to draw near.

Something that made him want to be as impulsive as he'd been earlier when he'd agreed to stay to help Bria.

Tory paused on the porch as Bria ran toward her car, carrying a bag of cookies and singing the chorus to "I'll Be Home for Christmas." The smile in Tory's heart matched the one on the child's face. Bria was going to perform as long as Valerie and Mac okayed it. And the directors of the center would. Bria singing with Kris held the potential for boosting the child's self-worth, something she'd been needing so badly. So many of the other girls at the center didn't respond well to Bria's rather abrupt and too honest assessments. She didn't have many friends, but Tory was helping her learn how to be a good friend.

"I'm so happy she decided to sing at Tinsel," Kris said following her out onto the porch.

"Thanks to you," she said, turning to him only after seeing Bria shove her earbuds in and slide into the front seat of her car. "Why did you do agree to stay in Charming and play for her?"

Kris shrugged, looking around at the porch. At some point, he must have hung the same big old-fashioned bulbs they'd dug out from the attic from the eaves. The festive lights swooped to form bright scallops from the freshly painted soffits. This little touch turned a simple country porch into something magical. Ah, the power of twinkling Christmas lights.

"I don't know. I just wanted her to do it. She has such a gift but is too afraid to share it. If I can make it easier for her, then I should. Besides, Tansy wants me to stay. That's why she's pulling out all this stuff and making us turn Trabeau Farms into something that rivals the Potts Christmas tree farm. I think the train arrives tomorrow."

Tory blinked. "Train? Seriously?"

"Nah, I'm joking, but she's dragged some linens down that she's been ironing at the table. They have poinsettias on them. I know because I received schooling in the origin of the poinsettia. Comes from Mexico, you know."

"I do. I'm a science teacher who loves botany," Tory said, admiring the way the lights glinted off his brown hair. He had auburn highlights that caught in the glow and his now clean-shaven face made him look younger and revealed the hardness of his jaw.

Danger. Danger. Masculinity alert.

"You are definitely a teacher." He smiled at her and that fluttery wonderful feeling burgeoned inside her again. *Dang it.* "You know, I thought I needed solitude. I thought if I withdrew from the world, I could find what I needed. Yet, ironically, being back here, doing this Christmas thing, and working with my hands has put me closer to finding just where my muse went."

"Muse?"

"You know, the pretend being who helps me find the words."

"She's been missing?"

Kris scratched his head. "For a while now. For some reason, living on the road, eating fast food and barely sleeping was attractive to the little devil. Ever since I've found success, my muse packed bags and left town. Can't say I blame her. Turns out success is harder than it looks."

Tory moved toward the porch steps. She needed to get Bria home, but a few more seconds alone with Kris was too tempting, especially when he opened up and shared his feelings with her. "I can imagine how hard it must be to do what you do. Your muse is probably hiding from the enormous expectation you've placed on yourself. Success has great benefits, but the downside is...well...you know, I'm merely guessing here. I only have pressure when I'm undergoing a teacher evaluation or, you know, taking on providing entertainment for a benefit a week in advance." She issued a dry laugh.

"Yeah, but you've handled that beautifully. Those kids will endear a lot of people into opening their wallets and making donations to help your center."

"And not to mention they get the benefit of seeing THE Kris Trabeau accompanying Bria on a Christmas song. As soon as that gets out, I bet we sell a lot more tickets." She paused, thinking about his sacrifice. He'd planned on solitude and writing his next hits. Maybe she'd been selfish in wanting him to stay. "Is that okay?"

He pulled his gaze from the stars trying to compete with the porch Christmas lights. "Is what okay?"

"That you do this. That you help Common Connection. I mean, I know sometimes agents or managers or whatever take umbrage with their clients doing things like this."

"No, Pres will be fine with it. Or not. I don't care. My life is my own and I…" His words faded away as he retrained his gaze into the night. Kris inhaled and exhaled. "It's all good."

But something in the way he said it made her wonder. He had a successful record, a burgeoning career (as best she could tell) and a reputation as a throwback which seemed to please a lot of country music fans. But his admission of a lost muse and his reaction to anything pertaining to his career or writing seemed to trigger an odd reaction.

"Good, because it's going to go a long way to help the center," she said.

Kris studied her face. "You know I'm happy to help you, Tory."

The way he said her name, as if he truly liked her, made her warm all over. She knew she shouldn't like it so much. He was staying for the short haul and would be gone like the wrapping paper on the curb the day after Christmas. He wasn't the guy to help her get over her heartbreak—a heartbreak that seemed to have miraculously lessened over the past week.

Oh, sure, some might say he was perfect—not looking for anything serious, gorgeous and nice, and, oh, yeah, famous. But he was also the kind of guy a woman fell hard for. She couldn't risk that again so soon, so she needed to take those warm feelings, ball them up like a pair of socks, and tuck them into the lost laundry basket inside her. Never to be found.

"Well, I should be going. Bria needs to get home."

Kris reached for the plate of cookies she held in her hands. "Let me carry this for you."

"It's just cookies. I'm pretty sure I can manage getting

them to the car," she said, smiling in spite of herself. *Silly man.*

He dropped his hands. "Of course. Don't know what I'm thinking."

"You're being polite."

"Or wanting to spend a few more seconds with you," he said, his mouth curving into a smile.

Tory's heart did a little drop into her stomach, like she was on the tilt-a-whirl and just hit a hard turn. Maybe she *was* on a carnival ride, but she needed to get off. Fast. Before she stayed too long and ended up sick on the midway. "Are you trying to steal my cookies?"

Kris laughed. "No. Is that what you think?"

She shrugged and started down the steps before she did something crazy...like kiss him.

What would that be like?

Probably as delicious as the Jingle Bell cookies she held.

"I should go," she said instead.

"You should," he said, watching as she descended. Just as she got to the bottom step, Bria blew the horn.

Tory jumped and nearly slipped off the step. Kris reached out a hand and bounded down the steps to take her elbow. "You okay?"

His hand was so warm on her arm. The chill of the night made her breath come in little clouds and a shiver run up her spine. "You seem to always be there to steady me. I really don't almost fall this much, I promise."

"I don't mind catching you. Not at all."

His flirty words flustered her. "I guess I better go before she wakes the neighbors. Oh, wait, that's me."

Kris merely stood there smiling at her, making her feel... warm...glowy...interested.

"I'll see you next week. Tansy said something about a projector and old reels of home movies. Not sure why I'm required to be there, but she's pretty insistent." Tory made it off the step and onto the walkway.

"Yep. That she is. Good night."

"Night," Tory said, heading toward the car and the child who obviously had grown weary of waiting. She slid into the cold car and looked at Bria. "Really?"

"It's cold out here."

Point taken.

"Well, you scared me so bad I nearly fell off the step. Here, hold my cookies," she said, handing the plate to Bria, cranking the car and putting it into reverse.

"Did you want to kiss him?" Bria asked.

Tory stepped on the gas too hard and ricocheted backwards too fast. She braked and looked at the child. "No. Of course not."

Bria smiled, her teeth white and somehow knowing in the darkness. "I think you wanted to kiss him."

Chapter Thirteen

TANSY THREADED THE FILM THROUGH the loop, lining up where it needed to be to catch the second spool. Her father had bought the home movie recorder and projector when she'd been a child. He'd filmed everything for a good two years. When Jenny died, he'd shelved the camera, and then when Robert was a toddler, he'd dragged it out again.

"He brought so much back to us," she said aloud.

Kris looked up from the box full of spools. "Huh? Who did?"

"Your father. He brought us all back into the light. I always said he was God saying 'I'm sorry.' You know, for taking Jenny so young. I know that's silly. Never thought God to be the kind who gives and takes away capriciously, but then again there is that whole Job thing. Anyway, your daddy was something special for sure." Tansy flicked the switch so that the film caught. She liked the hum and clack of the machine. Took her back to the times her parents invited their neighbors over to see their footage of the Grand Canyon or that one time they went to Canada. Her mother always called it "cocktails and a movie," though Tansy's cocktail was always sweet tea.

Kris's mouth curved. "Sometimes it's hard for me to remember him. I mean, I do. But his face fades away and I have to think hard to remember him. I mostly remember him working outside. He loved cutting the grass on his John Deere lawnmower."

"Probably reminded him of his days on the tractor, harvesting with our father. Robert never complained about work. He seemed to like being outdoors in the sunshine getting dirty and sweaty. Always up for adventure." Tansy smiled when the film started, ghostly shadows moving against the fireplace hearth. The room was too bright and she had yet to hang the white sheet she'd have to use in place of the screen. The tattered, moth-eaten screen hadn't been salvageable.

"He liked adventure. He was a good father to me and I miss him," Kris said, pulling out two other reels that were marked with Christmas 1959 and Christmas 1960. "But I'm glad you took me in, Aunt Tansy. Maybe I didn't say that enough."

Tansy's heart melted at those words. "You're so much like him, a most determined man. Besides, what was I supposed to do? Leave you in Texas?" She knew she said it like Texas was poison, but she'd been so angry when Robert had married Leah and moved out to where her family lived. Trabeau Farms was part of who Robert was, and he had just handed it over to Tansy and took off after that blonde debutante like a man who didn't have a dang lick of sense in his head.

But that was a man for you—a pretty thing could turn his head and have him doing things no one expected, like breaking promises, tossing over convictions, and leaving people behind. Her heart squeezed because her thoughts had shifted to Jack. Funny how she could forget about him for months and then something simple like happening upon a Dum Dum sucker or an old fishing cork could bring his memory back to her so fast and hard she couldn't remember how to breathe. Some things never heal. But some did. Take Tory. Her neighbor was looking fairly glowing and less sad-sack here lately.

She'd met Tory's fiancé once. Patrick was friendly enough, but Tansy could tell he thought he was smarter than everyone he talked to. She always disliked that in a person, intellectual superiority. She knew there were a lot more people smarter than she was. All someone had to do was ask her old English teacher Mrs. Hawthorne who was in The Willows retirement center, old as dirt but still able to relay that Tansy Trabeau had never been impressive in the classroom. Still, Tansy disliked people who enjoyed being smarter than everyone else in the room. It was something she'd drilled into Kris.

Kris had always been abnormally bright, working his way through gifted and talented classes, eyebrow-raising scores on the SAT and ACT. He'd excelled in school and even more in running the farm, which is why she'd been doubly incensed when he insisted on leaving Charming and following his passion. Trabeau Farms had needed him, and just like his father he'd chased after something that couldn't last.

She looked at her nephew sitting on the floor, organizing the reels of old footage, and her heart squeezed again, this time full because he'd said he would stay at the farm through Christmas. Thank goodness. *Job well done, Tansy.*

"Speaking about how you took care of me, I figure I owe you the same. I wanted to talk to you about the farm and..." Kris paused, looking up at her with cautious eyes. "Well, you never told me how much acreage was leased and how much you still have to take care of."

Uh-oh. Here we go.

Kris cleared his throat. "I guess I've been wondering because you're getting older, and with you falling—"

"I tripped. I didn't fall," she interrupted, sitting back in her chair and crossing her arms. She looked defensive so she made herself uncross them. Okay, so this conversation was long overdue. She could only redirect so many times before he forced information from her. Technically, Kris owned his father's half of the farm.

"Right, but the result was the same. You were out here alone with no one to help you."

"Joe helped me. That's how people do here in Charming. We help one another. Joe checks on me every time he delivers the mail. And sometimes he brings me some of Mary's strawberry fig jam. And tomatoes. The man can grow the heck out of some tomatoes."

Kris sucked in a measured breath. "I don't doubt Joe's a good guy, but my point is you're here alone and this is a big house. I've been working steadily for a week, painting, mowing and fixing leaks, and I still have a list as long as my arm of things that need to be done—things you can't do even if your leg was healthy."

"Bullfeathers!" Tansy crossed her arms and decided she didn't care if she looked defensive. "I saw your brochures, you know."

"What?" His eyes widened. "Where did you see brochures?"

"In your bag. I wasn't nosing around. Not really. I went into your room to smooth your covers that first day you were here and they caught my eye. So I know why you're truly here." Anger rose to replace the contentment she'd been feeling earlier. "How dare you come down here after having been gone for so long and try to get me to sell the farm?"

"I came to *visit* you, and those are just some options. I thought you may want a way out, a new start in a place where you could be, uh, more comfortable." Kris pulled his knees up and looped his arms about them. He looked far too casual to be discussing putting her in a home. "Wait, is that what this is all about? All this Christmas stuff? You're trying to, what, make me fall in love with Christmas at the farm?"

"And what's wrong with wanting you to see value in where you're from? This is *our* farm on land that was granted to my great grandfather back in the 1800s. You think I'll toss up a for sale sign and leave Charming like it's not a place I belong to? Besides, those brochures are *not* options. Those are putting me out to pasture and tossing away your heritage like it means nothing."

Kris pushed up from the floor. "Look, I know change is hard, Aunt T. But I can't leave you here by yourself any longer."

"It's not your decision."

"I'm your only living relative."

"No, you're not. I got cousins somewhere."

"Okay, I'm your *closest* living relative. Just be a tiny bit open to the possibility of coming to live near Nashville. Near me. The Hermitage is a great facility. There's a huge waiting list."

"Facility? Who wants to live in a facility? I want to live in a *home*."

"I misspoke. It's not a facility, it's a great community. They have yoga. You used to love to do yoga. And a pottery studio."

Tansy just stared at him.

Finally, he spread his hands apart, his brown eyes so much like her brother's. "Aunt T, I can't leave you here all by yourself. I know it's the family farm, but it's dangerous for you to be here with no one to check on you."

"I covered that. And if you're so worried, you can come visit more than, say, once every ten years."

"Okay, I can't leave you here without *family*. Without me.

I live in Nashville, and I have a very demanding career. I want you near me if at all possible. Besides, I finally have enough money to take care of you. Yeah, this farm has been in our family for a while, but it's just a place. You've already leased a lot of it and it's no longer a working farm. Our family—me and you—that's what's important, and that doesn't have to be here in Mississippi."

Tansy rubbed a hand over her face. "That's what you don't get. This farm is part of being a Trabeau. You can't sell your birthright. This is who you are."

Kris shook his head. "I know you're super attached to the house, but it's just a place like any other. This town is a town like any other. You can't tell me that you couldn't be happy at The Hermitage being with people your age and eating healthy meals and—"

She held up a hand and he snapped his mouth shut. "Maybe you're right."

"I know I am."

"But I can't believe you don't understand why Charming and Trabeau Farms are so special. I'm going to show you. In the next week, somehow, someway, I'm going to make you understand what being a Trabeau is all about. I'm going to show you why Charming, Mississippi, is your true home."

"Aunt Tansy," Kris sighed, shaking his head. "Making cookies and singing carols isn't going to make me change my mind. I wanted to do something nice for you. Because I felt bad about how I left all those years ago."

"I'm not mad at you, Kristopher. Back then, I was irrational because I wanted to protect you. Was I hurt that you stayed away? Yeah, I was. But I understood. I wanted you to feel like Charming and the farm was your home, but your desire to chase your dreams outweighed your need for a place to land.

Still, you're older and wiser, and I hope you can see that this is more than just a piece of land. So it may seem silly to you that I'm trying to show you what Christmas on the farm means to me, but there's something here that you need, whether you realize that yet or not."

At that moment, the doorbell rang.

Kris studied her for several seconds.

"It's okay. Get the door. We have more to say, but it can wait." Tansy turned back to the projector.

"Alright, we'll talk later," he said, sliding from the room looking not exactly defeated but willing to put off the conversation. The kid had never liked confrontation much. Honestly, she had hoped that over the last week, she'd shown him enough that he would let go of his plan. Obviously, she'd not done enough.

She heard muffled conversation and a decided whine of excitement. *Oh, no. Edison.*

"Hey, Miss Tansy, I hope it's okay that I brought Edison with me," Tory said, looking guilty as she came into the room. Edison walked next to her, tongue lolled out, brown eyes yearning. He no doubt wanted to eat Tansy. Or at least lick her to death.

"Why in the world?" Tansy asked.

Tory swallowed and then looked at Kris. Her nephew looked amused but didn't say anything. Tory glanced back at Tansy. "Uh, well, I've been over here so much, and Eddie's been lonely. He stays by himself all day so I hate leaving him inside all night. He's just had a nice romp outside, and he's promised to be good. Right, Ed?"

The dog looked up at her, his big hairy tail thumping on the floor. Then he looked at Tansy and woofed.

"That means yes." Tory smiled adorably. Tansy felt herself

moved by this neighbor who now felt more than a mere neighbor. And, okay, she liked the dog. Sort of.

"Fine. Just keep him on a leash and near you. I don't want his big tail knocking stuff off the tables." Tansy rose and reached for her crutches. When would she be able to stop using them? She had a doctor's appointment in a few days. Her hope was Dr. Jacobson would tell her she'd healed enough to wear a walking boot. She was tired of hopping around like a jumping bean, knocking into things. If she could ditch the crutches, Kris would see how capable she was.

She thumped around Tory and Kris, shooting the stink eye at Edison, who almost seemed to laugh at her. She patted his head before she could think better and earned herself a swipe of his tongue. The linen cabinet held a starched white sheet and impulsively she grabbed a dog biscuit from beneath the kitchen sink. When she went back into the parlor, Tory sat on the walnut armchair and Kris sprawled on the pink damask settee, an incongruity among the trellis of roses intertwined in the fabric. Edison had collapsed at Tory's feet, setting his big head atop his giant paws. When Tansy entered, the dog lifted his head and whined.

"Tory, hun, I need to sit in that chair. Could you sit with Kris on the couch? Hard for me to get up from the deep cushion."

Tory paused, looking over at the couch where Kris watched her. Tansy could feel the hesitancy and almost rolled her eyes at how silly they were acting. The dance they were doing around the obvious attraction they had for one another was both endearing and ridiculous. Maybe they needed a little nudge. "For heaven's sake, darling, Kris bathed today. I think. Did you bathe, Kristopher?"

"Aunt Tansy," Kris said, his voice holding a warning.

Tory turned the color of the new yarn Tansy had ordered off the internet, Hot Pants Pink. Tory glanced at Kris and said, "I'm not worried about…I mean, of course, I can let you have this seat."

"Good."

The younger woman rose, but Edison remained sprawled at the foot of the chair. Tory looked back at her beast, but the dog didn't budge. Just thumped his tail. Tansy rolled her eyes and slipped the mutt the biscuit he'd been waiting on before sinking onto the abandoned chair. "Okay, before you two get too comfy, take this sheet and stretch it across the hearth. I have two small pins to secure it. This will have to serve as our screen."

Kris rose and took the sheet, giving her a flat look that seemed to say *stop what you're doing*. Tansy smiled on the inside because she knew Kris didn't like her handling him, but there were times when a man had to be pushed off a ledge. Maybe if she could get him and Tory more interested in each other, her nephew would want to visit Charming more often…and would stop trying to talk her into moving to Nashville and selling their farm.

Tory followed Kris to the fireplace, and after a few dropped corners, they managed to secure the sheet. Tansy watched, noting the awkwardness between them, admiring how well they could suit if they stopped pussyfooting around their attraction. She also snuck a few pats on Edison's broad, soft head. She made sure neither of them saw her loving on the mutt.

"There," Kris said, pressing a second pin into the plaster. "I'm going to fix some spiced tea. Anyone else want some?"

"Me," Tory said.

"Auntie?"

"It's always good to have a man around to make tea," she said, giving Tory a wink. Kris made a face before shaking his head in disgust. Tory looked decidedly uncomfortable. Tansy decided that being old and meddlesome was a bit of fun.

Five minutes later, they dimmed lights and Tansy turned on the projector, its hum the only sound in the room as she started the spools. Two children playing in the snow appeared on the sheet. Two small girls. Her and Jenny. "That's my sister."

"Jenny, right?" Kris asked.

"Yes. Look how pretty she was. And, have mercy, I look like a boy with that bowl haircut," Tansy said, smiling at her and her sister tossing snow at each other. She remembered that Christmas well. They'd snuck their mother's good scarf to wind around the snowman, earning them a good scolding and no dessert. No dessert used to be a real punishment, especially for her and Jenny because her mother made the best rice pudding and strawberry shortcake. Her stomach had been very sad that day.

"Kris looks like you," Tory commented, sipping her drink.

"Like I said, I had a boy's haircut. I think that was because I had gone to sleep with chewing gum in my mouth and it got tangled in my hair."

The images shifted. Her dear mother wearing pearls and playing the piano on Christmas Eve. Aunt Ramona, Uncle Carlton, and a few neighbors joined in the singing. She and her sister danced. It could have been any family in the late fifties with a tinseled tree and punch bowl, but it was her family. And it was filmed right here in this room. In fact, the tree stood in the same spot, holding many of the same ornaments.

Raw, unshed tears gathered in her throat as she watched

the antics. There was no audio for these older films, but she could see the joy and that was enough. The strip ended and she picked up another spool and threaded it onto the projector. This time the film was in color and there was audio. Little Robert rode a stick horse, play guns strapped to his hips in a holster. He also wore a cowboy hat and mischievous smile.

"Mama, watch me," he said, dimples in his cheeks. Then a young Robert galloped around stepping on wrapping paper and trampling boxes. Then she appeared, a thin, awkward teenager, grabbing at Robert as he squealed trying to avoid her.

Kris leaned forward. "That's my dad?"

"Yep. Cute little booger, wasn't he?" Tansy said, unable to rip her eyes from her younger brother as a child. Lord, she missed him so. He'd been so fun, so full of life.

On the film, Robert turned. "Wanna see me play my guitar?" He bent and picked up a toy guitar and started singing an old Gene Autry tune.

"There's where you get it," Tansy said, laughing at the exuberance Robert portrayed. He'd had very little musical talent, but his showmanship couldn't be paralleled. Tansy had seen Kris perform. He had more of his daddy than he knew.

The film continued. Sweeping footage of buffets, pressed linens, flower arrangements of carnations and ivy. More of the family opening presents. Robert riding his bike. Tansy playing her guitar on the porch. A brief glimpse of Jack, which made her stomach flip over and her heart ache. The film ended with Robert sitting at the kitchen table with her mama, eating eggs and bacon.

"What are you going to be when you grow up?" her father asked Robert.

"A fireman. Or a cowboy. I'm not sure," her brother said,

looking into the camera. "But I'm going to live here with you and mama."

"Here?" her father asked, a chuckle in his voice. "You're not going to get married and build your own house?"

"Why would I do that? This is the house I'm getting and I don't like girls," Robert said, smiling and revealing a gap between his teeth.

"Hey, what about me?" a ponytailed young Tansy asked, buttering her toast.

"You can live here with me. This is our home. Dad said so." Robert turned away and the camera zeroed in on Tansy's mother.

Grace Trabeau's hair had been pin-curled and she wore a shirtwaist dress. Button pearl earrings nestled into her dark curls. Lipstick in place, of course. "See what you've done? He'll never leave now."

The film ended.

Tansy turned on the lamp next to her, careful to wipe away the tears swimming in her eyes before Kris or Tory saw her lost in the past and the memories of all who were no longer here...even though she carried them all in her heart. "Well, that's probably enough for tonight."

Tory blinked against the light. "What a lovely family you had, and what fantastic Christmases. I saw a lot of familiar decorations. Like the angel."

"Yes, Lord, as Kris is always saying, I don't throw near enough away. I tend to hold on to the past a bit too hard." Tansy didn't look at Kris. She figured he'd feel manipulated, but she hadn't known what had been on the spool. It had been well over thirty years since she'd watched those old home movies.

"Some things are worth holding onto, though," Tory said,

setting her empty tea cup on the coaster. Edison's tail started thumping and the dog rose and stretched. A yippy canine yawn followed.

Tansy had almost forgotten about the mutt. He had been pretty good, considering. His laughing sherry eyes and soft head made her miss the dogs of her past. Chickens were easy to tend, but hers didn't like to be held much. Independent chicks is what they were.

"I've always thought so," Tansy said. This time she looked at Kris. His mouth went flat and he looked away.

Good.

He should feel guilty for wanting her to sell the farm.

"I should get going," Tory said, picking up Edison's leash and delivering a scratch behind his ears. His tail cranked up and Kris just managed to snatch up a small bird sculpture from the Victorian end table before Edison's tail sent it careening to the floor.

Kris handed the figurine to Tansy. "I'll walk Tory out."

"You don't have to. I've got Edison to escort me home. He's a fierce protector, remember?" Tory said, clipping the leash to the dog's halter. The woman didn't look at Kris, and Tansy wondered why her neighbor was so quick to escape. She suspected—no, knew—that the woman was attracted to her nephew. Perhaps she was afraid to let herself go there. Tansy understood that inclination. She'd been in love with Jack for a year before she let him see a glimpse of her heart.

Kris looked as if he wanted to protest, but Tory didn't give him time. She walked over and gave Tansy a hug. "Thanks for inviting me to see some of your past Christmases. It was a treat. Oh, and the spiced tea was as good as always."

Tansy hugged the child back, giving her a little squeeze. "You helped me make Christmas mine again. Thank you."

Tory turned to Kris. "I'll see you soon. Bria said you were coming to the center to practice with her. I'm so happy you're doing this with her. She actually sounded excited, and she never sounds excited."

"It's going to be great. I predict the most successful Tinsel ever," Kris said.

"I hope so. Good night," Tory gave a wave and escorted her dog to the foyer. The front door shut with a soft bump.

Tansy looked at Kris. The man looked sad that he'd missed an opportunity to walk Tory home. "Sugar, I'm going up to bed. Too many memories for me tonight. I know you want to talk about the hermit house and selling Trabeau Farms, but I'd rather not. Let's talk after Tinsel. We both need time to think about the future and what we both want."

Kris nodded. "That's fair. I just want you to know that I love you, Aunt Tansy, and I want what's best for you."

"Well, sugar, I love you, too. Good night," she said, as she switched off the projector and turned off the globe lamp.

As she made her way through the dining room toward her room, Kris called, "And it's The Hermitage."

"And I ain't going to it," she whispered as she closed her bedroom door.

Chapter Fourteen

K RIS ARRIVED AT THE COMMON Connection Community Center, which was housed in a former bank branch, later than he'd planned. He'd intended on coming earlier but ended up having to fix the broken cupboard in the kitchen. Then he'd gotten a call from Preston that hadn't sat well with him. Seems his management was content to do exactly what the label wanted, which gave Kris reservations about not only the direction his career was taking but also his representation. He'd been with Preston for three years and had always trusted the man had his best interests at heart. But he knew Preston also felt the pressure to sell more records… and his mortgaged 6,000-square-foot house after his most recent divorce. Preston wasn't normally one to play nice, but maybe his desire to please Strata Records had colored his perspective.

"Nick's emailing me almost daily, man. He's worried because you're not giving them any feedback," Preston had said to him while Kris squeezed his cellphone between his ear and shoulder. The screws had stripped on the hinge of the cabinet door and he couldn't get them out.

"I've been busy."

"Just choose the ones you like best. Someone at Strata will go over your selections to make sure the album is balanced and then book the studio guys. The deadline is closing in, man."

"I'm not sure about what they've sent so far," Kris finally said after several seconds of silence.

"Dude, this is your dream label, right?"

"Yeah. Strata Records is the label I wanted more than any other, but I am not loving the stuff they're sending over. We've been over this. Those songs are not me, Pres."

"It's good music. These are tried and true songwriters whose shelves have to be refortified every awards season because they get too heavy from all the hardware. They write hits and Strata knows the market. Country crossover is trending big right now. We talked about this a week ago. Why are you still having doubts?"

Kris sighed. "Because that's not what I sing. I don't mind doing something a little bold on the album, but my fans are going to expect an old-school country vibe. That's what they like about me. You always say I should stick to what works, right? Dude, this could be as bad as KISS going disco back in the day. I don't want people burning my new record in the streets."

Preston laughed. "I'm not sure they're gonna do vinyl on this one."

"Okay, *virtually* burning the album, but you know what I'm talking about." Kris set the screwdriver down and contemplated his next move on the cabinet. He was stuck, and he knew this was a metaphor for his career, too. Strata had given him what he thought he wanted, and now he wasn't so sure it had been a good fit after all. His gut told him so. And most of the time he trusted his gut.

"I do." Preston paused, and Kris could visualize him tapping a pen and thinking of the right way to deal with a whiney entertainer. But Kris wasn't being irrational. He was looking out for himself, and Preston should be doing the same.

"Good. Then act like you're on my team."

Preston drew in a dramatic breath, making Kris roll his eyes. "Of course I'm on your team, K-Dawg. Look, I don't think the demos they've sent are as far off target as you think. Whatever ones you choose, you'll put your own stamp on. You can Kris Trabeau them right up."

"And the songs I'm writing?"

"They'll give them a shot. Wait, you have them ready? It's fine to send something rough recorded on your phone. I'll forward them to Nick and get some feedback for you."

Kris sighed, his stomach knotting because he hadn't even picked up his guitar since he and Bria had played on Saturday night. It was now Tuesday and the clock was ticking. "I'll have something soon."

"Okay. Sooner rather than later."

"I know."

"So are you good?" Preston asked.

"Yeah, sure." Kris lied through his teeth. He didn't feel good about any of this. Not to mention he never should have gotten so involved in the Tinsel thing. Sure, helping Bria was a good thing, but he'd derailed his original plans. And for what? Making cookies, fixing cabinets, and flirting with a woman he shouldn't be flirting with? He'd lost focus. He should have already talked Tansy into moving, then packed up and gone to Texas days ago. There was a cabin in Texas nestled in solitude, waiting to be filled with mind-altering lyrics and heart-wrenching melodies, and he'd traded that for trying to figure out how to pull a stripped screw from the oak cabinets his great grandfather had built.

He'd hung up, googled how to deal with stripped screws, and headed to Common Connection because he'd promised Bria he would practice with her today.

He climbed out of his car, eyeing the entrance, which was a glass-front door with a buzzer and camera. Pressing the button, he thumbed the strap on his gig bag and waited.

"Oh my gosh, it's Kris Trabeau," the voice said over the intercom. The buzzer sounded and he pulled the door open, a little nervous about the excitement shown in the intercom voice. He was pretty sure it was Valerie.

The woman flew around the corner with an alligator smile in place and gray-green eyes crackling with excitement. She wrapped him in a hug that took his breath from his body. "I'm so glad to see you again. I can't believe you're here and that you're doing this for Bria. And us. You're doing this for us. It's so exciting!"

Kris shrugged out of the pressure cuff named Valerie and smiled. "I'm happy to help."

Of course, that's not what he'd been thinking earlier. No, he'd been berating himself for missing out on his writing session in the quiet East Texas cabin. But he still had time. No matter what Preston said, he had time. Or he hoped he did.

"Hey," Bria said, stepping into the reception area, which was taken up by a huge bank vault which they'd tried to disguise with a large television set. Couches with stains, one with a hole in the arm, sprawled crooked in the empty space. A granola bar wrapper lay on the floor. "You're late."

"I know. I'm sorry."

"Most of the kids went over to the kitchen across the street. The church provides dinner every evening. Not always a hot meal, but something decent," Valerie said, securing the door behind him.

"Where's Tory?" Kris asked, stepping inside and lowering his gig bag.

"She's in the back practicing with some of the other kids who are participating in Tinsel. Mac's with the others at the church. Come on in. Can I get you a water? Or a soda?"

"No. I'm good. Where should Bria and I practice?" he asked.

Bria still hadn't stepped fully into the room. She looked upset. Maybe even aggravated. Kris glanced at his watch. He'd been only twenty minutes late.

"Come grab a study room. All the kids are done with homework and reading programs for the evening. We still have to take a few kids to basketball practice. I'll let Tory know you're here." Valerie left before Kris could say anything more. He felt a bit like a paper caught in a whirlwind, finally floating back onto the ground.

Bria started walking toward the door Valerie had disappeared through. She didn't invite him to follow but he went anyway.

The hallway was empty, but there were many bulletin boards full of art, one with pictures of all the students with a short bio, and inspirational posters. Bria opened up one of the doors and walked inside. He stood in the doorway of what had likely been an executive's office. Inside was a whiteboard, a table and a few chairs. A computer desk that held what looked to be an ancient IBM computer was shoved into a corner.

"Is this where you want to practice?" he asked.

Bria shrugged. "Sure."

Today she wore a sweater that was too small and jeans that were too short. Her braided hair was pulled into a high ponytail, and her sneakers had seen better days. Here he'd complained about not having his precious solitude so he could keep building his career, and this child was likely wearing second-hand clothing that looked more third-hand. Shame burned inside him.

"Cool," he said as he sat down, but he didn't shut the door. "Did you learn all the verses to 'I'll Be Home for Christmas'?"

"Yeah. They weren't that hard. I looked up some other songs, too." Bria paused. "What are chestnuts? Are they, like, pecans?"

"They're nuts. Up north people roast them. You can buy them on street corners in New York City." He unzipped his bag.

"People talk about them a lot in Christmas songs. And pie. They like to talk about pie, too."

That made him chuckle. "Well, eating is an important part of Christmas, I guess."

"Yeah, like them cookies we made. They weren't too bad. Sharon really liked them. She's my foster mom. She said she wanted the recipe, but I don't know why. She's not a good cook at all. She burned macaroni and cheese in the microwave. I didn't know anyone could do that." Bria shoved her hands in her pockets. "Can I close the door? I don't want people to hear me."

"Why not?"

"Because. I just don't." Bria crossed her arms and arched an eyebrow. She definitely had an attitude.

He hid a smile. "Sure."

They spent the next thirty minutes working on timing, inflection, and making sure the song was in the right key for her voice. There were times he found himself joining in and the harmony sounded good, but he didn't want to steal her thunder. Her voice was lovely, pure, and held the right note of wistfulness.

After a few minutes, he set the guitar on the table. "Often when someone sings a song, he or she tries to convey the emotion behind the words. What do you think about this song?"

Bria shrugged. "Dunno."

"Well, it's about someone saying she's coming home for Christmas, but in the end the song says 'if only in my dreams'."

Bria's squinched her face. "Like this person ain't getting to go home? Just thinking about it?"

"Right."

He waited a few minutes, letting the notion sink in.

"I don't really want to go back to where I used to live. Our house was so nasty after my grandma died, and my mama was always gone, leaving me and Marcus there by ourselves. Sometimes we didn't have food. No heat. She sold some of our good stuff to other people. One day I'd have something, the next I wouldn't. Now at least me and Marcus got someone to cook for us—even if she burns stuff—and wake us up on time for school. So I don't want to go home. Even in my dreams." Bria shrugged her shoulders, her topaz eyes so matter of fact. Like what had happened to her was no big deal. This was Bria's normal.

Kris wanted to cry. He'd been trying to get the girl to reach inside herself and pull forth the longing in the song, but instead she'd slammed him with a heavy truth. The kids at this center needed so much more than a new jacket or a toothbrush. They needed someone to make a sacrifice for them, to value them. They needed someone to stop worrying so much about his stupid career and worry a bit more about helping them. Bria was a reminder that he owed people more than just music. He owed people a chance to matter.

"Okay, so instead of thinking about going home, think about going someplace where people love you and want you there. Think about a fireplace, hot cocoa, and a big Christmas tree with pretty ornaments. Oh, and food. Lots of food. Just imagine a good place."

"Like Miss Tansy's."

Another shot to his heart. "Yeah, imagine Aunt Tansy's house."

"She said I can come over on Christmas Eve. You think she meant that?"

"She did. I hope you can come. And your brother Marcus and your foster parents, too, if they want."

"I'll ask." Bria opened the door and Tory stood on the other side, her fist lifted as if she were about to knock. "Oh, hey, Miss Odom. We just got done."

Tory smiled. "Everything go okay?"

Bria nodded. "Yep. I'm gonna kill it. Long as he shows up on time. He was late today."

"You're a tattletale." Kris shoved his guitar back into the black canvas bag and winked at Tory.

Tory's cheeks pinked, which made her look adorable. She wore a white silk blouse and tidy black skirt that fell to just above her knees. The woman had pretty knees...something he'd never noticed on a woman before. Her curly hair had been tamed into a low ponytail. And if she'd been wearing cute black-framed glasses, she'd be totally rocking the saucy librarian look.

Bria looked up at Tory. "Good news. I think he wants to kiss you, too."

Tory's mouth fell open. "Bria."

"What? It's true," the girl quipped, sliding past her and hurrying down the hall.

Tory turned back to him, her cheeks an even deeper pink. If Kris were prone to blushing, he'd likely be the same color. "Oh my gosh, she's a precocious child."

Kris shrugged. "She's astute."

Tory stilled, her gaze meeting his. "What do you mean by that?"

He ignored her question. "What did she mean by me wanting to kiss you, *too*?"

"Nothing. I don't."

He smiled. "You don't?"

"Of course not. I mean, that would be ridiculous. You're… uh, you. And I'm just a small-town girl."

"That's a prime set up for a Journey joke," he said, rising and shouldering his bag.

"What?" she drew back, looking confused.

"The Journey song? You know."

"Oh, yeah," Tory shook her head, still looking flustered.

"You don't know who Journey is, do you?"

"Uh, I'm assuming it's a band? I told you I don't know much popular music."

"Popular in the 1980s, and anyway, what does being a small town girl have to do with not wanting to—"

He paused at the scrape of metal beside them. They both turned as Bria climbed atop a folding chair and stood on the seat. The child reached up and taped a piece of mistletoe directly above Tory's head. Then she tossed them a smile and hopped down, folding the chair and taking it with her. Kris stood there with Tory, both of them apparently speechless.

Tory looked at Kris. "She did *not* just do that."

He started laughing. "I think she did."

"That child," Tory said, her eyes wide but reflecting amusement. She leaned out to look into the hallway then she leaned back in. "And she's hiding around the corner spying on us."

"Is she?"

"Yes." Tory's cheeks were still pink and she was somehow even more appealing than she'd been when he first saw her standing outside the door. That was the thing about Tory. She became more tempting second by second.

"We really shouldn't disappoint her," he said, looking up at the scrap of mistletoe, wondering where in the world Bria had found it. Then he remembered the sprawling oak that anchored the parking lot right outside the center door. Probably full of the stuff.

"Oh, don't be silly. You don't have to kiss me because of this," she said, glancing up at the bit of green taped on the frame.

"I think I do," he said, studying her lips. She had beautiful lips. A full bottom lip and a beautiful bow on the top. They invited odes to be written to them. No, they invited a kiss beneath the mistletoe.

"Kris," she murmured, glancing back nervously.

"Tory," he said, leaning toward her. "It's a perfectly good piece of mistletoe. We can't waste it."

She licked her lips, her eyes widening as he lowered his head.

Just as he was about to press his lips to hers, Tory reached up and yanked down the mistletoe.

He drew back surprised because her eyes had seemed to invite the kiss.

"We're at the center," she whispered, her gaze giving him an apology. "There are children around."

Disappointment socked him at the same time as the reality of her words penetrated his intent to kiss the daylights out of her. They *were* in the middle of the center and kissing, even at the urging of Bria, wouldn't be a good idea. Definitely not here. Probably not anywhere.

"Right," he said, shaking his head. "I don't know what I was thinking. Caught up in the spirit, I guess."

Tory pressed her lips together but not before a nervous giggle escaped. She put her hand over her mouth as if to stop from bursting into laughter.

Finally, Tory seemed to catch hold of herself. "So, anyway, I came to see if you would listen to the other participants. They've all been working on their performances and would love some feedback. I'll warn you though—they've been listening to some of your songs on their phones. You may have made some new fans."

"Sure. I can do that," he said, turning out the lights and shutting the door behind him. He glanced down the hallway where Tory had spied Bria. The girl stood with her arms crossed, looking disgusted.

"Dang," Bria said, before turning on her heel and disappearing around the corner.

"Nice try," he called out before pushing into another large room where ten or so kids sprawled at computer desks, awaiting him. All of them sat up straight and proceeded to look nervous.

"Everyone, this is Kris Trabeau. I know some of you already know who he is, but his songs can be heard on the radio so he's got some knowledge to share about performing," Tory said, glancing over at him. Her cheeks were no longer pink, but he could tell what had happened a minute ago had affected her. And that was strange comfort. They hadn't kissed, but if he were a betting man, he'd lay down a Ben Franklin that Tory Odom had sure wanted to.

Kris rolled up his sleeves and smiled. "So let's get to work. You guys are in charge of bringing in the bacon. Let's get that frying pan hot."

Chapter Fifteen

S HE'D NEARLY KISSED KRIS TRABEAU.

That was the uppermost thought on her mind when she showered. And again when she pulled on her flannel jammies peppered with kitty cats. And it was still there when she slid into the soft down bed and pulled her granny's quilt over her socked feet.

Two inches.

That was her best guess at the distance between his lips and hers. She'd felt his breath against her face. Spearmint. He'd probably had a breath mint minutes before. He seemed like that kind of guy—never smelling bad or sporting garlic breath. She, on the other hand, had just eaten a bag of Doritos. She hadn't pulled the mistletoe down because of her breath, though. No, she'd been too afraid that she would lose herself, and her heart, if she tipped over to the other side and met him under that mistletoe.

Mistletoe was a hemiparasitic plant that attached itself to a host, where it leached water and nutrients from the tree or bush. She had no idea why the poisonous plant had become a cultural symbol for Christmas, nor why anyone would want to kiss beneath such a, well, not so pretty plant. Probably some guy made it up so he could sneak a kiss and then the idea took off. Supposedly, it was bad luck to stand beneath mistletoe and deny someone a kiss.

But Tory didn't believe in superstitious nonsense. She believed in science. And reason. And making good decisions based on likely outcomes. The thing was, she couldn't deal with another broken heart. To let herself go through two in one year would be incredibly stupid.

So mistletoe or no mistletoe, she didn't need to kiss Kris.

Just as she reached for the clicker to turn on an old Christmas movie, her cellphone rang. She picked it up. "Hey, Mama."

"Hi, darling. I hope it's not too late. Your father and I were watching *Longmire* and the time got away from me. Have you watched *Longmire*?"

"No. I was about to watch *Christmas in Connecticut*."

"Well, your father loves the main character. He asked if I thought he would look good in a cowboy hat. Can you imagine your father stomping around town, delivering the mail in a ten-gallon Stetson?" her mother asked.

Tory thought about her friendly, gossipy father trying to look like a tough cowboy. It would be a like a toddler wearing a business suit—incongruous and probably hilarious. "Uh, I really can't, Mama."

"I'm just calling to check one last time that you won't come with us to Oklahoma for Christmas. Your brother said you can sleep on the pullout in the den and use the downstairs powder room. I wish you would abandon this ridiculous notion of skipping Christmas. That Patrick isn't worth skipping Presidents' Day over, much less one of the most joyful holidays of the year."

Tory smiled at her mother's ferocity. Normally a mild-mannered woman, Nancy Odom had taken a strong dislike to Patrick from the very beginning, something that had worried

Tory when she considered having to spend her life smoothing over her mother's passive-aggressive comments.

"You're right, Mama. Still, I'm going to stay here. Miss Tansy, my neighbor, invited me to Trabeau Farms for Christmas. I've been helping her decorate and plan a nice celebration. Plus, y'all are leaving the day after Tinsel, and I have too much on my plate right now to even think about packing. Oh, and boarding Edison. I don't want to do that."

Edison lay on the end of the bed and immediately his tail went thump, thump.

"I know, but I hate leaving you alone for Christmas. I guess it's good you have a neighbor to spend the day with. Your brother will be disappointed." Nancy was good at applying just the right amount of guilt. Tory was certain it was taught in Mothering 101.

But her brother Judd was not going to be disappointed. On the contrary, Judd loved having his parents all to himself. "Yeah, well, I'm sure he'll understand that with taking on Tinsel's silent auction and entertainment, I'm a bit swamped. I'll bring the presents for Jake and Mary Margaret when I see you Friday night."

There was a long pause.

"Mama?"

"Well, about that. Your father thought we might get on the road early."

Disappointment sank inside her. "You're not coming to Tinsel?"

"Well, I really wanted to, but you know your father. He wants to avoid traffic. I-20 is always so busy this time of year so he wants to drive at night. He's seeing so much better since his cataract surgery, you know."

Tory didn't want to act peevish, but she'd been looking

forward to having some time with her mother. Then again, ever since she took the reins from Valerie, it was unlikely that she would have much time to sit with her mother anyhow. Since she was the emcee for the entertainment portion, a task that still made her want to swallow her tongue in fear, she would be tied up, so maybe this wasn't such a bad thing. "I'll miss you, Mama, but I understand. Let Dad get a head start. I don't want y'all stuck in holiday traffic. I can give the tickets—"

"I already gave them to Henry Delmar and Sunny Voorhees. Do you remember them? Sunny used to babysit you?"

"Yeah, I remember her, but you didn't have to feel obligated to pass them on."

"I'm on the board of the Sunshine Animal Rescue with Sunny. Those two are dating again and I thought they might enjoy dressing up. Lord knows there's not much to dress up for here in Morning Glory. Everyone needs to put on a dress and heels sometimes. You don't mind, do you?"

"Of course not."

"And Henry said he would donate a weekend at his parents' lake house for the silent auction. Oh, they have a beautiful lake house with a big deck boat. He wrote up all that was included in the weekend."

"Are you serious?" Tory sat up and almost clapped. People loved to bid on escapes and no doubt the Delmars' lake house would fetch a nice price. Dollar signs and visions of new laptops for the center danced in her head. "Thank you so much, Mama. And thank Henry. That's such a lovely thing to do."

"Well, he's a lovely man. There are several lovely men here in your hometown. I know you adore your restored cottage and working at Common Connection, but won't you consider moving back home? I hate the thought of you living out in the country by yourself. And I despise the thought that Patrick hurt you so much. It's time for you to get back in the saddle, sugar. Life's too short to sit on the sidelines pining for a horse's patoot."

Tory smiled. "I'm good here in Charming. Edison is an excellent watch dog. Sorta."

At the sound of his name, Edison lifted his head and cast sleepy brown eyes at her. Then he lay his head back down as if accepting that he was, indeed, half a guard dog at best. Tory knew he'd likely lick a thief to death rather than bite him.

"Edison's useless, Tory," her mother said.

"No, he's not. He ran off a coyote a few days ago. Besides, I have neighbors."

"They're far away and that Tansy is old. I met her once, remember? And you've just been sitting home alone. Hey, what about one of those dating websites? A lot of people find dates on those. And something called Tinder. Daisy Albritton tried it out. She said all you have to do is swipe right or left or something, and presto-chango, you got a date!"

Tory widened her eyes, withdrew the phone from her ear, looked at it, and wondered what sort of alien had taken over her mother. Putting the receiver back to her ear, she said, "Isn't Daisy in her late sixties?"

"Well, older adults can use dating apps."

Her mother had just used the words Tinder and dating apps in the same span of forty-five seconds. This from a woman who still wore a slip, got gasoline at full service stations, and made Tory call her when she arrived home after every visit. Prim and Proper was her mother's middle name. Nancy Prim-and-Proper Odom. "Uh, sure, they can. Did Daisy have success?"

"Unfortunately, no. She developed painful bursitis in her heel and had to take a break from dating, but she's very determined to get back out there. That woman has a saddle on her horse at all times. I'm not saying you have to go on Tinder or sign up for eHearts or whatever, but maybe—"

"I'm sort of seeing someone," Tory blurted out before her mother went on FarmersOnly.com and filled out a profile for her only daughter. So technically she and Kris weren't *seeing* each other. They were merely seeing each other. So it wasn't a total lie. And, plus, they had almost kissed and that should count for something.

"Who? Do I know him?"

Do you listen to country music? Watch CMT? Read *People* magazine?

"No, and it's very new so I don't want to push things by making it public." Once Kris left and took with him any possibility of her falling in love with him, she'd tell her mother that things hadn't worked out. That should buy her some much-needed time from the sympathetic mother zone. Her mother had been more upset about Patrick jilting her than Tory had, and thus called to check on her heartbreak at least once a week. "Really, Mama, it's all very new, but there's a spark."

Definitely a spark.

But she'd douse it. Because once Kris got back to Nashville and got away from all the nostalgia Tansy was trying to drown him in, he'd realize that he'd had some form of Stockholm Syndrome when it came to Tory. He hadn't been kidnapped, but being held hostage by a holly-tossing, Christmas-carol-singing relative could have the same effect.

What it boiled down to was that she and Kris had nothing in common other than his aunt living next door. Tory was a small-town biology teacher and Kris was a big-time country music star. She wasn't interested in being a relationship with a man who was set on chasing fame and fortune. Been there. Done that.

Besides, she was certain Kris wasn't interested in dating someone who'd rather drink lemonade on the porch and watch her pansies grow.

"And you'll be seeing him at Christmas? Well, no wonder I can't talk you into coming with us to your brother's house. I'm so pleased you're trying, Victoria. So pleased."

"Thanks, I guess."

"Well, I have to go. Your father's paused the DVR. I wish he'd never learned how to operate that thing. Now he stops it and bellows 'Come on, dumpling' from the other room. I miss the good old days when you missed things and never felt obligated to watch them again. Sometimes what you don't see is a good thing. Love to you, my darling."

"Good night, Mama," Tory said, clicking off the phone and flopping back onto her pillows. Edison looked up and then slowly snuck off his doggy throw to inch next to her.

"You're not supposed to be off your blankie. I'll drown in dog hair, Ed."

Her furball issued a little whine.

"I mean it. I've already lied to my mother. I can't possibly break the vow I made that you would never sleep on my bed. You *have* to stay on the blanket."

Edison thumped his tail and peered up at her between his two fluffy paws with eyes an evil villain couldn't possibly turn down. Edison could end the threat of nuclear war with his chocolatey eyes. She rubbed his head and sighed. "Fine. My track record stinks tonight. Besides, a little dog hair never hurt anyone."

Chapter Sixteen

AFTER PLAYING "I'LL BE HOME for Christmas" so
many times Kris might never enjoy the song again,
he placed the capo on the guitar and handed it over
to Tansy. "How about you work some more with Bria? I'm
going to run over to Tory's place. I have some things to go
over with her. Uh, Tinsel stuff."

Aunt Tansy sat on the porch with him and Bria, reminding
him of the times he'd sat out here with her as she taught him
to play the guitar. He'd not brought up selling the farm or
having her move up to Nashville again. Tansy had asked to
shelve the conversation, so he was giving her space to consider
a new start. Bria held Tansy's guitar in her lap and practiced
the basic chords she'd asked him to teach. Of course, Tinsel
was three days away and there wasn't time to teach Bria to
play for her performance, but he couldn't resist doing for Bria
what his aunt had done for him—giving her an outlet for her
emotions.

A new melody had been haunting him. He showed it to
Bria, and the child tried to pick it out. She was like a duck
in water when it came to music, and he loved watching her
determination to learn.

His aunt looked over at him with a knowing gleam in her
eyes. "I'll be happy to practice some more with Bria. I guess
you remember how to get to where you're going, right?"

A loaded question. One that told him he was as obvious as a moose in a closet.

"I remember where Tory lives. Half a mile that way." He jabbed a finger toward Tory's place.

"Go. Bria and I will be fine."

Earlier that afternoon Kris had gotten lost in writing a Christmas song and forgotten the time. That happened sometimes. When the words flowed and the music came together, he was like Alice down the rabbit hole. Nothing but this delightful and sometimes scary new world existed. Like a vortex, he got sucked in it and lost all sense of the world he normally occupied. Maybe pitchers who threw a perfect game knew, or artists who went without sleep or food for days only to emerge with a masterpiece got it. But when his muse met him, grabbed him by the shirt collar, and dragged him into the zone, he had to stay there.

He loved the song he'd written, and the melody, something simple and almost vintage in its tone, kept running through his head. *More jingles in the bells, more magic in the tales, feeling more and more like Christmas.*

Ah, the relief that he'd actually written a complete song that wasn't garbage was almost tangible. He was so giddy after he completed the last of his chicken scratches, he literally stood up and danced around his room, punching the air.

Then he'd looked at the clock.

Thirty minutes late to practice with Bria at the center.

He phoned Tory and asked if there was any chance she might bring Bria to Trabeau Farms for a practice session. Tory worked her teacher magic and got permission once again from Bria's foster family and dropped her off at Tansy's an hour ago.

Tory had gone back to her house, professing the need to work on the script in absolute silence. He suspected it was more that she was afraid to trust herself around him. She was smart because he couldn't seem to stop thinking about the way her breathing had increased, the way her eyes had softened, and the way she'd nervously licked her lips beneath that scrap of mistletoe.

It probably wasn't the best idea for him to climb into his car and make the quick trip over to her house where she was very much alone...where there were no innocent eyes to offend....no nosy aunts to interrupt. Okay, there *was* a very exuberant dog, but if Kris threw the stick far enough...

He chuckled at the thought and fired the engine.

Go over the script for the event. *Hey, Tory. Bria is finishing up with Tansy. Thought I would come look over the script and give you some advice.*

Hmm...that sounded kind of contrived. She'd said she didn't want help.

But it *was* contrived. Maybe he should be truthful and tell her that he was into her. That he'd almost ripped that mistletoe from her hand and kissed her until her toes curled or she slapped him silly. That he couldn't help himself because he'd been intrigued by her since she first walked barefoot toward his car, restraining Edison, a twig in her hair, with resolute gray eyes that told him she was too prideful to ask for a ride but relieved that he had insisted.

What would she say to that sort of honesty?

He'd just pulled out of Trabeau Farms when his cellphone rang. Preston Kammer flashed on the car screen.

"Hey, Pres. Good news. I finished a song today."

His manager whistled. "Now that's a great way to answer the phone."

"Don't get too excited. It's a Christmas song. May not

make this album, but it got the juices flowing again. I'm feeling good about where I'm heading."

"Christmas song? Well, I guess every artist needs one. All the satellite radio and streaming channels like varied artists' versions for their Christmas channels, so that's not a bad thought. I'll see if we can't get it recorded. If Strata doesn't do it, we can go out on our own. As well as you're doing, it'll get airplay."

"Cool." Kris accelerated on the highway, smiling at the blow up Christmas decorations and light display across the highway. Lord, he felt downright cheerful. "So what's up?"

"I sent you some things you need to make a decision on, so please check your email and get back to me. I'm working with promoters on the tour that starts this summer, and the publicist wants you to weigh in on some things before she gets started. There's just a lot going on, bud. Don't leave me out here hanging in the wind."

Guilt played pinochle in his gut. He'd put off opening most of Preston's emails or anything that resembled dealing with his career. Which wasn't good. His career was everything, and the little bit of burnout he'd been experiencing had proved temporary. Hadn't he just written a complete song that rocked?

Why, yes, he had.

"Okay, I'll sort through them later tonight," Kris said.

"Now the main reason I called. I booked you on *Late Night in LA* with Rhett Bryan Thursday night. They had a guest fall through and you've been on their list for months. You're flying out of Jackson tomorrow afternoon, and they're putting you up at the Wilshire. I'll meet you there because after the show I'm going to try to get a meeting with the Strata execs about some of the promotions they've promised us. I want to push them hard on this second album and make sure you get lots of reach. Won't hurt to have you there, reminding them of their sizable investment in your career." Preston paused for a moment and then said, "You're right on the cusp of huge things, Kris. We can't get lazy now."

"I can't."

"Can't what?"

"Go to Los Angeles. I promised Bria I'd play the guitar for her performance at Tinsel," Kris said, turning into Tory's drive and hitting the brakes.

"What?"

Kris sucked in a breath. "Pres, you need to understand that I need this time off. I'm tired and that's why I can't write."

"See? That's the thing, chief. You don't *have* to write. Stop putting unnecessary pressure on yourself."

Kris sighed. "Preston—"

"No, listen to me. You can't pass up opportunities like this." Preston sounded perturbed.

Kris wasn't trying to be difficult, but he couldn't just hop on a plane and abandon all he'd done here in Charming. Even if staying hurt his career.

But at that last thought, he drew up short.

His career.

Preston was right. Kris didn't have the luxury of taking his foot off the pedal. That's how artists fell into the pit of anonymity, forgotten and labeled a one hit wonder. Kris wasn't at the finish line. No, he'd just gotten the first lap in on the track. So why did he think he could turn down *Late Night in LA*? Why had he let everything in Charming obscure his view?

Preston had been waiting for Kris's response. When he got none, he asked, "Who is Bria and what is Tinsel?"

"It's a charity event for a local community center. Bria's a student there. She's a foster kid with a phenomenal voice. I've been helping her, and I told her I'd play the guitar for her performance."

"Kris, I understand you're a good guy and may have committed to something you probably shouldn't have because you have a big heart, and, man, that's a good thing. I mean, I wish you would have told me. We could have done some press on it or something."

"I didn't do it for the press. I did it for the town. For the center." *For Tory.*

And maybe that was the problem. His emotions for Tory, the farm, his aunt and everything surrounding him had gotten in the way of his original goal. He'd gotten mired in nostalgia and it had him turned around. Preston was right. He needed to go to L.A. He needed to tend to his career.

"Look, I'll do the show. You're right. My career has to be first right now. Still, I have to be back in Mississippi by Friday afternoon. Have to."

"I'll try to make that happen."

"Not try. Do."

Preston blew out a breath. "Okay, fine, Yoda. But I'm going to tell you something you need to hear: If you're going to make it in this business, you have to make hard decisions. In three short years, we've made a hit album, won some hardware, and signed a deal with Strata. All that stuff is good, but it's the tip of the iceberg. We still have to hustle, and that means listening and trusting your label and going to gigs like *Late Night in LA.* And we need the Strata execs to throw money at your career. This isn't just about you. There are a lot of people banking on you. You understand?"

"I get it, but I need to be back on Friday, Pres. This is

important to me. I gave Bria and the people at the center my word. That still means something to me." Kris clicked the button on the car, hanging up on Preston, something he'd never done before.

He allowed his head to fall against the steering wheel, wincing at the slight honk that emitted. Well, there was one good thing about it. He now had a legitimate reason to talk to Tory. Shifting the car into Drive, he bumped up the gravel drive to her house.

She'd hung a Christmas wreath on her front door.

The security lights came on and he heard the insistent woof of Edison, likely at the front door prepared to protect his master. Or throw a party. With Edison, definitely a party.

"Kris?"

Tory popped her head out the door.

He climbed out of the car. "Yeah, it's me."

"Brrr!" She rubbed her arms. "Where's Bria?"

"She's still working with Aunt Tansy. I took a break. I thought I would come look over the script for you, but I just got a phone call that put a crimp in my plans for the next few days." He kicked a pebble and then glanced up at her. "Can I come inside? It's chilly."

"Oh, sure," Tory said, stepping back and opening the door. She wore fluffy socks, stretchy pants that might have been pajama bottoms, and a faded Henderson State sweatshirt. Her hair was knotted and she had a pen stuck behind one ear. He'd never seen a woman look so gorgeous. "Can I get you some hot tea? I just poured myself a cup."

"No. I'm good," he said, climbing the step and throwing up a hand just before Edison crashed into him.

Edison set his paws on Kris's stomach and swiped his face with a huge, very wet tongue.

It was not the kiss he'd anticipated.

"Edison. Down." Tory snapped her fingers.

"He's fine," Kris said, dodging Edison as he stepped inside her house. When she closed the door, sealing them in warmth, Kris shoved Edison into a sitting position. Then he ruffled the dog's head and gave him a good scratch behind his ears. The tail-thumping that commenced mimicked the entire percussion section of his band.

Tory's house was cozy, with white walls and dark beams stretching across the pitched ceiling. Bright museum prints hung on the walls, and a thick, fluffy rug anchored two leather armchairs with red pillows. A deep gray sofa that looked soft sat awaiting a good snuggle in front of the fire that cracked in the small hearth.

"I like your house."

"Thanks," she said, sweeping her hand toward the pair of chairs. "Sit down, if you'd like."

Kris sank into a chair, wondering why there was an awkwardness between them. Was it because she thought he had mistletoe in his pocket and nefarious motives for coming? Okay, so he had mistletoe in his pocket. But he'd keep it there if she were going to be so on guard around him. "Relax. No mistletoe." He waggled his empty hands.

"Very funny." She sank onto the couch, curled her feet beneath her and picked up her tea. Edison hopped up and curled onto the fleece throw that was likely intended for him. "Sorry, it's been a while since I had company, and my brain was wrapped up in working on this script."

A legal pad sat next to a small laptop on her glass coffee table. Several wadded sheets littered the polished length. "Not so easy being cheesy, is it?"

"Cheesy. That's the exact description of how this script

sounds." Tory made a face. "I thought it would be easy to talk about the center and each of the kids performing. I really think I should get Mac to do it. If he weren't being Santa, he could. He has such a great sense of humor."

"You'll be fine. Just speak from your heart. Say all the things you love about the center and the audience will be in the palm of your hand. Besides some of the kids are helping you, right?"

"Yeah, but that's easy for you to say. You stand in front of audiences for a living," she said, taking another sip of tea.

Silence fell, and again it felt a bit awkward.

Tory closed her eyes and shook her head. "Okay, so after yesterday, I'm a bit nervous. I don't trust myself around you."

Kris arched an eyebrow as something delicious wound through him. "Oh, really?"

Tory pressed a hand against her face. "I can't believe I just admitted that, but it's science really. You're an attractive man. I'm a woman who got tossed aside for a job in Michigan."

"I thought it was Massachusetts."

"Whatever. Michigan. Massachusetts. Up north somewhere." She shrugged. "All I'm saying is that we're two healthy adults, and my ego has been dinged. So, yeah, I'm attracted to you. It's just that..." She paused.

"What?"

"You're you."

Kris frowned at her. "I'm me?"

"You're a famous country music singer and you have women fawning all over you all the time. I'm just a Mississippi girl who is nothing extraordinary. I'm not your type. I'm not even close to your type. I'm just convenient because I'm next door." Her face was now as bright as the pillow he'd tucked beside him.

"How do you know my type?"

"I read stuff."

"Gossip?" He shook his head and settled back into the chair. "You're as bad as Aunt Tansy."

"No, it's just we don't make sense. That's all I'm saying." She set her tea down harder than she must have intended because it sloshed over the side.

He studied her for a few seconds. The way she looked so flustered, so adorable. She was absolutely right—he was attracted to her more than she knew. But those last words sat fat between them. *We don't make sense.*

Because she was right. They didn't. He'd paused his world for the last week and a half, but Preston had just hit the fast forward button to send him careening to the west coast and the life he'd shoved aside for a while. Yeah, he was coming back to Charming. He had promised Bria and still had to get his aunt to agree to move to Nashville. And then there were the songs he still had to write. How would Tory fit into his world?

"You said you had to talk to me about something?" she asked, averting her eyes. She didn't want to pursue the conversation.

"Yeah, but so you know, not everything has to make sense. You're into science, right? Most things have explanations, but some don't. Some things just are."

Tory studied him for a few seconds, her cheeks pink, her eyes a mystery.

"All I'm saying is think about the potential. What if all this has happened for a reason? Because maybe we were meant to be more than what we are now," he said, wondering if he'd just complicated things even more or if he was finally making sense. His world felt very upside down at present and nothing felt right. But for some reason Tory felt right.

"What was it you wanted to talk about?"

Okay, so she wasn't going to discuss their attraction. He'd give her some rope and stand back. It would either happen or it wouldn't. He was open to something as long as they didn't define it, but Tory had to decide if he was worth taking a chance on. "Yeah, I have to leave town for a few days, but I'll be back."

"You're leaving?" Alarm and maybe disappointment shaded her words.

"Just for a few days. I'll be back Friday afternoon." He sighed and rubbed his hands on his jeans. "I got booked on *Late Night in LA*. It will be my first appearance."

"Oh," she said, looking at her hands. "That's really great. It's a good opportunity for you."

"My label wants me to go crossover, so doing guest appearances outside the world of country music is key to getting me in front of new audiences. So I'm flying out tomorrow, but I should be back in plenty of time for Tinsel."

"Should," she repeated.

"I have to go to Los Angeles, Tory. Things like these are another step in building my career." Even as he said the words, he wondered why he had to make it sound like he owed an explanation. Why did she make him feel defensive about his career?

"And that's always been the most important thing." She said it as a statement.

"I've never tried to hide how important my career is. It's been a driving force in my life."

"Why?" Tory tilted her head. "Why do guys always feel measured by their careers?"

Kris blinked. "It's not just guys. Lots of people are invested in their careers."

"That's why I can't kiss you under the mistletoe, Kris. That's why I can't let myself feel anything for you other than affection as my neighbor's nephew. Because your main goal in life is to obtain money and fame. I've already been with a man who tossed me aside for all that glitters. I can't do that again."

"Who said I would toss you aside? Besides, if things between us worked out, you could come *with* me." It was a big assumption, yet he had to put it out there. Not everything was absolute. It wasn't as if he had to choose between his career and love. Tory could teach anywhere. She could come to Nashville...after they dated a while. Why was she putting him—and a potential relationship with him—in a box?

"Come with you? I live *here*." Tory spread her hands. "I like it in Charming. I like being a teacher, working at Common Connection. I'm even joining a book club."

"You sound just like Tansy. She's dug in her heels about moving to Nashville, too," he said, shaking his head in disgust. What was it with the women in his life? Why was wanting a career and security such a sin? What, was he supposed to cancel his new contract, move to Trabeau Farms, and learn to knit sweaters for his aunt's chickens? Why couldn't either one of them give one inch and try something different? Was he not important enough to take a gamble on?

"Wait, you're trying to get Tansy to move to Nashville?" Tory unwound from the couch and stood, rubbing her hands down her pants. She looked like a foot soldier preparing for battle. Even Edison lifted his head and looked concerned. "What about the farm?"

"It's valuable land. We'd make a nice profit on it," he said. Even as he uttered those words, he knew how it sounded.

Opportunistic. Heartless. Sacrilegious. Tory's eyes narrowed and Kris knew why a man facing the firing squad was given a blindfold. He really didn't want to see what was coming.

"*Sell* the farm?" Tory asked. She didn't raise her voice. No, her words were calm, measured, and static with anger. In other words, scary.

"It's just a farm. Just land. It's not holy ground."

"Are you insane? That farm has been in your family forever."

"I know that. Tansy has only told me that a million times. She started on the day I came to live with her. Jeez, if it's that important, we can keep it. Still, it's a money pit, and I don't want Aunt Tansy living there alone."

"You have money. Hire some help."

"Tansy doesn't want help."

"But you think she's going to agree to sell her farm and move to Nashville?" Sarcasm dripped from her question. He'd never really understood that idiom until now.

"Well, when you put it that way," he drawled. Two could play this game.

"What way? That you haven't been home in many years, and your solution to helping your aunt is to move her where it is convenient for you and sell the property that's part of who you are because it requires a bit of upkeep?"

Tory was good at this game, dang her. "You make it sound selfish. It's not. I want to give her the care she once gave me. This is a logical solution. It makes sense."

"But you just said some things didn't always make sense."

Touché.

Kris pushed himself up. He didn't want to fight with Tory. He'd wanted to kiss her. But maybe not as much now as when he'd gotten there. Her caustic appraisal of his situation had made him feel small. "I should be going."

"Running from the truth, are you?" Tory asked, parking her hands on her hips, looking very much like a teacher.

His inner teenager chafed at being fussed at. "No. But none of this is really your concern, is it?"

Tory physically recoiled at his words, which made him feel lower than a worm. No, lower than that. Of course, Tory would likely know what burrowed lower than earthworms, but she probably wasn't in the mood to share her knowledge of things that dwelled deep in the ground.

"You should probably go," she said, her words now more sad than mad. In fact, she looked like he'd taken a pin to her and deflated her. He decided he liked her better gloriously mad than defeated. A hurt Tory was one of the worst things he'd seen.

"I'm sorry. I shouldn't have said that."

"Why? It's true. I don't have a role in your life." She walked toward the door and opened it. Cold wind pushed inside, a chilly reminder that neither he nor Tory were secure in the warmth anymore. The strong words between them had chilled whatever he'd hoped to build. The fire was out before he'd even applied a match to the kindling.

"Only because you're afraid," he said, rising.

"No, because I'm not stupid," she said.

Kris shook his head. "I didn't want things between us to end this way. I like you, Tory, but this is who I am. The same way you are who you are."

Catching her lip with her teeth, Tory averted her gaze from him. "Nothing's ending, Kris. We never really started. Go take care of your business. I'm not telling Bria that there's a chance you won't be back. She's already nervous enough."

"I'll be back. At the very least, know that I care that much," he said, pausing before her. Edison had risen, hopped down and padded beside him. Kris took a small comfort in rubbing the dog's silky head. Edison licked his hand in silent brotherhood.

"Oh, darn. I forgot about Bria. I have to get her back home," she said, frowning at Edison, who seemed to stand in unity with him. Kris liked the dog more and more. At least, Edison didn't want to push him away, draw up rules, make him feel guilty or admonish him for wanting to reach his goals.

"I'll drive her home."

Tory nodded. "Thanks."

"I'm not a bad person," he said, wishing he didn't sound so pathetic. *Don't think badly of me. I'm a good person. Most of the time.*

Tory's eyes had taken on a sheen. Tears? Emotion? Trick of the porch light? "I don't think that, Kris. I know you're a good person, but that doesn't mean you're right about moving your aunt or selling your farm. It also doesn't mean you're right about me. You don't really know me."

At this, Kris smiled. "You would think that, right? But, somehow, I do know you."

With those words, he slipped from the house. Tory must have caught Edison's collar, because he heard the dog's nails scrabble on the hardwood floor. He didn't stop because he was a bundle of emotion. In the time he'd left Trabeau Farms and driven over here, everything had changed, and now he didn't know his up from his down, his right from his left. He'd never been more confused in his life.

Two weeks ago, his mission had been clear.

Presently, everything was as clear as the Mississippi River

bank on a cloudy night. The air was thick, his vision dark, and there was no light to see. The best he could hope for was to get on that plane, go to LA, and hope that some time away would bring clarity.

He shoved his hand into his pocket and pulled out the car keys. His fingers brushed the piece of mistletoe he'd swiped from the tree outside his aunt's house earlier. He'd planned on being cute with it. Saying something about no prying eyes now. Or something goofy about how he always carried a bit of mistletoe around in his pocket because he never knew when he might need it.

Crumpling it in his hand, he tossed it away and climbed inside his car.

Sometimes even mistletoe couldn't get a man what he wanted.

Chapter Seventeen

TANSY WATCHED AS KRIS CAME down the stairs, carrying the vintage briefcase that had belonged to her father. Her father had only used the leather attaché case when he went to regional agriculture meetings, so even though it was old, it was still in pristine shape.

"Thanks for letting me borrow this," he said, holding the oxblood leather case aloft. "It's a perfect overnight bag."

"You're leaving your suitcase?" Tansy asked, leafing through the *Charming Gazette*, her eyes landing on the photo of Mac and Valerie standing in front of the open guitar case holding the Stratocaster. The byline read "Local Charity Benefit Ready to Rock." She'd scanned the article already and knew that crack reporter Dandy Grigsby had hinted at Kris Trabeau making a special appearance. He'd also dug up an old publicity picture of her when she'd been with the Mississippi Travelers. The long braids, sad smile, and prairie dress made Tansy wince.

"I'm coming back. I told you that."

"Because you haven't gotten me to sign on that dotted line yet," she said.

Kris ran a hand through his chestnut hair, which made it stick up. That, paired with his frown, made him look adorably grumpy. "No. I'm coming back because I told you I would spend Christmas with you, and because I told Bria I would play the guitar for her. We said we'd talk about the farm and the future later."

"And Tory?"

"What about her?" His tone was guarded.

Tansy smiled. "Well, I'm not blind. I can see you care for her and that she makes you happy."

Kris drew in a deep breath. His eyes went toward the tree which stood in the corner holding court over the parlor. "No one has ever accused you of being blind."

"But you have accused me of being old. And infirm. And unable to care for myself."

"Aunt Tansy, you're really going to go there right now? Besides, I never said anything like that. You assumed, and now you're going to hold it against me that I care about you? That I want you closer to me?" He set the case down and walked around to the sofa. Sinking onto it, he set his hands on his jean-clad thighs and pinned her with a look of such utter incredulity that she felt a momentary wavering. "I want you to be safe. Surely you can see my concerns? You're stubborn, but you're also level-headed. You can squawk at me all you want about how independent you are, but everyone needs someone to depend on, to check on them, to help them when things go wrong."

Tansy wanted to rail against him and prove to him that she could still live alone. But she also knew there was truth to his words. She wasn't getting any younger, and over the past year or two, she'd found everyday tasks much more difficult. She'd even stopped going to church, even though she sent her tithe regular as rain, and she'd found all sorts of excuses why she couldn't have coffee cake with her old friends. When she'd come home to Trabeau Farms all those years ago after watching Jack Prosper drive away to chase his dream, she'd built a life that wasn't as full as she'd always hoped it would be—a life cluttered with kids, too much wash to do, and a husband bowing his head over supper every night. But she'd filled it with community involvement. She'd served on boards, volunteered at the library, and attended the Royal Ball every spring at the historic Duchess Hotel. She'd been a pillar of the community. But she'd also been much younger and had more energy.

"You're right. I can't do what I used to do, but that doesn't mean I need someone to take care of me. I've been living alone since you left, and I've been fine. Your concerns have merit, but honestly, I'm used to men leaving me. So you can move along without guilt. I can take care of myself."

"Aunt T, I wasn't leaving you."

"But you did. And that wasn't what I'm talking about anyway. I'm trying to say you're right. To an extent. I'll consider hiring some help."

Kris's lips twitched and he shook his head in disbelief. "You're actually admitting I'm right about something?"

Tansy shrugged and folded the paper. "Call it a Christmas miracle."

He snorted. "Will you at least look at the brochures and think about coming to live near me. Just be fair."

She wasn't moving to Nashville. Anastasia Beatrice Trabeau had been born in the upstairs bedroom, and she figured she'd just as soon go out in the same iron bed her granny had imported from England.

"I'll look at the brochures," she said finally because even though she wouldn't be moving to a retirement community, she could at least *look* at the colorful photos of yoga, pottery, and the ice cream machine in the Hermitage café. Didn't mean she'd change her mind. She wouldn't.

"Good." Kris looked pleased, like he thought he'd won a point. Guess it didn't hurt to let him think he had.

"Sugar, I want you to know I'm dang proud of you and what you've accomplished in your career. I didn't think you could do it. Not because you don't have the talent or the work ethic, but because you're a good person. Good people don't always last in the music business. I've watched greed and power chew up people and spit them back out. The life a musician leads while on the road, all that pressure, ain't easy. It's easy to get your ox in a ditch, and honestly, sugar, I didn't want that life for you. I just didn't."

Kris clasped his hands and studied them. In the hall the old cuckoo clock hooted out the hour. "Nothing worth anything is ever easy. Your concerns were valid. There were many days I almost packed it in and came back here, but I'm just stubborn enough to want to prove you and everyone else who ever doubted me wrong. Truth is, I love what I do. You gave me that. You taught me to love music and the gift it gives to others."

Tansy knew she was hearing her words back. So many times when they played, they talked about the power of music. He'd had so much anger and sadness inside him after losing his parents that she couldn't figure out any other way to reach him. That's why she'd tied a bow around that guitar and sat it beneath the Christmas tree all those years ago. She'd always worked her own feelings out strumming those strings. She figured it was worth a shot with Kris. The man sitting before her obviously understood the power in music. "You're doing that pretty well."

His shoulders rose, then fell. "I was."

"What does that mean?"

Kris stood and walked over to the window. "Well, writing

has been hard for me lately. I mean, you already knew that. I wrote a Christmas song the other day. It's good, but not what I've been looking for."

"And what have you been looking for?"

"I don't know. It feels like it's right there, almost within reach. It's like when you're trying to remember someone's name and it's right on the tip of your tongue. You can remember the color of their hair or the shirt they were wearing the day you met or even the song that was playing on the radio, but you can't remember the person's name. That's what my songwriting has been like lately. I feel something's so close and can't quite catch it."

"Mmm." Tansy fixed her eyes on the back of her nephew. "So being back where you belong didn't loosen your block?"

Kris turned. "Why are you so adamant that I belong here? I lived here for, what, eight years? Yeah, it's been my home but…" He left off and shook his head.

Tansy didn't have the words to convince him. How could he not know who he truly was? He was looking for a missing puzzle piece and it was right under his boot. Kris had come home. She was nearly certain it was because he had no other place to go. Oh, sure, he had an apartment in Nashville. But Trabeau Farms would always be his home, and the reason why it had taken him so long to come back was because he'd clenched his fist and vowed he wouldn't return until he had a fat record contract and his face on an album cover. Now he had that, but still he was looking for something.

Tansy could lead a horse to water, but she couldn't shove his darned head in the trough.

"I know things feel confusing. You had a plan, I've no doubt. But my mama used to always say there's many a slip between the cup and the lip. What you thought would work isn't always for the best. Life works in strange ways. Take Tory."

He jerked his head up. "What about her?"

"Well, some moron broke her heart and so she was dead set on skipping Christmas. Last I saw she looked to be enjoying Christmas pretty well. Strangely enough, she didn't look so brokenhearted either. In fact, I would say she looked happy."

"Not anymore," he muttered.

Tansy gave him a soft smile. She wasn't certain what had happened between the two. Last night he'd left with hope in his eyes and returned quiet as Sunday morning. After taking Bria to her house, he'd returned and mooned about looking like someone had kicked him when he was down. Finally, he'd spit out that he had to go to Los Angeles and begged her not to say anything to Bria. She'd asked about Tory, but he'd remained tight-lipped. She'd been around guys enough to know when to push and when to go on up to bed. "Well, we'll see how everything goes."

"I have to go. My plane leaves in a few hours." Kris stood and picked up her daddy's briefcase. "I'll be back as soon as I'm able. Don't forget to watch on TV."

"I'll watch. I always do."

Kris enclosed her in a hug, and even though part of her was as mad as a wet hen over his machinations, emotion choked her. It had been so good having him here. She'd gone so long living by herself that she'd forgotten how nice it was to have coffee brewed when she walked into the kitchen or how pleasant the sound was when her nephew whistled as he worked. He'd not only painted and repaired the house, but he'd brought life back to the place.

"Come home as quick as you can. We still have Christmas to do. I told Tory that I would host the after party for Tinsel.

Just a few friends back here for Jingle Bell cookies and hot cocoa. The house is decorated and I thought it was something I could do to help her. Everyone needs a wrap party, right?"

Kris finally smiled. "That sounds nice. I'm sure the kids will love having cookies and hot cocoa."

"And you can fix whatever you messed up with Tory."

Kris sucked in a deep breath. "Right now, I'm not sure I can fix anything."

Tory taped a bid sheet to the clothed table in front of a painting of an alpaca. She had no idea what to put as a starting bid. Sure, it was a cute painting, but how many people wanted a painting of a bright green alpaca?

Wren Daniels peeked over her shoulder. "Yeah, that's a tough call."

"Maybe $20?" Tory asked, tilting her head and staring at the painting. "It's sort of cute."

"Go with $10." Wren moved along the tables, pulling the brown envelopes that held gift certificates.

"But Miss Clarice painted it."

Wren paused and twisted her mouth. "Uh, go with $20 for the starting bid. Her friends will pay that much to spare her the shame of no bids."

"True," Tory said, writing the starting amount with the sharpie.

She and Wren were working on setting up the silent auction items for Tinsel. Luckily, the Duchess Hotel's grand ballroom had the capability of storing and securing the items that had been donated for the charity event. Tory paused and looked around. The mint green oriental carpet, huge glittering chandelier, and spotless beveled-glass mirrored columns looked more like they belonged in a European palace than a ballroom in a small Mississippi hotel, but the Duchess wasn't just any hotel. It was an historic landmark built in honor of Lady Eugenia Rose Everwood, the wife of Charming's founder Harold Horton. Lady Eugenia had also given the town its name. Legend has it that when her husband asked her what she thought of his land, she said, "Well, my dear, it's simply charming." The name stuck.

"What about the guitar?" Wren asked, standing in front of the table that would hold the items for the live auction. "We want to display it, right?"

"Yes, but I'm keeping it at my house until tomorrow afternoon. Just feels safer that way."

Wren nodded. "Good thinking. I don't think anything would happen to it, but better safe than sorry."

Tory was so glad to have the assistance of the owner of Little Bird Productions. Not only was Wren smart and organized, but she was Tory's age and had a good sense of humor. Tory wondered if it was because of her name. Like her namesake, Wren was tiny and seemed to flit from one thing to another as if she were expected to resemble the tiny bird.

"So, Kris Trabeau, huh?" Wren said after a few minutes.

"Huh?"

"The singer. What's he like? I mean, other than gorgeous and talented. I mean, please tell me he's a jerk or something. Aren't handsome, rich, talented guys always jerks?" Wren said with a laugh.

"Oh, well, he's not really a jerk. I thought he was pretty nice." *And I totally didn't cry over him on three separate occasions in the last eighteen hours.*

Which was really stupid because she'd known him for

all of one week and five days. How could someone possibly develop feelings for someone in that short of time?

But you did.

She didn't want to think something so silly as falling in LOVE or at least LIKE in a matter of days could be true. Because it sounded idiotic. Still, she'd known something was different about him from the very beginning. She felt like she knew him, like the connection between them was something binding. Like a covalent bond. *Hey, wanna share electrons?*

She rolled her eyes at herself.

The whole idea was ridiculous.

"Oh, well, I hope I get to meet him. He's still playing for the little girl, isn't he?"

Tory blinked. "Oh, yeah. Well, he's supposed to. He had to go to Los Angeles to do *Late Night in LA.*"

"Wow," Wren said, her blue eyes widening. "I love Rhett Bryan. He's a cutie pie himself. When will Kris be on?"

"Tonight," she said, ripping the bid sheet she'd written the wrong description on in half. Thinking about Kris always distracted her.

"You should come over to my house and we'll watch it together. My friend Dovey—do you know her?"

Tory nodded. "She's the one who has Fine Feathers?"

"Yep, that's her," Wren said, smiling. "My office is in the back of her boutique. She's been my best friend forever."

Tory found herself nodding. She wasn't sure if she wanted to do a girl's night to watch Kris on television, but it was the first offer to hang out with anyone remotely her age. If she truly wanted to be part of the community, she had to be willing to step outside her comfort zone and accept friendship. "That would be nice. Can I bring something?"

"Heavens, no. My mama has stocked my place with every

imaginable Christmas treat. She thinks it's the best way for me to attract a man." Wren rolled her eyes but managed a smile. "Do you think Valerie would want to come, too? I know she's married, and therefore has built-in companionship, but sometimes it's nice to get away and spend some time with the girls."

"She might. I know the CC basketball team has a game tonight, but maybe Valerie can come by later," Wren said.

"What am I doing later?" The voice came from the open doorway.

"Hey, Valerie," Wren called out, setting her clipboard on the table near the stage they'd set up earlier. Two huge red Christmas trees bedecked with gold tinsel glittered on each side of the stage and Mac had hung a huge swatch of gold lame cloth horizontally from chains that were attached to the ceiling. Across the front of that hung a foamcore cutout that spelled out "Tinsel" in a glittery red script font. Small lights had been set up to shine on the sign. The effect was simple, inexpensive and impressive. Wren had a great eye for design and an even better sense of what would give the biggest impact at the lowest cost.

Valerie trudged across the floor with boxes in her hands, huffing and puffing. "Hey, everyone. This is the last of it."

Tory took the top box so she could see Valerie's face. "Wren wanted to know if you wanted to come to her house tonight after we finish setting up here."

"For wine, Christmas cookies, and a little hometown country boy Kris Trabeau on a late night talk show," Wren chimed in.

"Oh, you mean my boyfriend, Kris Trabeau?" Valerie joked, setting the last box on the one empty auction table. "Because if that's the case, I'm in."

Wren laughed. "So greedy. You already got a man."

"I'm trading up, but don't tell Mac," Valerie joked, giving Tory a wink. "Though Miss Tory here might have something to say about that. I heard from a little birdie that our favorite tutor and the country music star found themselves standing beneath some mistletoe."

Wren turned toward her. "Reeeeally?"

Tory felt her face blaze. "No, that was Bria's whole idea. Nothing happened."

But it could have. It so could have. If only Tory hadn't chickened out.

Both Valerie and Wren grinned at her like two lunatics. Wren waggled her eyebrows. "You could have kissed him and didn't? What's wrong with you?"

Tory shrugged. "It's not like he's into me."

But he was. He so was. And they could have had something. Maybe. If she hadn't chickened out.

The question, though, was what would they have? A fling? She wasn't the kind of woman who could do a no-strings-attached couple of weeks. Some women could, but Tory wasn't one of them. Anything lasting seemed a far stretch. So she hadn't been chicken. She'd been sensible...even if it would have been nice to have the memory of that kiss.

Valerie snorted. "Um, sweet pea, I'm happy to break it to you—that man is into you. I grew up with three brothers and then had two sons. I know when a man is window-shopping, and he's spied a pair of Italian loafers that will make him look like a million bucks. And he wants them."

Tory made a face. "I'm more like sneakers."

Wren made a choked sound.

"All I'm saying is don't give me the 'he's just not into me.'

Heck, even a child is astute enough to see what is as plain as the nose on my face." Valerie tapped the end of her nose.

A flush of heat traveled the length of Tory's body and sweat rolled down her back. "Um, is it hot in here? Or just me?"

Wren burst into laughter and Valerie joined in with her.

Tory frowned. "What? Stop laughing."

Valerie's eyes twinkled like the lights on the Christmas tree next to her. "Come on, Tory. You aren't stupid. You know he likes you."

Tory shrugged again and averted her eyes to the tables Wren had set up earlier that morning. They had twenty tables that sat ten people each. Ever since word got out about the guitar and the possibility that Kris Trabeau might make a special appearance, ticket sales had shot up. They were near capacity and if they sold ten more tickets would be completely sold out. Valerie and Mac were on cloud nine. They'd never expected it to be even close since they'd had to move the event so close to Christmas Day. "I'm not sure what you're talking about. I mean, he's a male."

Wren blinked. "What does that even mean?"

"Well, the male species has an innate, biological response to females. He's a healthy specimen."

"I'll say," Valerie joked.

"You know what I'm saying. I'm a female."

Valerie rolled her eyes. "Okay, I'll give you that there are certain built-in responses. Thank goodness there are. The good Lord knew what he was doing when he made us, but I'm not talking about two bugs on a stick, Tor. You're both humans with brains, though I'm not sure yours is working all that well at present."

Tory didn't answer. Instead she picked up her marker and started finishing her work. She didn't want to have this conversation and hated having any focus on her. And both

Valerie and Wren were *way* too focused on her at present. Maybe she didn't need a girls' night out, if the girls in question were going to examine her life and find her lacking.

"Do you think you're not good enough for him or something?" Wren asked.

Arrow released. Bullseye found.

Deep down, Tory knew that her ego had taken a pummeling that summer. Patrick had been a good-looking, intelligent man who'd seemed perfect for her. Everyone had said so. When he'd proposed to her, she'd felt like the luckiest girl in the world. Patrick had wanted *her*. She'd found value in being on his arm. His colleagues respected him, and women turned their heads to look when he walked by them. In hindsight, she'd been unwise to put such worth in being with a man.

Now Kris Trabeau, hot country music singer, had spent the better part of almost two weeks flirting with her, making her feel things she wasn't ready to feel. And, yeah, maybe she felt like she wasn't right for him because he had legions of fans and she could barely keep the attention of the sixteen-year-olds she taught. As Valerie pointed out, she *was* human.

Nothing about Kris was perfect for her. She didn't even listen to country music, for heaven's sake. They didn't make sense on paper, on chalkboard, on any other writeable surface.

Some things don't make sense.

"No, it's not that. Not really," Tory said, but it didn't sound convincing.

Wren set her hand on Tory's arm and gave it a squeeze. "Hey, I understand being a little overwhelmed by someone like Kris being into you. A relationship with someone like him could be…daunting."

Tory looked at her new friend. In Wren's eyes, she saw the understanding she needed. "Yeah, it's overwhelming, and I'm not even sure if he's serious about me."

Valerie walked over and looped her arm around Tory's shoulders. "Hey, everyone gets afraid of taking chances sometimes. You got burned the last time, but you're not the kind to accept defeat. I've watched you over these past years and you're a tough cookie. Don't be afraid to leap."

"That's the thing. I always look before I leap," Tory said, issuing a wry smile. "I play it safe. I'm a scientist, that's what we do. You should see my lab safety procedures."

"But remember this, even scientists take risks. There's nothing wrong with being safe as long as it doesn't cripple you." Wren took the marker from her hand and set it on the table. "Let's take a break. I've been thinking about getting something new to wear for tomorrow night. Dovey texted and said she got a new shipment of things in. Let's go poke through the cocktail dresses."

Valerie gave Tory a last squeeze. "You girls go on. I'm going to finish up the rest of the auction bid sheets before I head back over to the center."

Tory nodded, not because she needed a new dress. Well, a new dress wouldn't be horrible. Her old black standby had lots of mileage on it. But because she needed a change of scenery and some time with someone like Wren. And Dovey. She'd met the tall, slender woman a few times and liked her sense of style and take-charge demeanor. Someone like Dovey wouldn't think twice about jumping into something with Kris Trabeau. "Sounds good. I still need to go over the script and take Bria out to Tansy's to practice. Dress rehearsals are tomorrow morning and I need to go over the script and make changes before that. But I would love to shop, and go to your house tonight."

"Perfect," Wren said, handing the clipboard to Valerie. "Let's go get something amazing to take a leap in."

Chapter Eighteen

K RIS LOOKED AT HIMSELF CRITICALLY in the mirror as the hairstylist sprayed his hair so his cowlick didn't poke up.

"There! You look pretty as a painting," the man drawled, giving him a wink.

"Thank you," Kris said, stepping from the chair, trying not to shove a hand into the hair that was now plastered to his head. He'd not done much on television and preferred interacting with an audience at his concerts. When he was on stage he didn't have to be clever or charming, answering questions and making witty observations.

But on *Late Night in LA* with Rhett Bryan, he did.

Preston appeared in the door way. "Hey, there he is."

Kris stood and smoothed down the black jeans the lady in wardrobe had insisted looked the best. He didn't do black skinny jeans. Or anything shiny. So he wasn't digging the plaid shirt with all the detail junk on it. And then there was the black bandana. He looked like a cross between Jack Sparrow and Liberace.

"Hey, Pres. Uh, this bandana around my neck. Axel Rose? Or Willie Nelson?" Kris asked, tapping at the offending fabric. This was so not him.

"Um, Kris Trabeau," Pres said, toothy grin in place. Preston Kammer looked like his name—compact, fit, and sharklike.

"Not amused," Kris deadpanned.

"Dude, you look good. You look like the hot country newcomer you are."

Kris stuck out a foot. "And motorcycle boots. I look like an urban biker."

"And you look fabulous," the hair and makeup guy said coming back into the dressing room, pulling a black leather jacket off a hanger and handing it to him. "One of those *Florida Georgia Line* guys wore one just like this last week for the St. Jude's benefit. It will look good over the plaid."

Kris figured the leather would disguise the bling on the cuffs so he shrugged into it. "I'd feel better in my old jeans and cowboy boots."

The stylist gave him a look. "This isn't *Hee Haw*."

Nope. It wasn't. It was *Late Night in LA*. Very California and very much an alien land for someone like Kris. Texas, Mississippi, and Tennessee, hadn't prepared him for LA living. Not that he was living here, but one night with Preston out on the town had shown him he wasn't cut out for Beverly Hills. He'd received grimaces when he'd asked for beer in a bottle at the fancy restaurant where they'd dined last night.

Someone who looked really hurried came to the door. "Need to get him to the green room."

"Okay, let's roll. Mention the new album and how much you like working with Strata Records," Preston said, draping an arm over his shoulders and steering him from the dressing area.

"I look like someone who has sold out. Might as well go all the way. Maybe I can wear a beanie and pair up with a rapper on the next album," Kris said.

"Not a bad idea. Drake has done some stuff with—"

Kris slapped a hand against Preston's chest, making him stop. "I'm joking. Surely you know that?"

Preston laughed. "Yeah, but you're easy to mess with."

Kris rolled his eyes and entered the room where guests stayed until it was their allotted time. There was a television where he could see Rhett Bryan giving his monologue. The set had palm trees decorated with lights and Christmas ornaments and a lime green tinsel wreath with a pink flamingo on the host's desk. Rhett had a tan, white teeth and hair that might have been highlighted or merely bleached by the sun. Good-looking and suave, Rhett's only redeeming grace was that he was a good Southern boy from South Carolina. Rhett Bryan had just been announced as the host for the next Oscars. His star was super shiny.

Kris grabbed a small bottle of water.

"Ah, vegan water," Preston said, taking one and dropping into an armchair.

"Vegan?" Kris repeated, looking at the beverage in his hand.

"That's a joke," Preston said, laughing in spite of the fact it wasn't really funny. Of course, Kris may have failed to get the joke because he was nervous.

Rhett pointed at the camera on the mounted TV. "When we return CMA Newcomer of the Year Kris Trabeau will be with us, so stick around. We got a great Christmas show for you."

Kris's stomach flipped like a bicycle hitting a curb. He was up next. *Lord, please don't let me say something stupid. Or trip. Please don't let me trip.*

Five minutes later he walked onto the set to thunderous applause. His mantra of *don't trip, don't trip, smile and look natural*, must have worked because he made it to the guest chair, shook Rhett's hand, and crossed his legs like it was the most natural thing in the world to sit on a carpeted platform wearing black skinny jeans and a bandana while cameras moved around him.

He got through the general questions about the awards and his career and then Rhett asked him about his hometown.

"So I grew up in East Texas, but when I was ten, I lost my parents in a plane crash. My Aunt Tansy took me in and I moved to Mississippi."

"Your aunt was a singer, too, right?"

"Yeah, for a while. She wrote music and sang in a folk group called the Mississippi Travelers back in the Sixties. She's the person who taught me how to play the guitar...and fetch eggs, bush hog twenty acres, and catch a lunker bass out of our neighbor's lake. I guess you can say I grew up country and surrounded by music, so it's no wonder I followed my dreams to Nashville."

Rhett smiled. "Ah, the delights of small-town life. You gotta love spending time in a place where you skinned your knees riding a skateboard and tried to ride a bull. But that could be me. Of course, it turned out the bull was a heifer. It was lacking certain parts." Rhett laughed at himself.

"Horns?" Kris asked.

Rhett laughed harder. "Right, right. Those, too. Now are you spending the holidays here? Or back in Nashville?"

"Actually, I'm heading back to Mississippi tomorrow. The town's doing a Christmas benefit for a local community center, and I volunteered to play the guitar for one of their talented kids, Bria Smalls. She's amazing, and I'm honored to accompany her as she makes her own debut."

"That's terrific," Rhett said, his blue eyes sparkling. The man managed to look cool and warm at the same time. "It's always good to give back to your community, and it sounds like you've found the perfect way to do that."

"I have."

"Well, it's been great having you on the show tonight. I understand you're going to stick around and sing a little for us?"

Kris nodded.

"Okay, we'll be right back with some furry friends from the San Diego Zoo right after this break. Stick around, folks," Rhett said into the camera.

The camera operator counted down and then he saw Rhett visibly slump. "Whew. Done with that segment. You good, Kris?"

Kris nodded. "That wasn't as hard as I thought. You made it easy."

The late night talk show host grinned. "Was this your first time?"

"On a national talk show? Yep. I was nervous as a pet raccoon." Even as Kris said the words, he felt country-come-to-town. Rhett was so sophisticated and cool.

"My grampy always says that. Country logic. Or something." Rhett smiled and then gazed off toward the wall holding framed posters of network shows. "Man, I can't wait to hop on that plane tonight and get home myself. I know you understand what it means to reconnect to the place that makes you who you are. Of course, it helps that I have a pretty brunette curled up on the couch waiting for me."

"Yeah, Summer. She and I wrote a song or two together back when she lived in Nashville. She's a good songwriter."

Rhett went from suave talk show host to proud new husband in front of Kris's eyes. "She's pretty great, isn't she? She's working on her first album, you know."

"That's great."

"Yeah, I'm so proud of her. Mostly because she's pursuing her dream but she's also keeping what's important in the forefront. Totally grounded and willing to sacrifice her career for what matters most. She always says she's just a girl doing what's right, but she's more than just a girl. You know what I mean?"

Kris nodded as something itchy tingled in his spine.

"And being out here is great. I love California, but there's nothing like being back home with her. You know, I found out home is more than just a town, too. So you enjoy Christmas at your aunt's house. And, hey, you're on your way up, but don't let fame and fortune blind you to what is really important. I learned that the hard way."

Kris shook Rhett's hand again, waved at the audience, and signed a few autographs as the cameraman counted down and the red light flashed on. Kris passed a man wearing a khaki uniform carrying a sloth in the hallway. There were cages that made him shiver as he passed them. One definitely held a python.

When Kris got back to the green room, Preston shoved the rest of the snack mix into his mouth and hugged Kris.

"Beautiful job, man," Preston mumbled with his mouth full.

"Thanks," Kris said, feeling both relieved and invigorated. And then there was that itchy feeling. Something Rhett Bryan said had hit him like a spinner bait. His words had snagged Kris and pulled something he'd been trying to find toward the surface. Home, a girl, the farm, who he was—all those things had been swirling around inside him, trying to find a way to connect, to rise, to crowd out all the noise and confusion of his life. The struggle to find the words and to ensure his aunt's safety had been pushing and pulling at him for longer than he wanted to admit. He'd called it burnout, but the thing was, he wasn't exhausted as much as he was turned completely around in his life.

Maybe that's what he'd been missing. Maybe that's what had been there all along and he'd been too obtuse to see it.

"I got a text while you were being interviewed," Preston said, taking a swig of water and clearing his throat. "Payne Reynolds wants to meet you tomorrow. He's in town for the holidays and he's invited us to brunch at his place in the Hills."

"Payne Reynolds? Are you joking?"

Preston grinned. "He likes what you're doing."

"You mean what I did," Kris said, easing from beneath the heavy hand of his manager. "The record that won me the awards is the record *I* wrote. So he likes what *I* did. Because the stuff Strata has been sending me is nowhere near what—"

"Okay, okay," Preston said, pressing his hands up in a "calm down" gesture. "I get it, but Payne has produced the biggest names in country music. I don't know how many times I have to tell you—trust the process and stop fighting me every step of the way."

"I have to be back in Charming."

"No. You have to go to lunch with the CEO of Strata Music. It's like being asked to lunch with the Pope or the President."

Kris glared at Preston. "Why did you tell him I was available? Do you even remember the conversation we had two days ago? Or maybe you didn't just hear me say in front of everyone in America that I'm playing the guitar for Bria?"

Preston made a face. "Look, it's not personal. It's business. You have to make the decisions that are right for your career. It's brunch. You can take an afternoon flight and make it to the charity thing, but you need to be at the meeting unless you want to sabotage your career. I mean, is that what you're doing? Trying to throw everything away because they want you to use some songs written by their guys? Because those are guys who write hits. So don't tell me this is a tit for tat sort of thing, K-Dawg."

"First, don't call me that ridiculous nickname," Kris said holding up a finger. The khaki guy carrying the sloth burst into the green room. Preston squealed and jumped behind an arm chair.

That at least made Kris smile.

"Sorry," the zoo guy said, putting the animal into a carrier that sat beside the hallway. He hurried back, leaving them and the animal alone. On the television, he appeared handing the guy Rhett was interviewing a python.

"If he comes back with that thing, I'm out," Kris muttered. He looked at Preston. "My career is important to me, so I'll do the brunch. But you better have me to the airport in time for my flight."

"Done," Preston said, scooping up another handful of snack mix. "I'll have a car waiting. You'll make it back to whatever that thing is you're doing."

Kris gave Preston another disgusted look. He liked Preston. Sort of. But the guy was definitely too focused on scoring. Kris had always been more of a team player, but being a team player didn't get a person where he needed to be sometimes.

But it at least made him the kind of guy he wanted to be.

Kris grabbed a bottle of water and sank into the chair Preston had abandoned. His manager was already back on his phone tapping, frowning, and tapping some more. Kris's mind tumbled around the words Rhett had spoken and then back to Preston's insistence that Kris dance the dance.

Time to decide who he was going to be, a puppet on a string or a man who forged his own path.

Tory set the wine glass on the coffee table, her eyes straying from the television where a guy in khaki handed off an adorable sloth to the guest from the San Diego Zoo.

Valerie looked like she'd landed on cloud nine. "I can't believe how much publicity we're getting. National TV, a feature in the Jackson papers, and they mentioned Kris playing at Tinsel on a Nashville fan site. This is like hitting a gold mine!"

Wren clapped her hands. "And he looked so gorgeous."

But the guy on TV had not looked like the Kris Tory knew. The Kris she knew would never dress like that or have been as smooth as the guy she'd seen on television. That guy had been untouchable, sophisticated, far, far removed from baking Christmas cookies in his aunt's humble kitchen. "Yeah, he did good."

"What's wrong?" Wren asked, sneaking another cheese straw. Her mother seemed to have a knack for baking: they'd eaten snickerdoodles, a cheese ball and crackers, and eggnog cheesecake bites. Oh, and mulled wine. Tory should have stopped at one glass of the powerful, festive brew, but she'd been so nervous about watching the guy she'd fallen for with new friends.

Dovey unfurled her long legs. "I really should be getting home, but these eggnog things keep whispering sweet nothings in my ear. I can't stop."

"My mom should sell those things. I use them as currency

all holiday season. That's how I got my neighbor to hang my Christmas lights. Pure bribery." Wren grinned.

Tory had enjoyed being there with Wren, Dovey and Valerie. All three women would be going to Tinsel and would also go to the after party Tansy was throwing. Kris's aunt had begged off attending Tinsel, saying she would be too busy prepping for the party and didn't have anything to wear anyway. Tory hated for the older woman to miss Bria's performance, but she'd promised her that Valerie would record it. She wanted to press Tansy into coming, but knew that she'd probably be unsuccessful. Her neighbor was as stubborn as her nephew.

Kris.

Her heart squeezed when she thought about him. She hoped he came back. She wasn't certain he would. That other world was a powerful one, and Kris had looked totally comfortable in it, too. Like he belonged on stage with Rhett Bryan. She felt like she'd been watching a stranger, not the man who'd thrown the stick for Edison or used his body as a stepladder so she could put the angel on his aunt's Christmas tree.

Her eyes darted to Wren's pretty tree. The event planner's townhouse was decorated in Scottish plaid and boughs of evergreen and holly. It smelled amazing, and the living area looked like something out of a designer magazine. Still, there were touches of whimsy throughout. Like a Santa frog peeking from behind the mantel display or a parrot ornament in the middle of the elegant glass ornaments. They were designed to make guests smile, and Tory couldn't resist her lips curving when she'd spotted them. The whole design seemed very much Wren.

"Oh, he's about to come on and sing," Valerie said, drawing their attention from the mulled wine and Christmas goodies spread on the coffee table to the television. Kris stood with Rhett smiling as the host joked with him.

"Turn it up," Dovey commanded, popping another eggnog bite in her mouth.

"So Kris is going to do a holiday song. What do you have for us, Kris?"

"Actually, this is something I've been toodling around with this past week, so not one person has heard it. But it came to me when I was with my aunt and some friends baking her super-secret Jingle Bell cookie recipe. All I need is a stool and my guitar," Kris said.

Someone came off the side and set a stool down. Kris walked over and picked up his guitar. The band behind him sat watching.

The camera panned to Rhett. "Well, this is going to put us all in the holiday mood. Remember *Late Night in LA* will be back after the New Year. We're going to say goodbye as Kris plays us out. Have a wonderful holiday, everyone."

The lights narrowed as Kris began to strum the guitar. The beat was quick and lively, and Tory fell back into that night. The laughter, the scents, the memories old friends always shared when they were together all wrapped around her as he sang.

"More jingle in the bells that ring,
More friends who gather round to sing
More presents on the hardwood floor
More people singing at your door..."

As he played, Tory found herself smiling. Worrying about his muse and not being able to write had been a huge obstacle for Kris, but it was obvious to her that he'd found his muse in his memories...in the spirit of the season...in the songs they'd sung around that old table that had been in his family for generations. She knew about the table because Tansy had told her all about it.

The camera went in and out on Kris. Sometimes it captured the band sitting and clapping along with Kris. Other times it was on a smiling Rhett. Or the silly flamingo Christmas wreath. But when it was on Kris, the look on his face made her heart flutter. He believed what he sang. The emotion was there, alive and powerful.

"Between the mistletoe and manger scene, it's getting more and more like Christmas to me," Kris sang, the last strums of his guitar fading as the credits appeared.

A commercial advertising carpet cleaning came on, breaking the spell.

"Wow, that was a great song," Wren said, pushing herself off the floor. She wore pajama pants with frogs on them. She seemed to have a thing for frogs. Or maybe that was coincidence. Scientific method beckoned for a closer examination. Or Tory could just ask her.

"That song was so good. And he wrote it in a week?" Valerie said, rising and scooping up her half-filled glass. She was Tory's ride, so she was glad the center director hadn't done anything more than sip the mulled wine. "The man's got talent."

"Sounds like his writer's block just got blown out of the water," Tory said.

"He had writer's block? Huh, so that's a real thing?" Dovey asked, eyeing the eggnog bites but rising instead of indulging. "Sounds like he's broken through. That was a good song. Made me feel excited about Christmas, which is a good thing since it's only five days away. I gotta run. I'll see you chickadees tomorrow. Oh, and Tory, wear the dress."

"I will," she said, trying to sound confident in her purchase.

The red dress she'd bought at Dovey's store was so not her typical type of dress. The dress hugged her figure and left her shoulders bare. It was simple and sexy and made her feel a bit vulnerable. Like maybe she needed a scarf or something. But that was silly. Wearing something that looked that good on her should make her feel confident.

But that was the whole problem, wasn't it?

Her confidence.

"Ready?" Valerie asked.

"Yeah. Thanks, Wren," Tory said, giving her new friend an impromptu hug. She surprised herself on that one.

Wren gave her a squeeze. "Anytime, Tory. It was fun."

She and Valerie rolled out of Tory's neighborhood with Christmas music on the radio and houses covered in Christmas lights to escort them. When they pulled onto the highway that led out to Tory's house, Valerie looked over at her. "Are you okay?"

"Yeah."

"You just nervous about tomorrow? Or is this about Kris Trabeau?"

"I'm fine." She didn't want to talk anymore about Kris. About his words to her. *Because maybe we're meant to be something more than what we are now.* Something more.

More.

Why was she so afraid to want more? More than being alone. More than what she thought she deserved. What made her think she didn't deserve to have a man like Kris? Because he was famous? How insecure did a woman have to be to shut down a man like that because she was afraid to hope for more than what she had?

Valerie said, "I know how you feel. On a smaller scale, of course. Growing up, I didn't have much. My mama worked as a waitress at a bowling alley and my daddy worked the oil fields. It was a humble life and when Mac came around, I didn't think I deserved him. He came from a good family. His daddy was a lawyer and his mama piddled with selling smocked dresses she made. She didn't have to work, but she liked her pin money. Anyway, I fell head over heels for that man, but I didn't think I was good enough. So I pushed him away. It was like he was offering me the moon, but I was too afraid to want it. Disappointment had been a way of life for me. You can call me a bald-faced liar, but I think you feel the same way I did."

Tory swallowed. "So how did you end up with Mac?"

Valerie chuckled. "Well, Mac's a man who is good at showing up. Every day, he appeared to walk me to class. One day he took my face in his hands and said, 'Baby, I can keep doing this for as long as it takes for you to understand that we belong together. I can take down that wall you've built brick by brick, but it would be easier if you'd knock 'em down yourself and save us both some time.'"

"What did you say?"

"I told him that I'd marry him, have his babies, and be the woman beside him when he closed his eyes every night. I mean, I'm not stupid." Valerie laughed.

And that made Tory chuckle. "You're definitely not stupid."

"All I'm saying is, don't try to figure things out so much, Tory. You're a practical woman, but there's nothing practical about love."

Tory shook her head. "It can't be love. We've only known each other for two weeks."

Valerie smiled in the darkness, her teeth so white, the tears gathering in her eyes crystalline in the light of the full moon, "Baby, I fell in love with Mac the day I first met him. We were walking together and he stopped and went over to a homeless man sitting on the side of the road. Mac pulled a sandwich out of his backpack, took that man's hand, placed the sandwich in it and prayed with him. My heart exploded. My ovaries, too."

Tory wiped the tears from her own eyes. "That's incredible."

"Yeah, so don't skip past incredible, honey. Life is too short to throw away something wonderful because you're afraid to grab on with both hands. Grab on, Tory. Grab on."

Valerie reached over and turned up the radio. Kenny Loggins crooned about celebrating his home, making Tory feel both nostalgic and maybe a little hopeful. Valerie's words had found a place inside her. Being scared wasn't something she normally had to contend with. No one would ever call her brave, but she was steadfast, determined, and constant. But Patrick had shaken her to her core, pulling the rug from beneath her confidence. Add to that the fact that Kris Trabeau was, well, Kris Trabeau, and her shaky confidence was too afraid to step back on the rug again. But that wasn't how she wanted to live her life.

"I'm going back to buy those strappy nude sandals, and I'm going to step on that rug again," she said as Valerie turned into her driveway.

"Huh?" Valerie turned to look at her.

Tory chuckled and gave Valerie a quick kiss on her cheek. "Don't worry. I know what I mean. I think I'm ready to leap, but I need some killer shoes to do it in."

Chapter Nineteen

TORY SMOOTHED THE RED DRESS against her torso and tried not to panic.

Kris wasn't there.

Valerie delivered a bright smile as she slid beside where Tory stood against the wall. The darkened ballroom held capacity and everyone's attention seemed trained on the high school drama club doing a few numbers from *Bye Bye Birdie*. The students were really adorable, but there were only three more acts before Bria took the stage.

Tinsel had gone off without a hitch thus far. Wren had ensured that the wait staff was attentive, the bartenders inventive, and the food as good as any top-notch party. The decorations were simple and the twinkle lights and flickering candles on the table lent a sophisticated, festive mood. The three-piece ensemble playing Christmas carols in the corner was way better than last year's piped-in music. Tory had perused the auction items and most were going for above estimated value. People seemed happy and generous—a perfect combination for a charity event.

"Bria's out in the hall asking for Kris," Valerie said under her breath, holding her smile so that the sold-out crowd couldn't tell anything was amiss.

"I know. I don't know what to do."

"Maybe call him?" Valerie asked.

Tory smiled and waved at a few of the teachers from her school. "I did. It went to voicemail. I called Tansy earlier. She said Kris had a meeting with the CEO of his record label but would still make it. But she doesn't know where he is." She tried not to sound disappointed in Kris, but she couldn't seem to help herself. He'd promised that he would be here for Bria. How could he not be here already?

But what had she expected? Compared to national talk shows and record label executives, Charming and Tory probably seemed like a huge mistake. How could a small town charity function and a geeky biology teacher stack up against LA with its glamour and gorgeous swimsuit models?

Stop it. Her mind was panicking and running amuck.

Something must have happened. Kris would have called. At the very least she knew that he wasn't the kind of guy who wouldn't show up without a very good reason. And he wasn't the kind who would have his head turned by buxom blondes or someone throwing money at him. Her insecurities were playing hide and seek with her emotions.

"What about Tansy?" Valerie asked.

"What about her?"

"See if she'll do it. I mean, I can't play the guitar. Can you?" Valerie pretend to chuckle, cupping her hand over her mouth. "Maybe if we beg her, she'll come."

"I have to go back and introduce the three divas. Here's my phone. She's in the contacts." Tory shoved the phone into Valerie's hand and moved toward the stage. The act ended, thunderous applause resonated and she climbed the two steps to the stage and walked to the microphone.

"Wow, wasn't that a treat? Thank you, Merry Players, for that wonderful preview of your upcoming performance of one of our Broadway favorites," she said, leading another round of applause. "Now, before we bring on our next performance, I've invited a few of our students to share with you why Common Connection is so important in their lives."

She motioned for the students who had tried out for the entertainment portion to come to the stage. Including them had been Kris's idea. Cole, sans frog, and several others traipsed up, looking adorable in their Sunday best. Out of the corner of her eye, she saw Valerie on the phone. Then Valerie slipped out. *Please, Lord, let Tansy come.*

Valerie and Mac had practiced with the kids about what to say. They were nervous, of course, but their nerves actually made them cuter. Tory glanced out into the audience and everyone was smiling.

Good.

Valerie slipped back in and gave her the thumbs up.

Tory announced the next act, the three diva girls. They were singing a classic Aretha Franklin song that had thankfully been covered by a modern singer so they'd already known the words.

"Tansy's coming?" Tory asked Valerie when she came off the stage.

"Yes, but I had to do some heavy guilting to get her here. I finally ended with 'get your butt in the truck and get here in the next ten minutes.' She wasn't happy with me ordering her around, but she'd started making excuses, saying Kris would be here, and I didn't have time to argue with her."

Tory sucked in a breath and breathed out. Glancing over her shoulder, she saw Bria frantically beckoning her through the narrow window in the door to the outside hallway. She hurried over and slipped into the hallway.

"Where *is* he?" Bria said, her little hands fluttering in the air.

"Okay, listen, Bria. Tansy's on her way. She'll be your backup guitarist. Y'all have practiced lots of times together."

Bria's face crumpled. "But Kris said he would be here. He said he would do this with me. He's late. I mean, he's always late. I should have known."

Tory's heart ached for the girl. She'd been disappointed too many times in her young life. "Bri, Kris had to have run into some trouble. I don't know what, but I know he would be here if it was at all possible. You mean too much to him."

Bria shook her head. "I don't mean nothing to him. I'm just a kid, and he's a star."

Tory glanced out the window into the ballroom. The girls were still singing, doing a synchronized sway with a snapping of their fingers. Tory turned back to Bria and grasped her shoulders. "Listen to me. You are an incredible singer. We need you tonight. Do you hear me? We need Bria Smalls to go out there and show everyone in this town how good she is."

Bria blinked. "You really think I'm that good?"

"I know you are. Everyone is going to love you. You don't need anyone to play the guitar for you. Your voice is the best instrument. But Tansy is on her way, so you don't have to do this alone. Okay?"

Bria clasped her hands against her stomach. She wore a deep burgundy velvet dress with black patent Mary Janes. Her braided hair had been caught back in a matching black satin bow. Small pearl earrings, a gift from Tansy, winked in her ears. "Okay. I can do this."

"Yes, you can," Tory said, giving her a quick, hard hug. "Now I have to go introduce Jack. Let's hope he breaks a leg."

"If he doesn't, I can do it for you," Bria joked.

"There's my girl."

Tory pushed back into the room and hurried to the stage

where the three girls had just bowed and scampered off. Tory needed to borrow a bit more time in order to give Tansy time to get to Tinsel. Testify. Yep, she needed to give her testimony on why Common Connection meant so much to her and the children it serviced. That would take a good ten minutes. At least seven. Maybe just five.

"Thank you, Divas. Nothing like a classic song from the Queen of Soul to get us ready for our next performer, but before we bring our class clown on stage to make you laugh, I wanted to share with you why I love Common Connection so much."

Tory talked about the programs from the standpoint of a teacher. The computer programs to help kids get up to grade level were expensive, as were the costs for the computer lab, facility upkeep, and the annual costs for gym rental and fees for league play. Intramural sports kept the kids busy and taught them invaluable life lessons about working hard, losing, winning, and playing as a team. Finally, she finished with what Common Connection had given her.

"Many of you know that I'm not from Charming, but being part of CCC has given me a way to belong to something that is worthwhile while becoming part of the community. Volunteering takes on a new meaning when you find yourself blessed by the collective determination to make our community stronger from top to bottom. It all starts with our children. When we make sure we serve those who will grow to be our new leaders, we're investing in Charming. We're investing in Mississippi. So I hope that tonight you'll not only bid generously on the items donated by the people in our town, but you'll consider being a true friend and giving your time and energy to making Charming a better place for all to live."

People applauded as Tory motioned Jack onto stage. "Okay, everyone. Prepare to have your funny bone tickled with some relevant Christmas observations by our favorite impressionist, Mr. Jack Jackson."

Jack, in true showman fashion, ran onto the stage, took the mike from her and did his first impression as Eddie Murphy, replete with the laugh. Then he launched into a story about wrapping presents that had everyone chuckling. The kid definitely had the timing and talent to be a comedian.

Tory hurried off stage just as Valerie escorted an out-of-breath Tansy into the ballroom. She wore a long black dress and carried her guitar. Her silver hair was in her normal braid and she wore hoop earrings and a bright red scarf. Thankfully, she no longer had crutches and instead wore a walking boot, which made her gait uneven but would allow her to get up the stage.

Tory grabbed her arm. "Tansy, I can't thank you enough."

Tansy pressed a hand to her heaving bosom. She was still out of breath. "I have never dressed so fast or driven so recklessly, but I'm here. Even though I don't want to be. I haven't taken the stage since I left the Travelers back in the late sixties. I don't know if I can do this."

"Just pretend you're in an orchestra. Um, no one will be looking at you," Valerie said.

Tansy shook her head. "I don't know. Now that I'm here, my mind is throwing up all kinds of blocks. Stage fright is a very real thing, you know?"

"I do. But this is for Bria," Tory said, sliding her arm around Tansy's thin shoulders as the audience erupted in laughter. "Besides it's just your friends and neighbors. Pretend you're on the porch with Bria. Just look at her when you play."

"Oh, God. I hope I can do this."

"Tansy, you've got to. Kris didn't make it," Tory tried to keep the emotion from her voice, but she knew her voice held the question *why didn't he make it?*

His aunt turned to her. "Kris took a later flight. His manager set up a meeting and Kris couldn't miss it, Tory. I know he wants to be here, but he's still fighting with himself over that whole success thing. You know men."

Yep. They sometimes got their lines crossed. Of course, it wasn't just men who did that. Plenty of people got sidetracked by glitter and strobe lights. "He probably has a good reason."

Tansy merely shrugged. "I can only hope."

"Go on into the hallway with Valerie. Bria's there and is nervous herself. See if you can calm her down."

Tory stood, trying to find a little calm as Jack wound down his performance with an impression of their jovial mayor, who had accidently dropped the blue-ribbon winner for biggest pumpkin at the awards ceremony at the county fair. Mayor Gardner was doubled over with laughter.

"Okay, get Bria. It's showtime," Tory said, moving toward the stage.

Jack finished his set to resounding applause. He'd set the audience up to love the beautiful gift that Bria was about to deliver.

"Isn't he the best?" Tory said, into the microphone, clapping along with the audience. Jack bowed. And bowed again. And again. And again. Mac came out in his Santa suit with a shepherd's crook and hooked Jack around the waist. The audience howled in laughter.

"And now, our honored guests, we've saved the debut of a young lady we know you will be hearing for many years to come. Accompanying her tonight on the guitar is former Mississippi Traveler, Tansy Trabeau." Tory clapped and smiled as Bria and Tansy, holding hands, came onto the stage. Tansy looked even more nervous than Bria, but the older woman pulled the strap of her acoustic guitar over her neck and settled on the stool Mac brought out onto the stage. The lights lowered as Bria walked toward the microphone that stood center stage.

Tory found that she was holding her breath, a prayer in her heart that Bria would be able to shine. That Tansy wouldn't pass out. And that she wouldn't break down and bawl like a baby when Bria sang her first note.

Everyone fell silent as Tansy strummed the opening to "I'll Be Home for Christmas."

Bria glanced back at Tansy, smiled and then pulled the microphone toward her.

Kris placed his hands on the counter of the rental car company housed in the Jackson airport and tried to look calm. "I understand, ma'am. But I need a car. Any car. I don't care if it's economy, luxury, or a blasted clown car. I needed to be somewhere thirty minutes ago. Please. I'm begging you."

"I'm very sorry, sir. It's the weekend before Christmas, and we just don't have anything. It's one of our busiest weekends," the clerk said.

"Nothing? Absolutely nothing?" he asked, glancing around, not willing to believe that he'd made it to Jackson only to be foiled by a dead battery or zapped alternator. Didn't matter which one it was. His Mustang wouldn't start. He'd called AAA, but all their towing companies were out on calls. They couldn't send anyone for forty-five minutes. Kris didn't have time to wait, so he'd sprinted toward the rental car counter.

"Excuse me, young man," an older woman said from the adjoining counter. She looked older than Tansy with blue hair and horn-rimmed glasses. She also wore a full-length raincoat knotted at the waist and honest-to-God driving gloves. "I am going right by Charming on my way to see my sister Gigi in Morning Glory. I can give you a ride. As long as you're not a serial killer. You're not, are you? A serial killer, I mean."

"No, ma'am," Kris said, stepping over to her. "I'm not even close to a serial killer. I don't even kill bugs. Well, except mosquitos. And roaches."

The older woman smiled. "You sound okay to me, and you're handsome as the devil. Plus, I need someone to carry my bag. You look like you got some muscles under that jacket." She winked at him and he wondered as desperate as he was to get to Charming if he better take a rain check on riding with a stranger who commented on his muscles.

"I'm Kris," he said, sticking out his hand, deciding it was worth the risk.

"I'm Mabel, but my friends call me Zsa Zsa." She slid the rental car keys from the counter and grinned at the woman behind the counter who looked genuinely concerned about this little blue hair getting in the car with a potential (lying) serial killer. "Come on, sugar. Let's get this show on the road. I don't see so well on account of my cataracts, but don't worry, I've gotten used to driving with those halo things."

Now the agent behind the counter cast an alarmed glance at him. "Uh, you sure this is a good idea?"

Kris looked down at the time on his phone. The entertainment portion of Tinsel was scheduled to start in ten minutes. It would take them at least thirty minutes to get to

Charming. Maybe more if there was construction. In Jackson, Mississippi, there was *always* construction. "We'll be fine."

Mabel shuffled at tortoise speed toward the parking lot. He followed behind, pulling her suitcase, which was surprisingly heavy. Bowling balls? Jars of fruit compote? Gold bullion? Who knew what she had inside, but he knew it was danged heavy. He slung his guitar over his shoulder and tried not to step on the back of her sensible low-heeled pumps in his haste to get moving.

Once they reached the small compact, he loaded her suitcase, prayed he didn't get a hernia from lifting it, and climbed into the front seat. Mabel took a good minute or two adjusting the mirrors and her seat. Finally, she looked over and said, "Ready to go, handsome?"

Um, yep. Like yesterday.

Of course, yesterday he'd been coiffed and coddled like a true star. Earlier today he may have crashed and burned. When he'd finally landed in Jackson, he'd turned on his phone to fifteen text messages from Preston. He didn't have to read them to know that Preston was panicked.

After leaving the set of *Late Night in LA*, Preston had tried to get Kris to go out for drinks with two pretty assistants who worked in the studio. Kris had begged off, claiming a headache, and took an Uber back to the hotel. His mind had been like a paper caught in a whirlwind, twisting, whisked to and fro. Images and conversations that had happened in the past two weeks kept pulling at him. Tory under the mistletoe. Aunt Tansy smiling softly as he played the guitar. Tug wearing that silly red nose. Bria biting her lip in determination. And Rhett's words about home. About a girl waiting. About discovering something more than bright lights and big city.

When he'd gotten back to his room, he'd tried to work his

emotions out the way he always did—he picked up his guitar. Twenty minutes into strumming a melody that had been playing dodgeball with him for a week, everything snapped into place. The words came so fast, so right, that he could hardly get one line down before the other was there. Two hours later, he had a song.

Not a song.

The song.

The one he'd been looking for since the moment he'd first started writing for his second album. That wisp of something he couldn't find, that empty place inside himself, that memory that couldn't be grabbed—all of it came to him in those words and melody.

When he'd woken that morning, he reached for his guitar and made sure it was as good as he remembered. It was. Then he sang it while he showered, while he shaved (yes, he'd nicked himself) and while he pulled on his button-down shirt and cowboy boots. Like a pilgrim in a strange land, he'd found the shrine he'd been looking for and his soul was at peace.

Finally. The words had come, his mind had cleared, and he knew exactly what he had to do.

When he'd walked out of the hotel and climbed into the car Mr. Reynolds had sent for him, he got a text from Preston. His manager had rebooked him on a later flight.

"No, no, no." Kris said out loud, drawing the attention of the chauffer.

"Sir?"

"Nothing. Sorry," Kris said, waving off the attention and then texting Preston. Not acceptable. I need to be there sooner.

Preston texted back. Sorry. Flight was overbooked anyway. First class confirmed on next flight out. Don't worry. You'll make it.

Kris slammed his phone down on the seat and fumed. He

and his manager would have a come-to-Jesus talk soon, but not today. Today he needed to make a favorable impression on Payne Reynolds. His career depended on that. Even though he had figured out what he needed, his career would remain a major focus in his life. His relationship with Strata Records and its CEO was paramount. *All in its time.* And at this particular time, he needed to dazzle and tend to the hand that fed him.

He'd make it back to Charming in time. He hoped.

When the car pulled up to the huge Mediterranean estate, flocked by palm trees and lush shrubs that were still blooming, Kris caught his breath at the grandeur. A fountain with a reflecting pool spouted in the center of the Italian rose marble entrance. The driver hurried around and opened the door of the car for him before he could climb out on his own.

"Thank you," Kris said to the driver before mounting the sweeping steps to the massive scrolled iron door. He rang the doorbell and a uniformed maid answered.

"Mr. Reynolds and his guests are waiting for you on the terrace," the woman said, closing the door and then escorting him through an opulent room to a bank of glass doors from which he could see a large swimming pool. He stepped outside and into an oasis. Statues of Roman gods peeked from the exquisite flowering shrubbery on both sides of the rectangular pool. Grecian columns held a pergola aloft at the far end, where Payne Reynolds sat with Nick, Kris's producer, and Preston. Payne wore a Hawaiian shirt and linen trousers, and smoked a fat cigar that Preston tried unsuccessfully to fan.

"Here's our star, now," Payne boomed, giving him a Churchill smile over the fat stogey.

"Hello, Mr. Reynolds," Kris said extending his hand upon reaching the table.

"Aw, hell, don't 'Mr. Reynolds' me. I'm plain ol' Payne," the CEO said, giving Kris a hard, businesslike shake.

Payne Reynolds was anything but plain. Born to a famous actress and director, Payne had shunned Hollywood in favor of New York City and making music. He'd found success with a band that had made a couple of hits in the sixties before moving behind the scenes. He started Strata Records in the 1970s and went on to produce some of the top names in the music industry. He started the Nashville label in the 1980s and hadn't looked back. Obviously, the biz had been good to him.

For the next thirty minutes, they ate and talked football, big game hunting and coin collecting—all Payne's favorite pastimes. All the while they dined on some of the best eggs Benedict, French toast and salmon Kris had ever tasted. Soft music played in the background, a compilation of artists Payne had made famous. The whole atmosphere was designed to impress. To give Payne an upper hand in negotiations.

But Kris wasn't there to negotiate. He'd already signed the contract.

"So Kris, how's the work coming on the album? Is my team getting you what you need?" Payne said, after he'd folded his napkin and tucked it beside his empty plate. Immediately one of his staff came and cleared it.

Was there condemnation in Payne's tone?

"It's going great, Payne," Preston said, looking as if he were about to launch into a normal Preston song and dance. His words died when Payne held up a hand to him.

"Nope. I'm asking Kris. He's the guy. You're the suit." Payne leveled eyes that looked as if they could see through any bull at Kris.

Kris smiled. "I'm very happy working with the label, Payne. Strata is exactly where I want to be."

Payne grinned around his stogey. "There's a 'but' in there somewhere."

"Now I can see why you've always been successful," Kris said, sipping the iced water at his elbow and giving the record executive his total focus. "You know how to read a room."

"It's a vital skill." Payne puffed, his sharp eyes on Kris. Several seconds ticked by.

"To be truthful, I have some concerns with the direction we're planning to take for my next album. I'm not interested in being a crossover artist unless the crossover occurs naturally."

Preston sounded like he was about to choke. Kris gave him a sharp look.

"Payne, I respect the label's desire to make money, but I also know what kind of music I need to make. My first album sold well because I have a particular sound. I'm not Luke Bryan or Eric Church. I dig what they're doing, but that's not who I am. I'm old school—my country music is a little Southern rock, a little gospel, a little R&B. That's what my fans want, and I want to protect who I am as an artist."

Payne sat his cigar down on a saucer and blew out a steam of smoke. Then he looked at Nick. "What you got to say on this, Nick?"

Nick shrugged. "I have a vision. I thought it lined up with what Kris wanted."

"Hey, hey, Kris is happy with Strata," Preston said, leaning up, getting that feral gleam in his eyes. "But he makes a good point. He—"

Kris pressed a hand on Preston's arm. "It's okay, Pres."

Preston sucked in a deep breath and exhaled, slumping back in his chair. Kris almost smiled at his disgusted acceptance.

Kris looked back at Payne. "I wrote the first album, and you liked it enough to offer me a contract. I made you enough money to offer a second contract. I'm not slamming the door on Strata, I'm merely asking to be part of the plan. I want to write some of the songs."

Payne arched an eyebrow but didn't say anything.

"Here's the deal. For a while, I got sidetracked by all the things that come with a hit record. I bought a loft in Nashville and ordered suits that someone tailored to fit me. I bought a Mustang and a Rolex. I won't lie, success feels good. But then I went home to Mississippi and I remembered who I am. I'm Wranglers, an old pickup truck, and a Timex. And that's okay because that's who my fans like. They like this good ol' boy who worked with his hands and made music that made sense to them. So I'm asking you to trust me on this next album."

Payne jabbed his cigar in his mouth, chewed on it for a few seconds and then jabbed a finger toward Kris. "Fine. Do your thing. Nick, support him, lend him your wisdom, but give this boy some creative space and control."

Nick nodded. "I'll be in touch. We'll come at this from a different angle. We'll go with your vision, Kris."

Relief hit him like a two-ton wrecking ball. "Thank you."

Payne bit down on his cigar and rose. "Now, anything else I can do for you?"

Kris took a deep breath and pushed his chair back. "Actually, there is. You have a private jet, right?"

And that's how he ended up back in Jackson...just a bit later than he'd liked. Payne's jet had to be fueled and his pilot lived in the San Fernando Valley, which meant a long commute on short notice. Then the plane had been rerouted. Then Kris's dang car hadn't started. So now he sat with Mabel, aka Zsa Zsa, tootling down I-20 in the slow lane. Seems Mabel didn't believe in going over 50 miles an hour. Even in the 75 miles per hour zone.

"Do you think the roads are icy?" Mabel asked, squinting through the windshield.

"Uh, no. It's right at freezing but there's been no precipitation."

"Well, they said it might snow. Every time we pass a highway light, it looks like snow," she said.

"That might be your cataracts?"

"Land's sake, you're probably right. I used to have such good vision. Back when I was a fashion model. I didn't used to be this old, you know. No, I was a hot little number."

"Fashion model?"

"Back in the fifties," she said as she increased her speed to fifty-two miles an hour.

Kris tried not to drum his fingers or tap his foot as they inched along. He glanced at his watch. Twenty minutes had already gone by since they'd started the entertainment at Tinsel. He hoped Tory had stalled. She hadn't answered her phone, and when he'd tried to call Tansy a few moments ago, she hadn't answered either. He hoped both of his ladies were okay.

His ladies.

Only if he could convince Tory that there was something more between them. That she was meant to be with him.

In his bones, in his gut, in his soul, he knew he'd come home to Charming for a very good reason. If he could just get there.

"Mabel, pull over," he said, unclicking his seatbelt.

Mabel shot an alarmed glance his way. "Is this where you kill me?"

Kris laughed. "No, of course, not. I think it would be best if I drove. As a gentleman should."

"I'm a woman's-libber."

"With cataracts. Just pull over and let me drive. Please. I have to make it to the Duchess Hotel, and, no offense, but at the rate you drive, Christmas might come and go before we get there." Kris pointed to the shoulder.

"Oh, fine. See what being a good Samaritan gets me? Insulted." But she didn't sound mad. She sounded pleased. Amused, even. Thankfully, she angled her tires to the right and put on her blinker.

One minute later, Kris took off from the shoulder, hitting seventy-five miles per hour in the rental. He pushed it to eighty. He needed to make up time.

"My, you *are* a fast driver. Don't wreck this rental. I didn't get the insurance," Mabel said, flipping down the mirror and getting out a shocking shade of hot pink lipstick.

And that's how Kris Trabeau arrived at the Duchess Hotel—with squealing wheels and an eighty-year-old fashion model beside him.

He couldn't make this stuff up.

Chapter Twenty

TANSY HADN'T BEEN PREPARED FOR the call that had come from Valerie. When the phone rang, she thought it was Kris. He hadn't returned when he said he would and had left her a message that he'd gotten tied up with a meeting. Seems the CEO of his label wanted to meet with him and he'd take a later flight out. Tansy had been outside feeding her hens when he'd called, and when she'd called him back, he'd obviously set his phone to *do not disturb*.

She'd prayed that digging out the ornaments, baking the prized family recipe, and stringing lights all over the farm would peel the blinders from her nephew's eyes and reveal to him what was important in life—a place to belong. She wasn't trying to get him to abandon his career. Hey, a man had to eat. But naked ambition had a price.

Sitting on the sidelines watching someone destroy his life because he could see nothing but dollar signs and his name in lights had been hard the first time. Jack Prosper had ended up homeless and beaten down by the very life he'd prized so much. The last time she'd heard, the man she'd once loved had fallen on hard times, and rather than wanting to say to Jack 'I told you so,' Tansy rather wished she could offer the man a cup of tea, a piece of her mama's pound cake, and a soft chair to rest his tired bones. Ambition could lead a person to a bad place, and she couldn't apologize for not wanting her nephew to find that out the hard way. Maybe she was being selfish to want him to clue in to what was important in life. Maybe she wanted to control him or bind him to her. Maybe she was the one grasping at straws that were meant to be tossed away. There was only so much a woman could do.

So when Valerie called, she'd been so surprised by the woman's out and out demand that she get her fanny down to the Duchess Hotel that she hadn't erected much of a defense.

"I can't do that," she said.

"Oh, yes, you can. Slap a little paint on your face, pull on a Sunday dress, and let your foot be heavy on the gas pedal." Valerie whisper-yelled.

"But I can't. I have everyone coming here for the—"

"Think of Bria. Of that little girl who is way more afraid to stand before a microphone than you are. All you have to do is sit in the back and play the guitar. She'll be in the spotlight. Give her that chance, Tansy." Valerie was good at moving mountains. Or maybe Tansy was tired of being stubborn.

"I guess—"

"Good." And then Valerie hung up, leaving Tansy standing there staring at the receiver. She hung the phone up and blinked at it.

Tansy hadn't been on stage since Shreveport in 1967, and even then, she'd shaken like a sapling in a summer storm. After losing her mama and then seeing the love of her life snuggling with a new singer in the wings, she'd been swamped with anxiety and couldn't remember any of the lyrics to the songs she'd written. That night had been horrifying and she avoided thinking about how she felt running out of that venue.

So the thought of climbing back on stage in front of people shook her to her core.

She couldn't do it.

But then she thought of Bria's sweet round face…the beauty of her voice…the desire to do something bigger than the child could ever imagine tore at Tansy's resolve.

Tansy had spent the last two weeks trying to convince Kris of who he was at his core. How could she expect him to own up to who he was if she herself ignored her own center? She'd been a singer/songwriter. A good one. Stepping on that stage wasn't about anything other than being a good neighbor and a friend to a child who really, really needed someone to sacrifice for her.

So instead of calling Valerie back and saying she couldn't make it, she climbed the stairs as fast at her new walking boot would allow. Luckily, she'd washed her hair and braided it earlier. She found a long black dress that covered her boot, shrugged it on, and swiped some coral lipstick over her lips. Then she hustled to the old truck, glad Kris had tuned the clunker up.

When she arrived at the Duchess, she parked illegally in the handicapped spot. She'd never bothered getting an official temporary sticker, but there was no way she could walk far in her walking cast. So even if she got a ticket, she had no choice.

Valerie visibly sagged when she saw Tansy slip into the ballroom. The woman quickly took Tansy's elbow and hustled her out the side door into the hall by the kitchen. "Thank goodness. You made it."

"Kris said he'd be here. Something must be wrong. Maybe the flight got delayed or…" Kris had sounded so certain. What if something bad had happened to him? What if… "Has Tory checked her messages?"

"She's been busy emceeing the event," Valerie said. "I tried earlier but I don't know her security code."

"You called me with her phone."

"Yeah, but she handed it to me," Valerie said.

Through the window, Tansy spied Wren Daniels and Dovey Horton directing servers and loading silver trays with hors d'oeuvres. She could see the packed ballroom, the stage where some funny kid stomped around acting like some overpaid actor, and the spotlight.

Her stomach plunged to her knees—knees that were knocking together. Tansy took a few measured breaths. In through her nose, out through her mouth.

"Tansy, are you okay?" Valerie asked.

"I'm trying to be."

Valerie touched her arm. "You don't have to, if you can't."

Bria walked toward her, looking adorable and serious. Tansy could see the nerves in the child. The way her gaze wouldn't light. Fidgety hands. Lip caught beneath her teeth.

"I can do it. I *have* to do it, for her," Tansy said as Bria reached them.

"Are you nervous, baby?" Tansy asked.

Bria looked up at her. "I'm about to puke."

Tansy suppressed a grin. Having stage fright was nothing to smile about. "Me, too. I always get so nervous. Look at my knees." She pulled her dress up so Bria could see her legs trembling. Well, sort of. The walking cast covered some of one leg.

"Your legs are shaking. Look at my hands," Bria held out hands that had the fingernails bitten to the quick. They trembled.

"Well, I guess if we can't sing we can do the gator."

"What's that?" Bria asked, her hands quieting a bit. Yes, distraction was the key. And positive thoughts.

"It's something silly frat boys would do back in the day.

They'd throw themselves on the floor and shake all over," Tansy said, mimicking the spastic dance.

"That's stupid…but kinda funny."

Right as Tansy smiled, they heard Tory introduce them. "Okay, that's us. You ready?"

Bria sucked in a deep breath. "I guess I got to be."

Tansy re-shouldered her guitar strap and held out her hand. "Showtime."

Bria took it and together they walked out and onto the stage. Someone had sat a stool behind the microphone, just slightly to the right. Tansy climbed the stairs awkwardly and looped her guitar strap over her shoulder. Bria walked to the microphone and stood. Before she began, the child looked back at Tansy, her beautiful eyes looking for assurance.

Tansy stilled her nerves and focused on the child. She smiled and nodded.

She would never forget Bria's answering smile.

Then Tansy positioned her fingers on the bridge and struck the first chord.

Kris ran into the ballroom, carrying his guitar and pushing past someone else arriving late. An older gentleman in a fedora he nearly knocked down. "Sorry. I'm late."

"Me, too," he called as Kris ran through the lobby and down the hall that led to the Duchess Ballroom.

He'd been running but forced himself to calm as he opened the door to the ballroom. Inside it was dark and quiet, only the occasional clink of a glass. Everyone was focused on the stage.

On the little girl standing at the microphone.

And the older woman sitting on the stool behind her.

Aunt Tansy.

Kris allowed the door to swing closed and stood stock still at the sight before him. His aunt was sitting behind Bria. On stage. Just outside the spotlight. The two were mesmerizing, almost as if there was a tangible aura surrounding them. It was a moment like in the movies where everything slows down, and you know, just know, that something special is about to happen.

His aunt struck the first chord, playing the introduction to the song.

Kris held his breath as Bria sang the first line, praying it was in the right key, and when she did it was with a voice so pure and rich, he felt the music in his soul.

"You can count on me," he mouthed as she sang the second verse. Then he realized the irony of those words. He hadn't made it in time, and they'd been counting on him. Still, his aunt had saved the night. A Trabeau had risen to the occasion.

The audience was entranced, their gazes pinned to the girl whose voice made chill bumps ripple up his arm. His gaze found Tory standing to the side, and though he was too far away to tell, he knew there were tears shining in those pretty eyes.

"Sir?" someone said behind him. "Ticket?"

He smiled. "I'm with the band."

Then he moved along the perimeter, making his way toward where Valerie stood with Mac, who wore a Santa costume. Both of them looked on like proud parents as Bria sang the Christmas classic. When he reached them, he had to actually tap Valerie.

"Oh, Kris, you made it...well, late, but you made it," Valerie whispered, clasping his arm.

Mac grinned and shook his hand then returned his attention to the stage, where Bria had closed her eyes and let the song carry her away. Tansy's smile as she watched the girl made his heart fill to the tip top with gratitude and love. He'd spent so many years avoiding her and his home, looking for something he thought he needed. Who would have thought he'd find what he was searching for right there in Charming, Mississippi?

But he had.

Bria sang the last notes and the audience broke into thundering applause. The noise seemed to startle Bria. Her mouth fell agape and her eyes grew wide as she looked back at Tansy. His aunt smiled big as Texas, her pride in the girl evident.

Kris walked to the stage, and Tory turned to him, tears streaking her cheeks. "Oh, you came."

"Better late than never."

"Wasn't she marvelous? She was *so* marvelous."

"She was the best," he said, climbing onto the stage.

Bria saw him and ran to him. "Kris. I did it."

He gave her a hug and winked at his aunt. "You were incredible. I knew you would be. Come stand with me."

Kris walked to the microphone and the applause died down. He could feel when the audience recognized him. Tansy stood and reached out her hand to him. He angled the microphone so he could speak. "Hello, everyone. Wasn't that amazing? She's the real deal, people."

Applause broke out again and Kris beamed at Bria. Then he turned back to the microphone. The audience quieted. "Most of you know me, probably because you were my Sunday School teacher, Cub Scout master, or lined up next to me on Friday nights. I was supposed to be here to accompany Bria, but I ran into some delays. Luckily, I have a talented aunt who could step in to fill my shoes."

People applauded again.

He paused, gathering his thoughts. "You know, I've had a little bit of success in the music business, but sometimes when you're chasing your dreams, you lose track of your path. You forget who you are. For the past two weeks, thanks to my Aunt Tansy and a few other special ladies ..." He looked down at Bria before lifting his eyes to Tory, "I've found that what I've been looking for has been right here in my hometown. I have an early Christmas present for my aunt, so if you're okay with it, I want to play a little something I wrote last night. It's a little rough, but indulge me and forgive me if I screw it up."

The ballroom erupted into applause as Kris played a few chords.

"It's called 'More Than Just a Town'," he said into the microphone. He patted the stool for Bria and winked at her. She slid onto it, grinning at him.

Kris fell into the song he'd written, opened his mouth, and let the truth he'd discovered pour out. "That's more than just a welcome sign, population 909. It's a welcome home when I've been on the road..." As he sang, he watched the audience, the way they responded to the words about coming back to a place that had made him. He was singing about *their* town. The place that bonded them ...and always would.

When he got to the chorus, his eyes found Tug and Honey in the audience. Their smiles fueled the emotion in his voice. "It's more than just a town. More than just a place where I grew up and ran around, where I got roots dug deep inside this Mississippi ground. After all this time, I don't know how I didn't know 'til now. This is more than just a town."

He moved to the second verse. As he sang, he turned to his

Aunt Tansy. "And that ain't just a family farm. It's a hundred-acre piece of my heart, four generations passed along."

Tears fell from his aunt's eyes as he moved back to the chorus, hitting the strings hard as he sang from his heart, eyes closed, feeling the words. Then he opened them and his gaze met Tory's.

"She's more than just a girl cause every thought in my mind keeps on running back to her. If she wasn't in my life, the world just wouldn't turn…"

In Tory's eyes he saw what he'd been looking for. Her face was a canvas of emotion— yearning, fear, desire, hope. The tears she'd shed during Bria's performance reappeared and she brushed them away, shaking her head. As if she couldn't believe he was singing them to her.

Kris felt like his heart might burst in his chest at the pure beauty of that moment. What they had between them was real, it was raw, and it was right.

But Tory had to believe him.

He pulled his attention back to the audience as he sang the chorus twice, each time more emphatically, as if he could make them feel the epiphany he'd had last night. As if they could become him and know the change in him.

When he finished, everyone stood, clapping and whistling. Kris could do nothing more than smile, because that was the exact response he'd needed after the words he'd given Payne Reynolds. He'd told the CEO to trust him and then he'd commandeered the man's private jet to fly back to the place he needed to be. The music had come to him and he knew that the words he'd been looking for had been inside him all along. He'd just forgotten to look in the right place.

Tory wiped her eyes, put on her game face, and walked out to where he, Tansy, and Bria stood. Tansy hugged her and

Bria wrapped her chubby arms around Tory's waist. Mac came out wearing the Santa suit and the after party started right there on the stage. The audience was on its feet, Mac was dancing to "Santa Claus is Coming to Town" and everyone joined in, laughing and dancing. It was one of those moments everyone lived for. Pure joy.

Kris looked over at Tory. "I think you can say Tinsel was a success."

Her smile was the only answer he needed.

Chapter Twenty-One

TORY STOOD ON THE BACK porch at Trabeau Farms, sipping her hot chocolate and staring at the fire Kris had built in the fire pit. The children from the center, including a now very popular Bria, were making s'mores and playing a game of tag. Not at once, of course, but suffice it to say they were having fun. Tug and Honey sat in two of the Adirondack chairs, helping the younger children toast their marshmallows while Edison reveled in chasing the kids playing freeze tag. Tory laughed when one of the frozen kids broke his pose when Edison licked his chin.

Well, Common Connection had done it.

The combined monies from the ticket sales, the silent auction, and the live auction had brought in almost double what they'd made last year. Mac and Valerie, who were inside with Tansy and some of the other volunteers, were over-the-moon. Kris had just put his twenty-thousand-dollar guitar upstairs in his bedroom. The bidding had gotten heated, but he'd prevailed by naming the price he'd tried to pay weeks ago.

"Hey," Kris said, opening the screen door to find her leaning against a porch column. "I've been looking for you."

"I needed a moment to decompress. Lots of energy in there."

His smile made her heart contract. "Yeah, lots of happy people."

"True."

"But you don't sound happy," he said, zipping up his jacket and walking toward her. He looked like he always did. Not like the man who'd gone on *Late Night in LA* the night before. Which man was he? The down-home boy or the crossover country pop star?

Moments ago, when he'd been on stage singing, she'd thought she knew. The way he'd looked at her when he'd sung those words about the town, the farm...and a girl. But she wasn't certain if his song was a reflection of how he felt about her. *What if he'd just needed to sing about a girl because it fit the song? So why did it feel like he'd sung it to her?* Maybe she was overthinking things too much. The last time she'd seen him, she'd been angry at him for wanting to move his aunt and abandon the farm. Not only that, she'd been fearful of falling for him, tumbling head over heels for a man who wouldn't stay but would go back to Nashville to pursue fame and fortune.

Now she wasn't so sure about what Kris wanted.

Or what she wanted.

"I'm happy. Why wouldn't I be? We made a ton of money for the center, Bria sang like an angel, and you made it back for Christmas. Your aunt is so relieved."

"And you?"

She hesitated. "Me?"

"Are you relieved I came back?"

She managed a smile. "Well, you didn't come back when you were supposed to, but you made it just the same."

Kris studied her for a few moments, and Tory tried to summon her courage. Valerie's words came back to her. Leaping and jumping. All those things seemed easier to do when Tory had agreed to do them. Now she felt vulnerable. Like a girl who might end up on her butt.

Kris leaned over and tapped the column she leaned again. "You see this?"

She pushed off and turned to look. Marks marred the white posts. "Are those measurements? Like marking a child's height?"

"Yeah, see, this one is my dad," he said, tapping the initials RT. "Here's Tansy's and this one is Jenny's. I'm right here."

She followed his finger to the initials KT. "Tansy measured you all the way until your current height."

"Yep, and that's part of the reason I had a change of heart," he said, lowering his gaze to meet hers. His eyes were so soft. She could fall into those eyes. The reasonable scientist inside of her tried to slap her back into reality. But Tory didn't want to examine the data. She only wanted to stare into Kris's eyes. She wanted to believe that he'd meant those lyrics. That he wanted to spend his life with her. Have babies together. Grow old on the front porch.

"You changed because of these marks?" she asked, rubbing his initials beside one of the marks.

His mouth twitched. "If we sold this place, someone would paint over them. Couldn't have that happen. I want to add my children's marks, so we gotta keep the farm."

She was too afraid to look at him. "Oh, well, yeah, if you want to do that."

At that moment, a brown ball of fur hurtled toward Kris. "Umph! Uh, hey, Edison."

Edison hopped on his back legs, issuing an excited woof. Kris caught Edison's face before he swiped him with a giant tongue. Kris ruffled the dog's fur. "What's up, buddy? You playing with the kids?"

Edison wriggled around, delighted at the love, his tail nearly knocking over an empty planter. The dog had been so happy to see her when she'd come home after Tinsel, she'd leashed him up and brought him along. He'd been in his element playing with the kids. Edison would be a great therapy dog if he could learn to control his enthusiasm. That would come. He was still a big puppy.

"Down, Edison," Tory said, stabbing her finger at her lovable mutt. Edison looked hurt,

And dropped to all fours. When Tory said "okay" and waved her hand, he bounded off after the squealing kids.

Kris straightened, but the smile didn't leave his face. "Walk with me?"

The night was cold, but she'd changed into jeans, boots and a sweater earlier, thank goodness. "Sure."

"Let's walk out front away from the noise," he said, starting down the back steps. Tug raised a hand and Kris waved back. "Be back in a bit."

Tory followed him around to the front. The lights of the porch illuminated the driveway filled with cars. Christmas music and laughter spilled out from the house. As they walked down the drive toward the clutch of oak trees sitting between her property and Trabeau Farms, a gentleman in a fedora hat walked toward them.

"Excuse me," he called out, lifting a hand. "This is Trabeau Farms, isn't it? It's been a while since I've been out here."

"Yes, it's Trabeau Farms." Kris stopped and she nearly crashed into him. He placed a steadying hand on her shoulder but kept his gaze on the stranger. "And you are?"

"Jack. Jack Prosper. Your aunt and I were friends once. Long ago."

Kris stiffened. "I know your name. You were in the Travelers."

"That's right," the man said, pulling at his collar. "I, uh, saw the benefit and the picture of Tansy in the paper. I live with my sister in Jackson now and …well, it's been a long time and there are some things I've needed to say to your aunt. I ain't getting any younger."

Kris studied the man, who was also dressed in slacks, a button-down, and shiny dress shoes. "Okay. I suppose that would be okay. Just don't give her a heart attack."

The man's smile transformed his face. "She may not let me inside. In fact, she could clock me on the head with a frying pan. We didn't part so well. I left her in Shreveport and she wasn't none too happy with me."

"Good luck, then," Kris said, motioning toward the house.

Tory's breath caught when Kris took her hand. He didn't speak as Jack Prosper's footsteps crunched toward the house. Instead, he moved farther away, taking her into the shadows of the tree.

He stopped suddenly and pulled her around. "Did you see that man?"

"Of course, I did. I'm not blind."

"He broke my aunt's heart years ago."

Tory looked back at the man who now stood on the porch. Jack's posture projected a bit of hesitation as he lifted his hand to knock. "Oh. Wow. He's the guy, huh?"

Kris grabbed her chin and gently turned her face back toward him. He didn't release her and his hand was warm against her skin. "Jack chose his career over Tansy. She came back here, but that rejection did something to her. I looked him up once. He had some success, but his failures far outweighed his victories. That man has lived a hard life all because he forgot about what was important. I don't want to be Jack Prosper."

"What are you saying?"

"That Tansy got through to me."

"About moving her to Tennessee?"

"That and selling the farm. Yeah."

Tory swallowed. "So you're…I mean…" She wasn't sure if he was saying what she thought he was saying. Hope had nestled inside her earlier. Now it woke and flapped around.

"I'm saying I don't want to be Jack Prosper." His words were emphatic and something swelled inside her.

"Am I the girl in your song?" she asked, finally taking the leap, spreading those wings. "Am I more than just a girl?"

"You're damn right you are," he said as he lowered his head.

Tory pressed her hand against his chest. "Wait. What does that mean? Does that mean you're staying?"

"It means that I knew from the very start that you were special. The more I was around you, the more I wanted to kiss you, talk to you, dance with you, kiss you."

"You already said that," she said smiling. How could she not smile? Kris was saying the things she'd only dreamed a man would say to her one day.

"Already said what?"

"That you wanted to kiss me," she said, looking up. Then her eyes widened. "Kris Trabeau, did you bring me out here because there was mistletoe in this tree?"

He looked up at the cluster they stood beneath. "It's bad luck to not kiss beneath mistletoe."

"You're serious about this? About me?"

He smiled and cupped her face in both his hands. "I've never, ever been more serious about anything in my life. Not about my career. Not about my baseball card collection. Not even about my lucky penny. I fell for you the day you told me chickens have a higher visual stimulus."

Tory laughed. "It's my best pickup line."

"Well, it worked," he said, looking deep into her eyes. "So I told you how I feel, but you haven't—"

"Told you about how I fell in love with you the first time you played the guitar for Bria?"

"You did?" he asked. His thumbs stroked her cheeks.

"I did. I was scared to trust my feelings. I was too afraid you couldn't love someone like me. I did a Carol Burnett Tarzan yell and admitted to collecting bugs. Not to mention all the times I almost fell down. I didn't think you could be into a dork like me."

His threw back his head and laughed, but he didn't let go of her face. "You're something else, Victoria Odom. And I do believe I've fallen in love with you."

Tory closed her eyes as his lips touched hers. She'd been waiting forever for Kris Trabeau to kiss her, and that kiss beneath the mistletoe in the sprawling oak under a glittering Mississippi sky took her breath away.

Eventually, Kris lifted his head. "That is what I need every day. Everything else we can figure out. Where I live, what our life looks like. But this, this I need."

"Just so you know, there is a lot of mistletoe in this tree," Tory said.

He grinned and kissed her again.

And there had never been sweeter music than Kris Trabeau holding her in his arms, kissing her madly, deeply, wonderfully under the tree his father had fallen out of and broke his arm. She knew this because it was another story Tansy had told them. One of a good thirty or forty stories. And the last thing Tory thought of before she rose on her toes again and kissed the man who loved her was that she'd probably have to learn to love country music.

An easy price to pay for loving Kris Trabeau.

Jingle Bell Fruitcake Cookies

In *A Down Home Christmas,* rising country music star Kris Trabeau goes home to Charming, Mississippi, hoping to convince his aunt to sell the family farm. Aunt Tansy's neighbor Tory Odom and a little girl Tory knows from the community center come over to help make Jingle Bell Cookies from a secret family recipe. Baking leads to impromptu Christmas carol singing, making the shared time even sweeter. Our updated version of Jingle Bell Fruitcake Cookies are a Southern-flavored treat that might just become a tradition in your own family.

Yield: 3 dozen cookies (36 servings)
Prep Time: 20 minutes
Cook Time: 25 minutes
Total Time: 45 minutes

INGREDIENTS

- ½ cup unsalted butter, at room temperature
- 1¼ cups brown sugar, packed
- 1 extra-large egg
- 1 tablespoon dark rum (or brandy, bourbon or apple cider)
- 1 teaspoon vanilla extract
- 1¾ cups all-purpose flour
- ½ teaspoon baking soda
- ½ teaspoon kosher salt
- ½ teaspoon ground cinnamon
- ¼ teaspoon ground nutmeg
- ¼ cup buttermilk
- ½ cup chopped pecans (or walnuts)
- ¼ cup chopped pistachios
- 1 cup Medjool dates, pitted, chopped (or chopped figs)
- ¾ cup glacé-candied red cherries, halved
- ½ cup dried apricots, coarsely chopped
- ¼ cup glacé-candied fruit mix (such as candied pineapple, citron, orange peel, red cherries)

DIRECTIONS

1. Preheat oven to 400 degrees F.
2. In the bowl of an electric mixer fitted with the paddle attachment, cream the butter and brown sugar on

medium speed until fluffy. Beat in egg; add rum and vanilla extract and mix until fully blended.

3. In another bowl, combine flour, baking soda, salt, cinnamon and nutmeg; whisk to blend.

4. Alternately, add dry ingredients and buttermilk to batter and mix until blended.

5. Fold the chopped nuts and fruit into batter by hand. Chill dough 10 minutes.

6. Drop dough by rounded tablespoons or with a small ice cream scoop, about 2 inches apart, onto cookie sheets lined with baking paper.

7. Bake each cookie sheet for 8 to 9 minutes, until lightly golden.

Thanks so much for reading *A Down Home Christmas*!

You might also enjoy these other books
from Hallmark Publishing:

Journey Back to Christmas
Christmas in Homestead
Love You Like Christmas
A Heavenly Christmas
A Dash Of Love
Moonlight in Vermont

For information about our new releases and exclusive
offers, sign up for our free newsletter!

You can also connect with us here:

Facebook.com/HallmarkPublishing

Twitter.com/HallmarkPublish

You might also enjoy…

At the

HEART *of* CHRISTMAS

JILL MONROE

Chapter One

QUINN HARDWICK FOUGHT BACK TEARS as she clutched the documents in her hands. When her grandmother had asked for Quinn's help checking on the old farmhouse, she'd never expected to be reading through paperwork. The deed to the family farmland. Another for the house. And finally, a copy of her beloved grandfather's will, listing her as the new owner of the Hardwick Ornament Company.

"I'm a travel agent. What do I know about running an ornament company?" Quinn dropped the papers on the picnic table her grandfather had built himself while she had helped with the very important task of fetching nails. She breathed deep and wished she'd brought a coat. The air was growing chillier as fall changed to winter and the sun set earlier each night.

Gram took Quinn's hand in hers, her hazel eyes warm. "That's the great thing about learning. You can always begin. When you quit is when the trouble starts."

Quinn glanced from the old mint-painted farmhouse, a color no one in the family had dared to change, to the red and white barn, and finally to the workshop she'd first explored with her grandfather when she was a little girl. "Gram, I'm not sure I can take this."

"You're the only one of your generation who's ever shown any interest in this place. Why not you?" she asked with a shrug, sending her large red and orange leaf-shaped earrings swaying. "Because you think your brother and sister will want to do it? Landon is married to the law and Emmaline is enjoying college. Maybe too much. She won't want to bear this responsibility. And don't worry about your cousins. Chloe is in Boston being the reporter she's meant to be. Alara isn't going to shack up here in Bethany Springs unless that man of hers proposes. Silas is probably on a baseball diamond even as we speak."

Quinn's gaze strayed from the dear, familiar scrawl that only a doctor could get away with, the paperwork representing her grandfather's last wish of gifting her with the Hardwick Ornament Company. His passing four weeks ago had left her devastated. After the funeral she couldn't bear to attend the reading of his will. Her heart ached at his loss, but she was also blown away that her grandfather had believed in her so much. She took a deep breath and tried to focus on anything other than the tremendous gift she'd been given.

"So you think Derrick's going to propose, too?"

The older woman wrinkled her nose and tucked a strand of her gray hair behind her ear. She picked a piece of lint off the cuff of her black and brown patchwork sweater. At some point, she'd appliquéd leaves and bright red cranberries to the pullover, a staple of Gram's fall wardrobe.

"Honestly, I don't know what's taking that boy so long. She's perfect for him."

Alara might be her goofy cousin, but Gram was right. Derrick wouldn't find anyone better.

Gram cupped Quinn's cheek. "And you stop trying to change the direction of this conversation." Her grandmother's hands dropped, and she gathered the documents into a pile and stuffed them into the large manila envelope where she'd retrieved them earlier.

"It's so much easier to worry about someone else's problems than your own," Quinn pointed out.

"Don't I know it," Gram said. "I can fill an entire day with just my six grandkids alone." She tucked the envelope back into her oversized purse and tugged the strap over her shoulder. "Walk with me," she invited as she looped Quinn's arm through hers.

Quinn smiled as they walked side by side, the fallen leaves crunching beneath her boots. Even though the farm was right outside of Bethany Springs, Massachusetts, visiting here had always been a special treat, reserved for splashing in the creek in the summer and sipping hot chocolate around the fire when it grew cool. She always felt lighter here. Carefree and creative.

"I do love it here," Quinn said with a sigh as they walked along the wooden fence line, eyeing the rolling mountains of the Berkshires in the distance.

"Your grandfather wanted you to have this land and the workshop. I know you have ideas."

Quinn gave a hesitant nod. She *did* have ideas. But none she'd ever shared. Gram's eyes narrowed, and she practically vibrated with expectation. Quinn's parents had instilled pragmatism and solid skills, like typing and paying bills on time...but her grandparents? They'd gifted all their grandchildren with the permission to dream.

Quinn fought off the melancholy threatening to take over. "Seeing all this unused land and the old workshop makes me think about how much of the past we've lost. Not that I'm against progress."

"That phone that's rarely out of your hand clued me in," Gram said with a wink.

"I would like to bring back the Hardwick Ornament Company."

Gram wrapped her arms around Quinn in a tight hug. "Your grandpa would be so proud. Now tell me your plans."

Her mind raced with the many ideas she'd considered over the years when she daydreamed. "First I'll have to modernize the workshop and bring it up to code. If I sell my condo in town, I could move out here and live in the farmhouse. That should give me enough startup money."

"Good idea." Gram's face turned thoughtful as she studied one of the outbuildings, its roof caved in and a side listing. "It's too bad the old storefront is falling down."

Quinn pointed to another building, its paint peeling, but with a far sounder foundation. "What about using one of the bunk rooms in the old Berry House? I thought maybe we could repurpose a bedroom to set up an area for memorabilia, showcasing old designs and catalogues. You still have all that stuff, right?"

Gram made a scoffing sound. "Like I'd get rid of any of that. You'd pore over those collections for hours as a kid. I had to practically drag you out of the attic to play in the backyard with your cousins."

"Not that Landon or Emmaline would ever tell you this, but our cousins could kind of be pains back in the day. Although they're pretty cool now," she said, nudging her grandmother's arm.

Gram's shoulders began to shake, and her earrings rocked back and forth as she laughed. "It would probably surprise you to learn they felt the same about you guys."

Quinn gasped. "No way. We were way too cool for them," she defended, although a small part of her suspected her Gram was right about their cousins. Those three had probably tried to ditch them as much as she and Landon and Em had tried to find the best place to hide.

"My attic is open to you any time. No one's moved anything since you've been up there. I like the idea of a mini-museum. It'll be nice for others to enjoy the history."

Quinn's thoughts ran wild, and she allowed herself to dream for a moment, as her grandpa always encouraged her to do. "Once we're up and running, we can give tours of the workshop, demonstrate the old techniques of glass blowing. Maybe even offer classes."

Gram rubbed her hands together and grinned. "Now tell me about the ornaments. You adored those as a little girl, so I know you have plans there, too."

Quinn's gaze focused on the horizon. The sinking sun set the sky ablaze with color. "That's the harder part. Lots of dreams and ideas, but I can't draw or design. Well, I can, they're just…not that great. I'll have to hire someone who can take my scattered concepts and design them into a workable glass mold."

Gram wrapped her arm around Quinn and stared at the glowing reds and yellows and oranges in the sky. Her voice lowered. "Well, between you and me, the Hardwicks always worked better in sales and planning than the artistic side of the business."

"That's what I was afraid of. No matter how many how-to videos I watch on the internet, I'm missing the creator gene." Her head dropped forward. "Where do I find a person who's an expert glass blower, *and* who's willing to relocate and design for next to nothing?"

Read the rest! *At the Heart of Christmas* is available now.

About The Author

A finalist in both RWA's prestigious Golden Heart award and RITA award, Liz Talley has found a home writing contemporary romance with a Southern accent. Liz lives in North Louisiana with her childhood sweetheart, two handsome children, three dogs and a mean kitty.

CPSIA information can be obtained
at www.ICGtesting.com
Printed in the USA
LVHW042227230519
618853LV00001BD/1